PRAISE FOR W

"Incredibly steamy, passionate, exciting and downright delicious!

Want a period romance with bite? You've found it.! Full of high angst, danger and a wickedly delightful love story that would rival many modern set plots this is an absolute joy to read especially seeing how the Devil in question succumbs to his fate! A wickedly entertaining read." Amazon review

A beta readers quote: *"Y'all, I'm doing a beta read right now and this book is amazing. Holy crap. Just plan on staying up all night to read it when it comes out"*
Nilambari K.

Delicious
Reviewed in India on 7 March 2023
Wren St. Claire is a new-to-me author. Her writing is fun and witty. This story moves swiftly forward with nary a dull moment.

- The best part was the meet-cute. I won't give away the spoiler, but Diana and Anthony's meeting brought Jess from Lord of Scoundrels and Eva from Outrageous to mind. This scene had me well and truly hooked. What followed was an amalgamation of delicious moments involving, but not limited to, dramatic encounters, wild chases, emotionally charged experiences, scorching assignations and heartfelt declarations of love. What more can you ask for?

- I freaking adore a strong heroine and always have. Diana fit the bill to boot. God, considering her early experiences, this girl was unafraid in the face of danger, saved herself (not a damsel, this one), saved him (twice), and was kind, acceptant and optimistic. She was just sugar and spice with Anthony, and I loved it.

- Anthony, ooh la la. Not having read the previous book, I was not aware of his transgressions, and it allowed me to look at him with a fresh set of eyes. And what I saw wasn't half bad at all. In fact, it was utterly delectable. He saw her. He wanted her. He went after her and refused to let her go. Consequences be damned (a man after my own heart). The way he fought to keep her in his life by brow-beating the circumstances to make her life easier had me falling in love with him. This man, this devilish man, was well and truly tamed.

- The plot was ripe for a sensual engagement, and Ms St. Claire delivered. The romance was super swoony with a more than generous helping of tender, loving, caring and comforting steamy goodness. Diana and Anthony's absolute inability to be without each other made their love perfect. They grew together, learnt to trust one another and found togetherness in their loneliness. Sigh.

*This book put Ms St. Claire on my authors-to-read list, and it intrigued me enough to read the prequel and all the other books that will follow.

TAMING THE DEVIL

A STEAMY REGENCY ROMANCE

VILLAIN'S REDEMPTION SERIES
BOOK ONE

WREN ST CLAIRE

THE DEVIL'S MISTRESS
A REGENCY ROMANCE

WREN ST CLAIRE

Copyright © 2023 by Wren St Claire

All rights reserved.

No part of this book may be reproduced in any form or by any electronic or mechanical means, including information storage and retrieval systems, without written permission from the author, except for the use of brief quotations in a book review.

Created with Vellum

❦ Created with Vellum

To all my Beta Readers who so very enthusiastically read and loved this book. You loved Anthony as much as I did, and you gave me the courage to move forward with this series.

Thank you. Wren, 27 June 2024

ABOUT THIS BOOK

She destroyed all his plans with one shot from her pistol... now he will turn the world upside down to have her.

Miss Diana Lovell is a woman thirsting for revenge. She blames the late Duke of Mowbray for her father's demise and ruining her life. She reasons that the current Duke is cut from the same cloth as his grandsire and she means to get what is hers by right, no matter the cost. But she doesn't bargain on the magnetic attraction that sparks between her and the current Duke and finds herself drawn into an intimate and dangerous proximity with a man she cannot resist or get away from.

Sir Anthony "Devil" Harcourt is now the 7th Duke of Mowbray, but with the title comes a mountain of debt and a reckoning, as the sins of his grandfather come crashing down upon him in the form of a beautiful virago bent on revenge and obtaining what is hers. Anthony's cold heart is not easily softened, yet the moment he sets eyes on Diana he knows he will never let her go. The trouble is the lady has other ideas.

Passion explodes when these two souls collide and bitter,

cynical Anthony discovers that love may be possible after all, if he can only redeem himself sufficiently to deserve it.

Taming the Devil is the sizzling HOT second book in the Villain's Redemption, Steamy Regency Romance series. If you like wicked heroes with a dark past, spicy, passionate romance and feisty heroines, then you'll love Wren St Claire's deliciously wicked romance.

Author's quote: "Anthony was the villain in Book 1 of the series, but I was so enamoured with him I had to turn him into a hero and write his love story. I needed a strong heroine to match him, and Diana fits the bill nicely. She certainly won't take any crap from him and brings the former rake and bad-tempered misanthrope to his knees."

CHAPTER 1

*I*t was just before midnight and Lovell's gaming hell in St James's was humming as usual. It was a popular and rather exclusive gentleman's club patronised by many of the more hardened gamesters of the ton. It was certainly no place for a single lady of birth and breeding.

A game of faro in full swing on the second floor, was presided over by an attractive young lady of slender build with dark curls and grey eyes. She was dressed in a low-cut gown of blue silk, laced at the front in the old-fashioned style and designed to show off her excellent figure, which was much appreciated by her audience judging from the quips and compliments thrown her way.

"Did you hear the old Duke of Mowbray finally passed on?" remarked the gentleman in a puce waistcoat, to her left.

Miss Diana Lovell, in the act of shuffling the deck of cards for the next round, pricked up her ears at the name and glanced up.

"Both his sons are dead, aren't they? Who will inherit? Not Barrington?" the gentleman in the blue swallow-tailed coat across the table asked. Diana flinched internally at the mention of Barrington, and glanced up under her dark lashes as a third gentleman seated to her right entered the conversation.

"No, Anthony Harcourt is next in line, son of the younger son."

"Oh, yes, was forgetting him," replied blue coat.

"Aye, he's been living on the expectation for years," remarked Mr Ashley Morton, a tall, lanky gentleman seated beside him and one of Diana's regulars. Diana, poked a loose brown curl back behind her ear and placed the cards in the shoe, smiling round at her group of players.

"Place your bets gentlemen." Her soft command interrupted the chatter, and the men began moving rouleaux about on the green baize surface of the faro table. When all the bets were placed, she drew three cards. The first, a two of diamonds was discarded, the second, representing the banks bet, was a king of clubs and the third, the players bet, was an ace of hearts.

Cheers and groans greeted the revealing of the cards as the players learned their fate, winner, or loser.

"Kings lose, aces win," announced Diana, reeling in the losing bets for the bank.

"You're stealing my heart, my lovely!" said the corpulent gentlemen next to Morton.

Diana smiled at this sally and quipped back, "It's the king that has my heart sir!"

This provoked a laugh from the table and a request for another bottle.

"Place your bets, gentlemen."

She was in the act of dealing the second hand of the rubber, when her uncle Garmon, the proprietor of this exclusive gentleman's club, appeared at her elbow. He was a well-made man of above average height and regular features, with a touch of grey at his temples. He waited until the cards were drawn and the bank reeled in its share, before murmuring in her ear, "Rooke will take over, I need you." Addressing the table, he said with a jovial smile that didn't reach his eyes, "I trust you're enjoying the evening gentlemen?"

Ayes and groans sounded, depending on who was winning or losing.

"I am going to steal away your fair goddess for a few minutes, Mr Rooke will continue the play."

This was greeted with protests from the players.

Diana curtsied to them and said, "I shall be back momentarily, sir's, pray continue, and may your luck improve."

"Nay, you are my luck!" exclaimed a red-faced young man, the worse for drink.

Diana laughed at this declaration, a smile curving her lips, and followed her uncle across the room, past a noisy game of rouge et noir and a tense game of hazard, to the corridor. Here they passed through a door at the end into a service passage and thence to the office, where the manager, Connor Mor, met them.

Connor's dark, Irish good looks, magnificent physique and penetrating blue eyes, cut a swath through the female population, and scared the living daylights out of unruly males, the latter a useful skill in a place like Lovells.

"What's to do?" asked Connor as they entered and Garmon shut the door.

"Sir Nathaniel Conant, the Bow Street Magistrate, is on our doorstep with a search warrant and ten constables. We're going to convince him it's a bad idea."

"How would we be doin' that?" asked Connor.

Garmon smiled, and Diana shivered. It was what she called his reptilian expression. His hazel eyes looked green in this light, and the hint of silver in his hair reinforced the air of authority he wore like a cloak. He was still a handsome man at forty, lean and taught of build, and in her experience, he seldom left anyone in doubt that he was in command of the situation. "Just fetch him here. Carlos has him detained at the door. And make sure the constables stay outside!"

Connor bowed in acquiescence and left the room with his usual swagger.

"What is my role?" asked Diana.

"Witness." Garmon spoke curtly as he took a seat behind his desk and pulled a folded paper towards him.

Diana took a seat in the corner of the room and had just settled her blue silk skirts when the door opened, and Connor ushered Sir Nathaniel Conant into the room. The man was middle-aged and may have been handsome in his youth. He was spare of build, his hair generously flecked with grey.

"Come in sir and take a seat," said Connor, offering him a chair. "Sir Nathaniel Conant, Mr Garmon Lovell, the proprietor of this establishment."

Garmon rose, bowed to Conant, and offered his hand. Conant bowed in return and took his hand. From what Diana could see, the handshake was firm on both sides. Conant kept his back straight and his expression tight. It was not hard to divine that he was not happy about this interview.

Garmon waved him to the chair in front of the desk and resumed his own seat. Conant however swivelled to bow in her direction, "Ma'am."

"My niece, Miss Lovell," remarked Garmon.

Diana bowed her head in return.

"Charmed, Miss Lovell."

Connor Mor took up a position against the wall with his arms crossed, his stunning blue eyes watching the proceedings like a hawk.

The amenities dealt with, Conant took a seat and shucked his cuffs. "Mr Lovell, you will be aware of the purpose of my visit."

"I am sir, you would also be aware that such a move would be bad for business."

"That really isn't my concern, Mr Lovell. My concern is for the law-"

"Perfectly understandable sir. But I have something that has come into my hand that may interest you." He passed the paper across the desk, and Conant took it, clearly startled at this turn of events. He opened the paper and read it. Diana watched his colour rise and his fulminating expression as he raised his eyes to Garmon's was a sight to behold.

"How did you come by this?"

"That is something I prefer not to reveal." Garmon smiled and Diana shivered again. "I think that you will agree, this puts a different complexion on the matter. You would not care for this to ah- fall into the wrong hands or to appear in the Hue and Cry Police Gazette, I'm sure."

Conant huffed for a moment, chewing on invisible cud. Finally, he said softly, "How much do you want for this?"

"It's not for sale, sir, nor would it do you any good if I sold it to you. It's a copy. The original is in my safe, where it will stay. As will its contents. If you and your men leave quietly, there will be no need for this state of affairs to change one iota."

"I understand you."

"Good. I do hope you understand that I bear you no ill will, Sir Conant. I am merely a businessman protecting his interests. And incidentally, yours. If this were to fall into more unscrupulous hands than mine..."

"Hm. I take your meaning Mr Lovell." He rose to his feet. "Good evening to you. And you Miss Lovell."

"Mr Mor will show you out," said Garmon with a smile.

The door closed on Connor and Conant, and Garmon sat back steepling his fingers. "And that, my dear niece, is how you achieve your ends with no blood spilt." He went on with a frown. "Now to find out who betrayed me!" She shuddered as his eyes darkened, and his hands clenched on the arm of his chair.

She must have moved because he looked over at her and his expression cleared. "You can return to the faro table now my dear, the patrons miss you."

"Yes Uncle," she rose, shaking out her skirts.

"You're an asset to this house you know." He added, a rare compliment. "Were the men bothering you?"

"I can handle them," she said serenely.

"Good girl, I've taught you well."

She inclined her head and left the room to head back to the salon.

On the way she met Connor returning and he smiled. "You look very fetching tonight, darlin'. Is that a new gown?"

"You know very well it isn't," she said, knowing better than to fall for Connor's blarney. It was automatic with him, she doubted he was even aware he was doing it. "I'd best get back to my table, the men lose more when they're looking at my décolletage."

"I'll be up before supper to relieve you."

"Thanks," she passed on and turned at the door back into the front of house, to see him re-entering the office. No doubt he and Uncle had things to discuss. Pushing open the door she reflected on the tidbit of gossip she had caught earlier. The old Duke of Mowbray was dead. *Was there any hope of retrieving her property now? And if so, how? She needed a plan.*

CHAPTER 2

The newly minted Duke of Mowbray, formerly known as Sir Anthony Harcourt, glared at the man who had served his grandfather as Steward for forty years.

"His Grace didn't hold with spending more on the tenants than strictly necessary, your Grace."

"Which is why the tenant farms are in such a poor state!"

"His Grace always said-"

"I don't give a fuck what his Grace always said! I'm the bloody Duke now and, it's my fucking responsibility to fix this fucking mess he's left me with. Now are you going to offer me some solutions or would you like this damned register shoved up your arse?" He said waving the book he'd been staring at all day.

Mr Garston turned red. "It's not fixable your Grace. It would need a great deal of money-"

"I'm aware of that!" The Duke rose from his seat and paced to the window. The prospect was dismal. The snow that had covered the ground for most of December, January, and half of February, was beginning to thaw and making a hasty pudding of the grounds. The trees were bare and the sky leaden. So dark that he had been forced to light candles inside for days. "Once I get the money, what is the first step to repairing the neglect?"

There was no answer, and Anthony turned, prepared to launch another verbal attack at this criminally stupid man but stopped short. Garston had tears coursing down his cheeks. "I'm sorry your Grace! I don't think I can do this. You'd best have my resignation." And before Anthony could say anything further, the man left the room.

Anthony stared after him with mixed feelings. The man was clearly incompetent if not corrupt, but he knew the land and Anthony didn't. He would just have to find someone else. *Another task to add to the growing pile! There was no end to it.* None of this improved his temper or his mood.

"Your Grace?" a timid voice from the door interrupted his train of thought.

"Yes?" he snapped.

"Pastor Bridgeforth has called to see you."

"Pastor-" Anthony erupted. "Tell him I'm not home, imbecile! What part of, I'm not to be disturbed, did not penetrate your thick skull? The last person I want to see is the blasted Vicar! Now get out and bring me the damned brandy!"

"Yes, your Grace."

Pack of idiots the lot of them! He fumed. *He should sack the whole damned household and start over. There wasn't one he could trust among them.* He'd have brought his own servants from his house in Bedfordshire if he hadn't already sent them to make the London house habitable.

With a sigh, he rummaged his flaming red hair with agitated fingers. Returning to the ledgers, he once more applied himself to the task of trying to understand the size of the debt he had inherited, and what, if anything, he could sell to defray it.

CHAPTER 3

Peace reigned in the sitting room of the Earl and Countess of Stanton's London house, in Berkeley Square. The only audible sounds were the ticking of the ormolu cloak on the mantelpiece and the crackle of the generous fire in the grate. The soft glow of candlelight set just so to afford my lord excellent vision of the printed page and my lady of her embroidery. The Earl was a handsome man in his early thirties of slim build and just above medium height, the Countess a tall slender lady with striking red hair and green eyes. Both were dressed as tastefully as their surroundings and appeared completely at ease in each other's company.

"Ow!" exclaimed the Countess sucking her thumb.

"What is it my dear?" The Earl looked up from his book.

"My concentration lapsed, and I stuck myself with the needle," her ladyship used a handkerchief to absorb the drops of blood from the needle prick.

"What were you thinking of love?" he asked with a fond smile.

Lady Anne put her embroidery aside with a sigh. "I heard the most awful tale of Anthony today, and I am trying not to believe it, but I fear it is true."

The Earl put down his book and wrapped an arm round his wife's shoulders.

"I fear you are right love. Most of the tales about my lamentable brother-in-law are true, the unsavoury ones at least."

She sunk her flaming head onto his shoulder and sighed again. "That he killed Sir Barnabus Maltby in a duel last year."

"It is true." He looked down at her ruefully.

"And you never told me?" She said accusingly.

"Neither did Anthony," he pointed out.

"He's just my brother. You're my husband; you're supposed to tell me everything."

"Everything, sweetheart?" He cocked an eyebrow.

"Everything that matters."

"It's not a tale for a lady's ears, and in any case, it occurred before we met." He frowned at his boots, crossed at the ankles.

"What was the point at issue?"

"I understand the offence related to a lady."

"I expected as much. Who?"

"Maltby's wife."

Anne snorted. "Typical! Are there any other skeletons in his cupboard I don't know about?"

"Several I should think, Maltby isn't the only man he's killed."

She sighed. "Do you think the Dukedom will improve him or make him worse?"

"I've no wish to offend you my love, but I fear worse. His grandfather was no pattern card of rectitude."

"Grandpapa was as bad, if not worse than Anthony. They used to positively delight in fighting with each other." she snuggled closer to Denzil. "I am so glad you are not quarrelsome, love. They made my life a misery the pair of them." The Earl kissed his wife's flaming curls and hugged her tighter.

"As I am glad you did not inherit the Harcourt temper."

Silence followed this for a few moments before the Earl remarked. "I forgot to tell you. I got a letter from my brother today. He and Viviana are coming home. It appears she is in the family way, and despite her declaring she doesn't mind giving birth in a tent, Jack won't have it. He tried to persuade her to come home alone, but you know Viviana." The Earl glanced down at his wife to see how she was taking this news. "She refused to leave him. So, he plans to sell out to come home and settle down."

"That's marvellous! How do you feel about it?" probed Lady Anne with a mild look of anxiety.

"Love, whatever feelings I may have thought I had for my former fiancé have well and truly evaporated. They did so the moment I clapped eyes on you."

Anne settled back into his arm with a satisfied smile. "Well then it is a fortunate thing that our son will have a play mate."

"Our-" the Earl sat up with a shock. "You're not!"

"I am. I think." She rested a hand low on her belly.

"When were you going to tell me?" The Earl asked with an edge of mild exasperation.

"When I was certain, but the doctor seems to think it is likely. It might be a girl of course." She smiled with shy pleasure.

"Anne, my dearest!" the Earl enveloped her in a kiss that took some minutes. When the Countess could speak again she said, rather flushed, "You're pleased?"

"Of course, I'm pleased! As long as you are well?" he asked with an anxious survey of her face.

"Fine as a fivepence so far." Her smile widened.

"I think," said the Earl softly, "We should have an early night."

CHAPTER 4

Garmon slid down the bed, to commence what he planned to be a thorough exploration of Genevra's delightful body. He began with the ravishing of her breasts. These luscious globes made him salivate with longing, and he had entirely neglected them earlier, driven by an overmastering desire to just get inside and fuck her.

The problem had been his inability to stop thinking about doing precisely that all day. Despite the slight distraction of his unsatisfactory meeting with Diana, he had been walking around with an erection for the duration, remembering and anticipating.

Having her back in his arms had completely destroyed his plans for a slow seduction, especially when she responded so immediately and wantonly to his kisses. It was obvious she wanted the same thing and from that point on it was a frantic rush to the finish line. He was pleased and mildly flattered by her response. A mutual attraction this strong was rare and to be savoured and enjoyed to the full.

His mouth made a meal of her hard nipples, nibbling, licking, sucking first one and then the other. His hands cupping, squeezing, stroking and caressing the lovely, round, soft flesh. Her legs moved restlessly on the bed, signalling her arousal from this treatment. *Could he? Would she?* He decided to try.

Lifting his head he said, "Spread your legs and keep them spread. Wide as they will go."

She gaped at him.

"Trust me," he said coaxingly.

She nodded and obeyed. He looked down and groaned at the sight of her spread out before him, her breasts lolling heavy, with her nipples jutting up pink and hard, her stomach a lovely curve and her quim revealed to him in all its pink, satiny glory, damp and dressed with strawberry curls.

"Now, no touching yourself unless I say so, hmm?"

She nodded, and he grinned. "I am going to play with your breasts, just your breasts. And you are going to keep her thighs spread wide and clench your inner muscles as I do so. You understand what I mean by that?"

"I think so," her voice was a husky croak. She swallowed, her tongue licking her lower lip.

"The idea arouses you, doesn't it?"

"Yes," she whispered.

He pushed a finger inside her. "Try to clench," she obeyed, and he groaned, imagining what it would feel like if she did that while his cock was inside her. "Yes, like that." He withdrew his finger and licked it grinning at her. Her eyes widened and he kissed her lips. "Now clench and release while I play with you."

He bent his head to her breasts and nuzzled and licked and kissed one mound while he cupped and squeezed and fondled the other. He kissed and suckled, using his tongue to swirl over and tease the hard nub, feeling her arching up into his mouth as he widened and took more of her breast, sucking harder.

She whimpered, her hands clutching the sheets, and he transferred to the other breast giving it the same treatment, soothing the first with his fingers. He sucked hard on her nipple, pinching the other at the same time. Then soothed and repeated the process, each time getting a little harder.

Her sounds got louder and more urgent and her hips rolled, her thighs trembled and her back arched. A deep groan tore from her throat and she cried out panting.

She collapsed back on the bed trembling her thighs snapping together and rubbing, her panting breath audible. He kissed each pink breast soothingly and sat up, his cock jutting up hard against his belly.

She lay limp and pink against the pillows a dazed expression in her eyes.

"I didn't know that was possible."

He grinned. "I told you I would show you pleasure you have never dreamed of." He leaned over her and kissed her, slow and deep. He couldn't seem to get enough of her mouth. Sitting back on his haunches he said, "Would you do me a favour?"

"Of course, what?"

He waved at his belly. "Suck my cock with that luscious mouth of yours?"

She smiled and sat up. "I'd love to."

He groaned again. "Genevra I'm going to die of pleasure, and it will be your fault!"

She laughed and leaned forward.

"No stay there I want to-" he moved to straddle her. "Lean back against the pillows." She obeyed him, and he knelt before her, resting his hands against the bedhead behind her. He leaned forward, and she circled his girth with her fingers, and pulled down the foreskin to reveal the head of his cock. She took him in her mouth, and he groaned at the sensation of her tongue against his flesh and the hot wet cavern of her mouth.

He closed his eyes the better to appreciate the exquisite sensations and thrust slowly in her grip, driving himself deeper into her mouth, careful not to choke her.

He savoured the experience for several minutes mindful not

to push beyond a certain point. This was purely for the pleasure of it, he had no intention of ejaculating yet. He wanted a lot more pleasure before he reached that point. An advantage of having climaxed so quickly the first time was that he could delay the final event for longer now, allow them both to wring the most from the experience.

He thrust into her mouth with agonising slowness, teasing himself and resisting the urge to go faster. *God that was good!* Her tongue swirled over the head, sending shivers through his body and tightening his balls. He panted, groaning softly. *So good...*

*Too good...*Pulling out of her mouth with a muffed groan, he sat back on his haunches and regarded her.

"What's wrong?" she asked.

"Nothing, I don't want you to make me come yet. That was a pure piece of indulgence."

"You like it?"

"Oh yes, very much," he leaned forward and kissed her again. "Now I'm going to pleasure you."

"But you already have," she protested.

"Not half, sweetheart. You won't be able to walk by the time I've finished with you," he said, moving down her body until he was between her splayed legs.

"That will be very awkward, I have to work tomorrow," she said playfully. Then she jumped and uttered a kind of squeak as he plunged his face into her delicious fragrant cunny and licked and kissed her. Spearing her with his tongue and lapping at her flesh.

He worked her relentlessly until she was feverish with wanting to come, writhing and clutching the sheets while he pushed his fingers in and out of her and lavished her bud with licking, sucking and kissing.

"Garmon!" She pushed up into him frantic, panting, moaning. His cock twitched and ached forcing to him bear down into the mattress with his hips to ease the aching.

He renewed his assault on her flesh and pushed her ruthlessly over the edge into a climax, savouring the cries of her pleasure and the pulsing of her flesh under his tongue.

Barely allowing her a moment to recover, he pushed her again to the peak and through another fall with his tongue, and his fingers. More gentle but relentless he pushed her into another and another until she was panting and limp and cried out in protest.

"Garmon please!"

He raised his head and grinned. "Had enough?"

"Please," she put out a hand.

He shook his head. "I don't think you've had enough yet."

"I have really!" she protested breathless and trembling.

"You want my cock? You want me to fuck you?"

"Ohh!" she collapsed back on the pillows, her legs falling open. "Yes! Yes! Fuck me!" she said to the ceiling, her lovely neck arched and her breasts on full display.

His cock leaked copiously at this display of debauched wantonness, his balls already tight, throbbed painfully. He rose over her, grabbing a pillow to fit under her bottom and gripping her hips, he speared her hard with his cock. She lay splayed below him, while he fucked her with hard deliberate strokes, his eyes feasting on the sight of her laid out and helpless in his grip.

"Do you like it, Genevra?" he asked his voice cracking with barely controlled lust.

"Yes!" she rolled her head on the pillows and clenched the sheets, her breasts bouncing with the movement of his thrusts as he jarred her whole body with the force of his fucking.

"God, Garmon, yes!" her voice rose, and then he felt it. The clench of her inner muscles as she strained against him, arching her back. He moved one hand to rub roughly over her bud to bring her off and the result was spectacular.

Her muscles pulled taught, and she groaned loudly, her body shuddering and the internal clenching became a ripple that made him groan helplessly and his cock quiver, teetering on the edge of coming.

He wrenched himself free of her grip, squeezed the base of his cock hard to stop himself coming and panted, watching her roll slowly sideways off the pillow, her legs coming together as she curled into herself moaning softly.

He leaned over her, stroking her hair off her face. "Are you alright?"

"Hmm," she nodded, her body writhing on the sheets.

He smiled. He recognised the signs. She had reached that point of over stimulation where her whole body was afire. He had hoped to achieve that with her but was surprised it had happened so quickly. He rolled her gently onto her stomach and pushing her tangled hair aside, kissed the back of her neck, which made her moan and writhe on the bed.

"It's all right sweetheart, I know what is happening. Your skin feels hypersensitive, doesn't it?" He stroked her back gently.

"Hmm." She rubbed her face into the pillow, pushing her bottom up.

"You feel all coiled up inside, don't you?" he swallowed the groan the sight of her wet swollen peach pushed up into his view provoked.

"Y-yes," her voice breathless, broken.

"Oh Genevra," he groaned leaning over her and kissing her back, her shoulders her spine, his hands caressing her skin. He gently lifted her beautiful round bottom up and placed the pillow under her tummy. Her hips writhed on it, she seemed almost insensible of what he was doing, lost in some erotic dreamscape of her own body's sensations.

Her breathing came in erratic pants, punctuated by little mewls and moans that made his sorely tried cock leak and twitch. Moving between her writhing legs, he slowly lowered his body on top of hers and slid the head of his cock along her wet swollen flesh.

He groaned with the pleasure of the sensation, and she jerked beneath him and gave an answering groan. Pulling back a fraction, he found and notched the head to her entrance and pushed gently but firmly inside her. She gasped and her back arched, he groaned and gripped her hips, kissing her back and then stretching forward and taking his weight on his hands and knees he lay on her full length. Rocking slowly, he pushed into her, leaning down he found her mouth, and kissed her. Then he reached under her to rub her gently while he slid in and out of her slowly and she moaned helplessly into another climax.

"That's it," he whispered kissing her neck and her cheek and her shoulder, rocking himself inside her and swirling her inexorably into another peak. She shook beneath him, her limbs tensing and going limp and tensing again as he wrung yet another surge of pleasure from her. She was panting and their skin was slick with sweat where they touched. The slap of their flesh meeting was audible between their laboured breath. He was perilously close to losing all control.

It was time, he couldn't hold back the nagging ache to come any longer. He gripped her hips and pulled back onto his haunches bringing her up with him onto her knees.

He massaged her gorgeous bottom, enjoying the feel of her buttocks in his hands, his thumbs separating them so that he could see himself pushing in and out of her wet cunny. His cock was red and glistening wet, swollen and veined and so fucking hard it hurt.

He pushed deeper, gripping her hips again as he sped up his thrusts, *God yes!* The pleasure, held at bay for so long, surged up and up and wound itself into a tight knot of exquisite, agonising, ravening, joy. And burst. His cock jerked within the confines of her hot tunnel and spilled his seed in a series of blissful shots that left him gutted and limp, collapsing on her back and pushing her back down onto the bed in a panting heap.

. . .

SHE WAS RUINED. She couldn't move. He rolled off her and lay panting beside her. But she couldn't even turn her head to look at him. What he had done to her, she couldn't begin to describe, or comprehend. Her body was jelly, boneless. Her lady parts were mashed, wet, swollen, beyond tender.

His hand on her back made her flinch. "Genevra?"

She swallowed. Her throat hurt.

"Genevra, sweetheart?"

She opened her mouth, but nothing came out but a huff of breath.

He removed the pillow and her body collapsed onto the mattress. He turned her over, and she flopped onto her back.

His expression of concern made her force out. "I'm all right." Her voice cracked.

He stroked the hair from her face, and then he disappeared from her view. She felt him get up from the bed, but she couldn't summon the will to turn her head and watch him.

He returned, sitting down on the edge of the bed and lifting her head with one hand, he offered her a drink. It was whisky, potent and fiery, it caught the back of her throat and made her cough. But the spirit brought some sense back to her limbs and when she had stopped coughing, she took another sip. He eased her head back onto the pillow and stroked her cheek.

"Better?"

"Hmm." she cleared her throat. "Yes. Thank you."

"I did warn you; you wouldn't be able to walk." he said with a smile.

"I didn't think you meant it literally," she said, attempting to match his light tone.

He put the glass on the bedside table and kissed her forehead.

He then climbed back into bed and eased her into his arms. "I think you have earned a rest."

She huffed a weary laugh, resting her head on his chest and closed her eyes. "I have to leave before dawn, my staff..."

"Hush, I'll make sure you get home in time, rest."

"Hmm..." sleep took her over the edge into darkness.

Garmon lay awake for some time listening to her breathing and wondered how a week was going to be enough to explore everything he wanted to with this woman.

He woke at half past two. A habit he had formed in childhood, when sleeping was hazardous at the best of times, was the ability to wake at a time he nominated to himself. Getting out of bed quietly, he pulled on a robe, poked up the fire and set a kettle on to boil some water.

He returned to the foot of the bed and watched Genevra sleeping. She lay on her back, her glorious light copper hair, a tangled halo round her head, her face relaxed. He would wake her at three. That would give her sufficient time to get home before her staff arrived.

Glancing at the clock he moved quietly into the sitting room where he rekindled the fire that had gone out and picking up the novel he was reading, he sat and lost himself in the fantasy world of Mrs Gaskill's Mysteries of Udolpho for twenty minutes.

Putting the book aside and rising at just before three, he went back into the bedroom. The kettle was boiled and taking a cloth he poured the hot water into the basin and turned to the bed. Sliding under the covers, he watched Genevra's sleeping face for a moment longer. A flash of his childhood surfaced, of his mother sleeping exhausted and of his reluctance to wake her as instructed. Pushing the memory aside, he bent his head and kissed Genevra's lips gently.

She woke with a start, her eyes springing open in alarm.

"Good morning," he said with an amused smile at her shocked expression. He could see the moment she recalled where she was and how she got there and what had transpired before she slept.

"What time is it? I have to go-"

"It is 3:00 am, and you have plenty of time." He watched her scrambling out of bed and added, "There is hot water in the basin."

"Thank you," she said going to the basin and making a hasty toilet, shivering slightly despite the fire.

While she was doing that, he gathered up her strewn garments and when she turned from the basin he said, "Let me be your maid." He had done this often enough as a lad in the brothel for the girls and his mother.

She stared up at him, slightly dazed and watched as he knelt to offer her a stocking. She put out a foot, balancing herself with a hand on his head. His fingers lingered momentarily as he fastened her garters into place. And he resisted the temptation to kiss her sweet mound. If he started, he might not be able to stop, and she really had, had enough tonight and besides he didn't want to make her late.

Rising he helped her on with her chemise, laced up her corset and then her dress, knelt again to help her on with her boots. She clutched at her hair. "Do you have a comb?"

He nodded and produced a comb and brush, when she went to take them from him, he said, "Let me."

She turned her back in acquiescence, and he carefully worked the tangles out of her hair before plaiting and pinning it for her. Dressing a lady's hair had been another of his duties. "There, perfectly respectable," he said turning her to the mirror on the dresser, his hands on her upper arms.

She looked up at him over her shoulder. "Thank you."

He smiled and kissed her hair. "You're welcome. My carriage will pick you up at eleven tonight. You will find it out the front now waiting for you."

"You–you want to continue, tonight? You wouldn't prefer a break?" she said turning towards him.

He shook his head. "No, but we will explore other things tonight, I shan't tax you so, I promise."

She nodded, lowering her head.

He tipped it up, with a finger under her chin and kissed her lips gently. "Thank you."

She swallowed. "Thank you, I didn't know- I've never-"

"I know. I'm sorry if I pushed you too far-"

"No!" she put a hand on his chest. "No, it was wonderful, just overwhelming. I feel strange this morning, light and sort of out of kilter. I can't explain it."

He kissed her forehead. "You had better go before I forget my good intentions. Until tonight." He cupped her face and kissed her mouth again. Letting her go reluctantly, he stepped aside and escorted her to the door. He helped her on with her cloak and then escorted her down the stairs and out into the street, where he handed her into his carriage. He watched the carriage turn the corner before he went back inside.

He had a great deal to accomplish today, because he had achieved fuck all yesterday, he'd been so distracted by thoughts of Genevra. Today he would do better.

He didn't.

CHAPTER 5

Six weeks later

Diana wiped down the gaming tables with a damp cloth and moved the chairs back into place, working her way round the room, tidying as she went. The large chamber was empty, it being eight in the morning and the last of the clientele having left at seven. The air was stale with sweat, tobacco, alcohol fumes and the faint acrid smell of fear that men who'd lost everything left behind. The windows along the outer wall stood open in an attempt to shift the stale odour and refresh the room ahead of the new influx of clients to be expected just after noon. She gathered up a pack of cards that had been strewn across a table and fallen on the floor. She was just tidying them neatly into a stack when Connor Mor strode through the archway from the front salon. He came over and slid an arm round her waist.

"Good mornin' my lovely," he said with a smile creasing his handsome features. "Have you seen Garmon?"

She eased out of his embrace and nodded to the door at the back of the room. "He's in his office, waiting for you, didn't Carlos tell you?"

"Yes, but I was busy."

"You know Uncle doesn't like to be kept waiting." she said patiently, avoiding his second attempt to kiss her.

He sighed and inclined his head. "Any idea what he wants?"

She shrugged and went back to wiping tables. His expression tightened with displeasure, and he headed towards the door to Garmon Lovell's office. Passing into the room, he flicked the door behind him, but it didn't close completely. With a glance round to make sure no one else was about, Diana scuttled over quietly and put her ear to the crack.

There was silence for a few moments, only the scratching of a quill on parchment which told her, that her uncle was keeping Connor waiting just as Connor had made him wait. Her lips twitched at the games men played to assert their power over one another. Connor was on the losing end of this one. It was Uncle that held the reins and paid their wages. Connor was as hostage to Garmon's whims as she was. Her role was to grace the tables for the entertainment of the guests. As Uncle Garmon covered all her living expenses and gowns, he didn't see the need to pay her an actual wage. Fortunately for her, the tips were generous. Not that he stinted her on dresses and such, but it was nice to have some money to call her own. She had been saving as much of it as she could for her plan if she ever got the opportunity to execute it.

"I have an assignment for you, Connor." Her uncle's gravelly drawl came to her clearly through the crack in the door.

"Aye?"

"The 6th Duke of Mowbray is dead and his debts haven't been paid. He owes me thirty-five thousand pounds, and I want my money."

"A bit difficult if the man's dead."

"I want you to collect it from his heir, Harcourt. I understand he's holed up in Leicestershire at Harcourt Place. I have it on the best authority that he is planning on coming to London with a collection of jewels worth at least as much as the debt his grandfather owed me. I want you to get those jewels and bring them to me. My informant tells me he plans to ride, alone. He should be easy pickings."

The loud thudding of her pulse in her ears obscured Connor's response to this request as Diana, leaned against the wall, her legs weak with excitement. At last, an opportunity to secure what was rightfully hers and put her plan into action. She removed her apron, draped the cleaning cloth over a chair back and left the room rapidly, almost running up the stairs to her room.

Changing quickly into breeches, boots, and a heavy serviceable cloak, she picked up the bag she had already packed for this adventure and stole down the back stairs to the mews. Here she swiftly saddled her horse Sugar, a gift from her father, and urged it quietly out of the back alley and into the London street. She needed to be away from St James's before anyone noticed she was gone.

CHAPTER 6

Anthony was not in a good mood. But then, when was he ever? His thoughts on this occasion were darker than usual. He knew he was not a good man and had spent most of his life not regretting it. But his crowning iniquity, shooting his sister Anne, had given him pause. Admittedly it was an accident. In fact, it was Anne's fault for getting in the way of two men in the throes of a duel. But the act, accident or not, caused him some angst. It had come at the end of a day of heinous acts, for which he had been resoundingly punished by a beautiful woman and the man she loved. That rankled. For a man who never admitted to loving anyone, he had come whisker close to loving Viviana Torrington and the loss still itched like a healing wound.

If he believed in God, which he didn't, he would think the almighty was trying to punish him. For on top of all of the misfortune that dogged him as a result of his attempt to force Viviana to marry him, he was now saddled with the biggest problem of all.

Refilling his glass of scotch and staring morosely into the fire, he loosened his lace cravat and sighed. He should be happy, he'd inherited his grandfather's title and estate, which he had long coveted, but it was a poisoned chalice. For the estate was mortgaged to the hilt and drowning in debt, a debt he had no way of servicing as he had just discovered, after two months of attempting to break the entail. He was saddled with it, he couldn't sell any part of it. He had made a list of everything he *could* sell, yet he feared it still wasn't enough to put a serious dent in the looming pile of debt he was facing. But he had to try.

Tomorrow he would ride to London to sell the most precious items in his grandfather's collection. A set of heirlooms that miraculously, through all his vicissitudes, the old man had hung onto. He could have given the task to his grandfather's man of affairs, but he didn't trust the old devil. He wanted to see for himself how much the haul would realise. But he knew it wouldn't be enough. He needed another way to restore his fortunes. His original plan to marry an heiress was still the most likely way out of this mess. Albeit one, he was strangely reluctant to embrace, after the disastrous failure with Viviana.

He smiled sardonically at the flames, remembering the damage she had inflicted on him. Remembering the fire in her eyes and her stunning beauty, her luscious figure that drove him wild with wanting her. *Could any woman ever eclipse her?* He doubted it. He'd kept a string of mistresses and had affairs with multiple married women and none had come close to trapping him. Until he fell victim to Viviana's wild spirit and stunning dark beauty.

But then again, when had he ever expected to find love in marriage? He knew better than that. Love was an illusion, at best a fleeting thing of physical passion, soon burnt out and turned to bitter ashes. The example of his parents' marriage had taught him that. His mother's affaires, his father's fury, and retaliatory flaunting of his mistresses. The crocodile tears and shouting, the broken furniture, and in some ways, the worst part of all: the brief peace when they made it up in passionate and extravagant style. All the while Anthony waited for the next betrayal to tear it all down again. His parents passionate, on again, off again, love affair had made his childhood a roller coaster of drama and bitterness. It engendered both a deep-seated anger towards the world and a bitter distrust of women in particular. *There was only one woman he trusted, his little sister Annie, and he shot her for fucks sake!* He winced internally and swallowed another fiery shot of whisky. *Love was an illusion and not for the likes of him.*

But the happiness Annie had found with Denzil Elliot, the Earl of Stanton, caused a persistent thin thread of hope to rear its head, only to be quashed with a resounding slap. He neither needed nor wanted love. *Because,* whispered a voice softly in the back of his head, *you don't deserve it.*

His lip curled viciously and, he threw his glass at the fireplace. This did little to assuage his feelings. He picked up the decanter and took several large swallows of the fiery amber liquid. It burned his throat and warmed his stomach, a familiar temporary peace spread through his body, chasing the shadows of doubt away. For now.

~

MID-MORNING THE FOLLOWING **day**

Connor Mor approached the dairy at Harcourt House, via a circuitous route as he had no desire to advertise his presence to anyone of note in the household. In his experience, his best informants were chambermaids or dairy maids. In this case the dairy, located at the rear of the premises away from the immediate view of the house seemed an ideal location to find an obliging maid to give him the information he sought.

Propping himself against the door jamb of the dairy, he enjoyed the view of a young woman bent over, reaching for something on a low shelf. She located a large earthenware dish, and straightened her face slightly flushed, and turned humming a tune. At the sight of him she squeaked, almost dropping the dish. He leaped forward to save it and said with his trademark smile.

"Don't be alarmed, my dear! I mean you no harm."

"Who are you?" she asked, her eyes going wide as she took in his face and form. Setting down the dish absently, she fiddled with a curl that had come loose from her bun, and he stepped closer to capitalise on the effect of his presence.

"I was wonderin'," he said stepping closer. "If you could tell me if the Duke was at home?"

"You've just missed him. Left at the crack he did, well on the road to Lunnon by now."

Connor suppressed a curse and produced a coin which he flipped carelessly. "Was he riding or did he take the coach, given the weather."

"Oh, he was riding, mad he is. Worse than the old Duke, and he was a curmudgeon and no mistake! The new Duke though," she grimaced." Glad to see the back o' him we are! Nastiest temper this side of hell if you ask me. Allus was according to Mrs Graves, she's the housekeeper. All of the Harcourts are hellraisers. Seemed to me though he was like a wounded animal, snarling at every one and snapping their heads off for no good reason."

"Was he riding alone?"

"Oh aye, mighty fond of his own company he is. Mind you, I daresay nobody'd abide him if they didn't a have to. The neighbours all tried to call, and he wouldn't have a bar of any of 'em."

He flipped her the coin which she caught and pocketed expertly. "Thank you my sweet. Got a kiss for a traveller?"

She dimpled and offered her face with a smile. He lifted her chin with a finger and kissed her pretty lips. "You've not seen me aye?"

She cocked her head and said saucily, "For another kiss I'll undertake to be as blind as Mother Hubbard."

He grinned and took her in his arms to execute a thorough kiss.

He left her pink faced and swollen lipped, waving him from the door of the dairy as he picked his way back to his horse through mud and remounted, heading out into the gathering gloom. It would be pissing down in sheets before the day was over he predicted morosely. The Duke wasn't only one suffering from a bad temper. Connor's normally sunny disposition was suffering mightily for this wild goose chase.

∽

THE DUKE WAS WELL on the road to London by mid-morning, riding his gelding Midnight. It was beastly cold, and threatening rain. There was still no sun, the skies being leaden and dark like every day before it. He had sent his valet with the coach and his luggage ahead of him, content to ride in spite of inclement weather, it suited his mood, which hadn't improved overnight.

Once he reached London, he would sell the collection he had in his saddlebag and then turn his attention to finding an heiress to marry. It was the only course open to him at this juncture; he didn't have enough funds to win back a fortune at the tables, as much as he would prefer that avenue. The prospect of tying himself for life to a woman he would no doubt despise in a matter of months, filled him with a depressing lack of enthusiasm.

He'd call on his sister Anne and seek her assistance in finding him a suitable bride. There must be an heiress or two in this year's crop of debutantes. *But none to rival Viviana*, the voice in his head taunted. With an internal growl of frustration, he pushed thoughts of Viviana away. She was out of his reach now, but acknowledging that, didn't stop him from indulging a pleasantly distracting dream of spitting her spouse, Captain Jack Elliot on the end of a rapier. But no, killing Jack would make her loathe him all the more. Viviana was never his, despite his deeply held conviction at the time that she was made for him.

He shook himself out of his melancholy, taking in his surroundings. The road was muddy, rutted, and narrow at this point, with thick brush on either side. The light was poor, despite it being only midday and looking at the sky he was likely to get a drenching before long. He pulled his hat down over his face and hauled his thick woollen cloak round him against the sudden flurry of icy wind. It might even snow, he concluded morosely.

He was rudely jerked out of his thoughts when a cloaked and masked youth on a grey, dappled mare emerged into the road in front of him. The slender figure was brandishing a pistol and rasped in a high-pitched voice, "Stand and deliver!" Utter surprise made his jaw drop.

DIANA, her heart thumping wildly in her breast, held the pistol steady and repeated her command.

"Stand and deliver, Sirrah!"

Her quarry brought his mount to a halt and sat looking at her. He was very like his grandsire by all accounts, but then red hair, those distinctive dark brows and blue eyes were hard to mistake. At least she had the right man. She hadn't expected him to be so big however, he seemed huge, swathed in a dark cloak on the back of a large, black horse.

Tightening her grip on the pistol, she said grimly, "Dismount, step away from your horse and put your hands behind your head."

Her victim's lips twitched in amusement. "And if I don't?" His voice was deep and an involuntary shiver ran down her spine. No doubt prompted by the chill wind.

"I shall be forced to shoot you, Sir."

"It's your Grace actually," he said slightly apologetically, but infuriatingly still not budging from the back of his horse.

She clenched her teeth and said, "Mowbray, please dismount and do as I say. Or I *will* shoot you!"

"You know who I am." The smile evaporated slowly from his handsome face, and he frowned.

"Of course, I do. Now get *down*!" She said with growing asperity.

"I don't think so," he said with a drawl, his right hand, which had been resting on the pommel of his saddle, slipped beneath his cloak. She caught the movement, and guessing that he was going for his gun, took aim and fired.

The report of the pistol was loud in the damp air and smoke wafted from the weapon making her nose twitch as the horse reared and its rider lurched in the saddle. Bringing the horse under control with his knees, he brought his hand up to his shoulder. "You hit me!" his indignant voice made her bite back an hysterical laugh.

"I told you I would!" she said, reaching for her second pistol and raising it. "Do I have to do it again?"

His hand came away bloody from his shoulder and the growing stain spread through the fabric of his cloak. He swayed in the saddle, his face blanching with pain.

"Damn! Not again!" His voice was hoarse and faint.

She watched in alarm as he sagged sideways, and she leaped from her own horse but could do nothing to stop him sliding off the horse into the mud. He was too heavy for her to hold and all she could do was ease him onto the muddy ground. He smelt of something spicy, sandalwood? A little shiver skated over her skin as she took in his pallor and the lines in his face that spoke of pain.

She had meant to graze him, but it seemed she may have hit a more vital spot than she intended. She bent over him, lifting the cloak to inspect the wound as panic skated along her nerves making her breathing erratic and her vision blurry. The bullet had torn through the cloak, coat, and shirt beneath and his arm was bloody to the elbow, the wound in his shoulder seeping conspicuously.

His hat had come off as she lowered him to the ground, revealing the full glory of his red hair. His pallor was alarming, and he appeared to have lost consciousness. Her heart contracted with near panic, but the purpose of this ill-fated event was at her hand. Forcing herself to rise, she stepped over him and went to the saddlebags searching through them feverishly for the object she sought.

In the first, she found a shirt, stockings and two neck cloths, in the second one, under another shirt and waistcoat, she found a heavy drawstring bag. She pulled the neck of the bag open and looked inside. A collection of jewels met her gaze, necklaces, bracelets, and the piece she was looking for, her mother's brooch. A large four-leaf clover design with emeralds for each of the leaves set in gold. She slipped the brooch into her pocket and seized the two neck cloths, refastening the clasps on the saddlebags.

Returning to the Duke, she bent over him, her pulse thumping wildly, and pulled back the cloak to reveal his torn jacket. As she had already noted, the arm was soaked to the elbow. Using one neck cloth as a pad, she wrapped the other as tightly as she could around his shoulder. He came round just as she was tying it off. His eyes fluttered then suddenly opened widely, and a big hand grasped her upper arm.

"Who are you?" His breathing was laboured and her pulse skipped and jumped with fear. His blue eyes bored into her, fierce and dark with a smouldering rage that hit her in the solar plexus. She swallowed, striving to cover the flutter of heat that went through her like a bolt of lightning. But she couldn't stop the flush that rolled up her neck to her cheeks. Fortunately, the mask covered the upper half of her face and the light was dim enough that he might not notice her embarrassment.

Had he penetrated her disguise? Divined her gender? She was

conscious of a strong sense of his masculinity, despite his seemingly helpless position, lying prone in the middle of the road. He was exceedingly handsome and angry. Very angry. Her stomach muscles tightened with a thrill of fear and something else. His mouth, those beautifully carved lips, showed a grimace of pain.

"My name would mean nothing to you, your Grace. The tourniquet should stop the bleeding." She pulled at his grip, but his fingers tightened, digging into her arm painfully.

"Help me up," he said squeezing her arm savagely.

She shook her head and reefed her arm out of his grip. It pulsed, aching from his tight hold, he would have left bruises. Backing away she said, "I will send someone to help you."

"Damn you, come back here!" He tried to get his feet under him and fell back into the mud cursing.

She scrambled away from him, her heart thudding, how could she do this? She mounted her mare, Sugar, and turned her, setting off down the road at full pelt. Just before the bend in the road hid him from her sight, she looked back to see him on his knees, one hand reaching for the saddle strap to pull himself up. Rounding the bend, she urged the mare into a gallop. She scanned the hedges on either side of the road for sign of a house or hostelry where she could leave word of his plight, hating herself for leaving him. If he should die... Her heart thudded in time with the mares' hooves, and she resisted the urge to turn back. She had what she came for, she just needed to get away. If he caught her, she would hang or at best be transported. Neither fate was how she planned her life to go. Touching the brooch in her pocket with one gloved hand she sent a prayer to her mother's departed soul and spurred Sugar onward.

ANTHONY SWAYED IN THE SADDLE, his vision darkening and for a moment he thought he might pass out again, nausea rolled through him in waves. Cold seeped through his sodden cloak making him shudder, and pain radiated from his shoulder like a lighthouse beacon, pulsing with his heartbeat. By some damnable mischance the confounded miscreant had hit the wound Viviana gave him three months ago. The shock and searing pain of the bullet hitting his left shoulder had made him reel and lose consciousness, he barely remembered sliding from the saddle to the ground. When he came to, it was to the tug of the makeshift tourniquet the villain had tied to his shoulder. He supposed he should be grateful the young varmint had done even that for him, but what possessed the creature to hold him up in the first place?

He checked his pockets for his fob watch and wallet. Both were still there, as were his heavy signet ring and the pin in his cravat. Not simple robbery then. He slewed round in the saddle reaching for the saddlebag that contained the jewels and feeling with his good hand he found the bag and hefted its weight. The jewels were there too. What in damnation did the devil want? What was worth shooting him for? Was it some enemy he had wronged? But who? No one that fitted the youth's likeness occurred to him. Surely no one would hire such a stripling to shoot him in the middle of the day on the London road? It made no sense. But then his mind was fuddled with pain, perhaps something would occur to him when he was clearer headed.

Reaching into his pocket he took out his flask of whisky and took a generous swig. Ignoring the screaming pain in his shoulder, he kicked Midnight into a walk. The horse had been remarkably docile throughout the proceedings, he patted him in gratitude and increased the pace, which jarred his shoulder abominably. He had to catch the damned thief and make him talk. He would get to the bottom of this mystery and the menace would be strung up for his knavery. He had balls though, he must give him that. He'd shown no fear, just a kind of desperate exasperation.

The jolting pace of the trot was unbearable, and he spurred Midnight into a canter. Could Midnight catch the mare? He was a bigger animal with longer strides. A strange horse for a highway man to be riding. More a lady's mount than– the memory of a scent of rosewater underlying the faint salty tang of sweat and leather that clung to the thief as he- no she! bent over him. Below the mask, the soft jaw line, innocent of any hint of whiskers... the shapely lips, rose pink and kissably full... The body had been swathed head to toe in a long cloak, boots and breeches hinted at beneath, a jacket, waistcoat and neck cloth, gloves on his hands and that damnable loo mask. A female though under all that, he'd swear.

What would drive a woman to such a desperate and foolhardy act? He didn't know, but he was damned well going to find out. He urged Midnight into a gallop as great drops of icy rain began to fall and the crack of thunder reverberated round the hills to either side. This was followed almost immediately by the slash of lightening forking to the ground up ahead. The Duke bared his teeth in a grimace and hunkered down in the saddle. That little wretch was going to pay for putting a hole in his shoulder, and she wasn't going to like the price!

CHAPTER 7

The rain was torrential and the road soon awash with mud, the intermittent thunder and lightning made Sugar jumpy, forcing her to slow to a walk. Diana was soaked to the skin in short order. She removed the velvet mask so that she could see. Not that it helped much. The rain was so heavy and the light so dim it was like riding through a waterfall at dawn when the sun had not yet breached the horizon. Visibility was barely a foot or two in front or behind and to make it worse, rain lashed her face, making it impossible to see anyway. She was shrouded in a curtain of icy water in a grey and muddy landscape. She kept doggedly on, her head down to protect her face from the incessant rain, fervently hoping the tempest would ease soon; such a heavy storm couldn't last long, surely.

Minutes later, Sugar baulked, tossing her head and neighing but refusing to budge one step further. Squinting through the rain Diana made out the shape of a fallen tree, its great trunk and thick branches blocking the road.

"Damn and blast!" she muttered. There was no help for it, she would have to leave the road to get past the tree. Backing Sugar up, she sought the edge of the road and a break in the hedges that bounded it. She had to go back a fair way to find one and then persuade a reluctant Sugar to jump the water filled ditch to reach the field beyond. The ditch was almost a small stream by now, muddy water eddying around stones and clumps of grass, overflowing onto the road and into the field, turning it into a marsh. She got Sugar over it safely, and they splashed through the puddles towards higher ground.

The rain began to ease slightly, and she spied a stand of trees ahead that offered some hope of shelter. She set Sugar in that direction just as another thunderclap and lightning strike rent the air, it was so close it made her body jolt and Sugar screamed with fright, bolting for the trees. She shouted trying to bring Sugar under control, but the mare ignored her, heading hell for leather towards the spinney. They reached the trees and Sugar slowed and then stopped, dropping her head, her sides heaving. The canopy lessened the fall of water and muffled some of the sound. It also blocked most of the ambient light, what there was of it. Diana dismounted and patted the mare, trying to soothe her, even though her own pulse was jumpy and her nerves shredded. That last lightning bolt had been too damned close for comfort.

The thunder rolled again, but this time it was further away and the rain noticeably eased a bit more. The storm was passing, Diana heaved a sigh of relief and finding a large tree root above ground, she sat down on it, a sudden weakness flooding through her limbs. She began to shake and realised dimly that she was suffering from the effects of delayed shock. She wrapped her sodden cloak more tightly round her and clenched her teeth against their chattering.

She shouldn't have left him, not in this foul storm. Even if he managed to get himself into the saddle, he would likely pass out again. What if her bandage hadn't stopped the bleeding? He could bleed to death. He needed medical treatment, the bullet was still lodged in his shoulder. He could be dead by now! Thoughts stabbed at her, accusatory, blaming. Her stomach roiled and she swallowed bile. She closed her eyes, rocking herself in her distress, tears seeping out and mingling with the rainwater on her cheeks.

The mare snorted, forcing her eyes open in a sudden premonition of danger. Her heart thudded with alarm, her nerves seemingly shattered as another distant roll of thunder sounded, followed by a distant flash. In the snatch of light, a shape moved in the darkness. She rose to her feet slowly, trying to track the movement of the shape, which resolved itself into the outline of a horse and rider, heading in her direction.

Sugar tossed her head and neighed, shifting her feet restlessly and the other horse answered, moving more swiftly towards them. A great black shadow with a swaying figure atop its back, swathed in a dark cloak and a wide brimmed old-fashioned hat. It was him! How he had found her she didn't know, but the fact that he had, meant he was still alive and that consideration outweighed all others for the moment. Even the threat he represented faded in the face of her relief at not being a murderer–yet!

"Found you!" said that deep, delicious voice hoarsely as he swayed dangerously in the saddle. She went to his stirrup as he dismounted heavily, leaning against his horse's flank. It was too late to run and concern for him kept her still in any case. Would he recognise her?

"Sir, you're hurt!" she said, tipping her head back to look him in the face. She was right he was big, well over six foot and broad through the shoulders.

"Aye and it's your fault!" he said, his hand reaching out to grab her arm. "But you won't escape me again, you little wretch, what did you mean by it?"

"I don't know what you're talking about sir," she said, trying to pull her arm out of his iron grip. She would have bruises all up and down her arms before this day was over. The man was a brute. He was clearly not at deaths door as she had feared. But that didn't mean he wouldn't die of his injuries if he didn't receive medical attention, and soon.

"Don't lie to me, I recognise your horse. There can't be two women masquerading as boys loose on the London road on a day like this!" He hissed, shaking her.

She sighed and shook a wet hank of hair out of her face. The pins had come loose and her hair was tumbling out from under her hat.

The rain had stopped and the cloud cover lightened sufficiently that they could now see each other's faces.

"Who are you and what the bloody hell do you mean by holding me up and shooting me?"

Her heart thumped and skipped, and she swallowed, trying to think of a reason for her bizarre behaviour other than the truth. "It was a wager!" she blurted.

His eyes widened, and he surveyed her face with cynical scorn. "I don't believe you. If you were the stripling you counterfeited to be I might, for young boys are monumentally stupid, but no girl would do such a thing for such a paltry reason."

She shrugged and looked away. "Believe what you like, it's the truth."

He shook his head, the movement of which caught in the corner of her eye. He let go of her arm and reached with his good hand to turn her face up to his. "You're a lady by your diction, young and-" his eyes surveyed her face, his mouth twitching up in a slight smile that, made something warm bloom in her centre of her chest. "Very pretty."

She flushed and tried to move her head, but his fingers held her still and his eyes burned into hers with a look that sent that rush of heat lower.

"Ladies don't normally get around in breeches and shoot strangers on the highway. I repeat, who are you, and what are you about?"

She bit her lip and looked at him mulishly.

"Well, I suppose they don't need your name to string you up!" he said viciously, squeezing her jaw.

"Ah!" she cried out in sudden pain.

He let her go instantly, an expression she couldn't read flitting across his face. He turned away a moment, his good hand clenching by his side. The other hung uselessly, bloody water still dripping off the cloth and staining his hand. "I'm sorry, my damnable temper!" he muttered. His words so low she had to strain to hear them.

Her stomach muscles tightened, and she wondered what it would take to get away from him. He was dangerous, he was also wounded and that was her fault. He could have her arrested, yet she needed to ensure he got proper medical attention before she escaped his clutches, or she would never be able to live with herself. She swallowed, a plan beginning to form in her head.

"Is your wound still bleeding?" she asked watching him warily.

"I don't know," he said, sounding tired. "It hurts like the devil. You hit a previous wound and reopened it."

"Oh, well you must have moved, I only meant to graze you. I'm quite a good shot as a rule."

"Are you now?" he turned back to face her, his expression sardonic. "Quite the accomplished damsel, aren't you?"

She grimaced. "I've no end of accomplishments, Your Grace, none of which belong in the drawing room."

"I gathered as much." he scowled at her in frustration. "At the risk of repeating myself, what is your damned name? You obviously know mine."

"I do, your Grace. Sir Anthony Harcourt, 7th Duke of Mowbray."

He bowed in acknowledgement and waited. She sighed and curtsied in return. "I am Diana Lovell. Miss Diana Lovell."

His eyebrows rose, and then he frowned in effort of recall. "Lovell? The only Lovell I know is Lord Peter Lovell-"

"My father," she admitted, a flush she couldn't suppress rising to her cheeks. "He's dead -"

"Killed by my grandsire!" He glared at her. "So, that is it? Revenge? Did you mean to kill me then?"

"No! Of course not!"

"I don't think I believe you. You're just not as good a shot as you claim."

"No! I swear, I'm no murderer. Why would I bandage your arm if I meant you to die? I could have left you to bleed out, I didn't do that."

"Then what reason did you have for holding me up?" He reached for her again and the horse shifted nudging his injured shoulder.

"Fuck!" he cursed loudly, clutching his arm, his eyes closed and his teeth bit down on his lower lip. His face was appreciably whiter than moments before, and he swayed on his feet.

She grabbed him round the waist, taking some of his weight as he sagged, his breathing hoarse. "Damn!" he swore, putting an arm round her to steady himself. "There's a flask in my breast pocket, get it out, will you?"

She reached in under his jacket, her hand encountering the cloth of his waistcoat and the heat of his body, the muscles beneath. Her fingers stayed over his chest a moment and then turned to find the pocket and withdraw the flask. His arm tightened momentarily about her waist and a wave of heat rolled through her body, staining her cheeks. She pulled back, unscrewed the cap, and offered him the flask, his good hand came up to take it from her.

"Thank you." He took a draught, his eyes closed. After a second sip, he opened his eyes, and offered the flask to her. "Here, it will warm you, you're soaked and freezing."

Could he feel her shaking? It wasn't the cold but his proximity that had her trembling like a ninny. This man was big and dangerous, even injured as he was, he could overpower her if he chose. She had met many men through the gaming hell over the years but none who affected her as he did. She took the flask and tipped it up taking a long swallow. The fiery liquid filled her mouth and slid down her throat, exploding in a warm burst in her belly, fanning out from her solar plexus and steadying her nerves.

She wiped her mouth with her sleeve and offered it back. "Thank you."

"Put it back in my pocket," he said, his voice husky and low. She blinked up at him, her lips parting slightly as he tightened his grip on her waist with his good arm. She rescrewed the cap, reached up and pushed the flask back into the pocket. Her hand slid out and dragged across his stomach to come to rest on his hip. Her pulse beat faster and her ill-disguised bosom swelled as she pulled in a desperate breath, her fingers flexing on his hip. His eyes, molten blue, blazed down at her, holding her mesmerised. "You make a very pretty youth, Miss Lovell," he murmured, lowering his head.

His intent was clear, he meant to kiss her, and she should be shoving him away, kneeing him in the cods even. She'd had plenty of practice evading unwelcome advances from men since she had entered her uncle's employ at the gaming hell. But with dawning comprehension she realised she didn't want to push him away. Just for once she wanted to feel what it was like, to be kissed by an attractive man who knew what he was doing. And she had absolutely no doubt the Duke would know what he was about, his reputation was every bit as bad as his grandsire's had been.

And perhaps that was his weakness. She needed some way to dissuade him from handing her over to a magistrate to be sentenced.

. . .

Anthony, dizzy with loss of blood and pain, wondered for a moment if he had lost consciousness again and had fallen into a fever dream. How else to account for the sensation of being burned alive, by the press of her body against his? The heat between them was palpable, and he knew the moment she realised it by the change in her eyes, which he discovered were a disconcerting violet grey. It was impossible to tell the colour of her hair, for it was wet, but he suspected an unremarkable brown, like her eyebrows. Her skin was flawless and soft, as soft as her enticing mouth. His arm tightened around her slender waist, pressing the soft cushions of her breasts against his chest. Everything about her was damnably, deliciously soft. Without further thought he lowered his head and pressed his lips to hers.

The tingling explosion of pleasure took his breath and poleaxed him with a surge of lust that thickened and lengthened his cock in instant burning need. The pain in his shoulder was forgotten in the avalanche of pleasure flooding his body, as her lips pressed back and parted for his tongue. Miss Lovell was no innocent it seemed. His hand moved lower to cup her bottom, moving up under the skirt of her jacket to clasp and squeeze through the fabric of her breeches. He pressed her closer against his rigid cock, straining behind his falls.

His lips moved over hers, teasing and persuading, his tongue delving and tasting, provoking an unexpectedly fierce response. The lady moulded herself against him, and kissed him back with bold hunger, eliciting an involuntary groan of appreciation. Unthinking, he attempted to move his injured arm to hold her closer and a shot of excruciating pain took his breath and made him break the kiss.

"Bloody hell!" he swore, closing his eyes momentarily. He breathed through the pain which subsided into a dull throbbing ache that made him feel sick.

"Sorry, Miss Lovell," he managed after a moment. "I'm in no fit state for dalliance."

Her eyes, cloudy with desire, cleared, and she pulled back, visibly composing herself, only her heightened colour and swollen lips gave away what they had been doing moments before. He swallowed a curse, what he wouldn't give to have her under him, he'd make her sigh and gasp, moan, and scream. But right now, he was struggling to stay upright. The desires of his cock would have to wait.

"You need that bullet removed," she said, with a frown of concern, every bit the demure damsel again. An odd contrast with her shocking attire.

"You're right, I do." he admitted.

"Can you ride? We need to find a doctor." He noted the use of the word 'we' with satisfaction. She intended to stay with him for the nonce. That was good news, if she chose to elude him now, he doubted his ability to chase her down. But chase her down he would if it killed him. He was going to get to the bottom of the mystery that was Miss Diana Lovell, and in the process, he was going to have her, in every possible way his imagination could conjure.

"Yes, the village of Markfield should not be far from here." He congratulated himself on the calm tone of his voice. It wouldn't do to let the lady know how much he craved her; if he was right, and she was as experienced as he suspected, she could use that against him. He turned to Midnight and placed his foot in the stirrup, hauling himself into the saddle one handed.

She mounted her horse easily, swinging a leg over the saddle and urging the mare forward. They emerged from the trees and crossed the sodden field back to the muddy, badly rutted road and set themselves towards the village of Markfield.

During the ride they composed the story they would provide when they arrived at the only hostelry that Markfield boasted, the Bull's Head. She would be his young cousin and ward, Dean

Collier. "Sent down from Eaton and entrusted to my care while your sire is on the continent. I will leave it to your fertile imagination to devise the cause of your expulsion." said the Duke with a slight smile.

She liked his smile, she decided.

"We were set upon by highway men, but your enthusiasm with a firearm saw them off, and we were saved from the indignity of being robbed. Although not before one of the miscreants managed to wing me. Are you happy with that version of events?" he said.

She nodded. "You do not intend to have me charged?"

He looked across at her with a sardonic curl of his lips. "Not yet, I may change my mind, it really depends on whether you decide to tell me the truth. And what that truth is." His tone made her shiver. Or perhaps it was just the cold wind slicing through her soaked garments. The heat they had shared briefly under the trees had faded leaving a stale achy feeling in her pelvis. She could use his desire for her against him, but she needed to be careful she wasn't caught in her own web. She couldn't deny the fire his kisses had ignited in her. He was dangerous to her in a way she hadn't anticipated.

CHAPTER 8

It was nearing four o'clock when they arrived at the Bull's Head. Dusk was closing in, storm clouds had regathered, threatening more rain and the sky's meagre light was largely swallowed up by the grey mass overhead.

The Landlord, a portly middle-aged man tsked over their news and lamented what the world was coming to.

"I will send my young man to fetch the doctor at once. But we are full as we can hold your Grace, I've only the one room to offer you..."

"That will be fine, my cousin can sleep on the floor, he is young!' The Duke threw her a smirk and she visibly bit back her fury.

"You may regret that coz, I snore!" She said with a look that promised retribution.

"I expect I'll sleep like the dead, after the day we have had," he retorted. And added for her ears only, "Unless you plan to smother me in my sleep?"

She shook her head and murmured back, "You deserve I should, but I won't. I told you I'm not a murderer."

"If you'll follow me, your Grace?" the Landlord led them

towards the stairs and Diana followed carrying a saddlebag over each shoulder. "You're in luck your Grace, our best room was just vacated this morning, I hope you will find the accommodations satisfactory. I'll have food and hot water sent up straight away, and the doctor as soon as he arrives."

Anthony took the stairs slowly, trying to hide the effort it took just to put one foot in front of the other. He felt damnable and feared he had lost more blood than he'd realised. He was also beginning to feel uncomfortably cold. The sort of cold that presaged a fever.

The landlord brought them to a halt before a door at the end of the corridor, and using the large key, unlocked and flung the heavy oak door wide. The room was large as Inn rooms went, dominated by an old-fashioned tester bed draped in heavy red brocade. Two sash windows in the far wall featured matching curtains and the bedside tables and dresser were made from the same deep cherry mahogany as the bed. The fireplace was centred on the wall opposite the bed. Two armchairs, also upholstered in the brocade were positioned in front of the fireplace. The preponderance of red was overwhelming, but Anthony was not in the mood to be fussy; the prospect of lying down was more than welcome.

The landlord bustled in and began lighting the candelabra with the candlestick in his hand and the maid, who had followed them up the stairs, knelt to light the fire. The landlord and maid withdrew with the former making promises of food and his best wine. Anthony shed his cloak and sank down onto the bed, which gave under his weight, indicating a smotheringly soft mattress. He didn't care. "Remove my boots, will you?" he asked sticking out a mud encrusted boot.

She knelt and performed the office then rose and began helping him off with his jacket. Which was easier said than done, as his arm was useless and every movement sent excruciating pain through his shoulder and fresh blood down his arm. The makeshift bandage was soaked. A knock at the door heralded the return of three maids, two with jugs of hot water and towels and the third with a tray of food.

When they had left, Miss Lovell returned to the task of removing his jacket, having discarded the blood-soaked bandage. Easing it over his shoulder and down his arm she got it free. She turned away to lay it over the back of one of the chairs, while he fought the waves of pain and nausea the exercise had caused. The pain eased back to a dull throbbing, and he opened his eyes to find her looking at him with concern.

"Now we need to get your waistcoat and shirt off. The waistcoat shouldn't be difficult, but I think I will have to destroy the shirt."

"Don't worry about that, it's ruined anyway."

She nodded and helped him out of the waistcoat. Then took up a knife from the dinner tray and ripped the shirt from collar to cuff on his left arm and from armpit to waist. She could then peel it away from the left side of his body without disturbing the injured shoulder. She worked swiftly and efficiently, and while she appeared a little pale, she maintained her composure and showed no signs of outward distress. He admired her strength and competence and was grateful for it. She might have caused his discomfort, but she seemed to be doing her best to make amends for it.

With the wound finally revealed, he could see the blood running freely down his arm. She had put down a towel to catch the drips and had poured some of the water into a bowl and was gently washing the skin around the wound. The water in the bowl was already dark red with his blood. The salty, metallic tang, caught in the back of his throat and made him feel sick. He swallowed and closed his eyes, his head was beginning to feel light, he feared he was going to pass out again.

At that moment a knock at the door followed by its swift

opening, revealed a short grey-haired man carrying a black bag who proved to be the doctor.

Tutting over the wound and the temerity of highwaymen to shoot innocent people in broad daylight on the King's road, the doctor set to work. He cleaned, stitched, and bandaged the wound, able assisted by Diana, still in her guise of his young male cousin.

The pain was bad enough that Anthony missed bits of what ensued, and at the end of it, his skin was slick with sweat, he felt sick and his shoulder was on fire. He opened his eyes to discover Miss Lovell bent over him, her face creased in concern. The doctor had gone.

"Here," she offered him something cool in a cup, and he drank it greedily as she held his head up. He sank back on the pillow, and he must have slept for when he next surfaced, she had removed her hat, and her hair, a dark tumbled mass, was loose round her shoulders. She had shed her jacket and waistcoat and was wrapped in a blanket over her shirt. She sat on the side of the bed and wiped his face with a damp, cool cloth. His body was a raging furnace and his shoulder burned hottest of all.

Seeing he was awake, she offered him more to drink.

"Please," his voice was rusty.

The water was soothing to his raw throat and blessedly cool, as was the cloth on his skin. He shuddered with a sudden bone cracking chill.

He closed his eyes enduring the wracking shivers, his teeth clattering uncontrollably. His body ached, his joints burned, his shoulder throbbed, his head pounded. Constant thirst plagued him. Each time he opened his eyes, she was there with water or a cloth to soothe him. He sank back into oblivion.

He was in hell, he'd died and gone to hell for his sins and he was burning in eternal torment. He opened his eyes and blinked. A figure bent over him, the most beautiful creature he had ever seen. The candlelight behind her threw her hair into a halo, *she was an angel! What was an angel doing in hell?* She had tears on her cheeks and she whispered.

"Don't die. Please don't die."

He wanted to say he was already dead, but his tongue wouldn't work. She gave him more water, and he clutched her hand.

"Don't leave me my angel," his voice was raspy, desperate.

"I won't," she said, squeezing his hand back. Comforted, he slipped back into the hot darkness.

ANTHONY'S FEVER WAS SEVERE, and Diana didn't dare leave him for long while it raged at its worst. She bathed him with cloths to keep his temperature down and fed him sips of water between bouts of shivering when his teeth chattered so badly he couldn't swallow. He was out of his head for most of the time, only surfacing briefly for lucid moments, rapidly lost. She kept herself swathed in the blanket when the maids came or the doctor and kept to the shadows of the room to avoid scrutiny. When they were alone she curled up on the bed beside him and caught snatches of sleep when she could. The days and nights blurred together, and she had ample time to bitterly regret her split second decision to shoot him. Her constant fear was that he would die.

Stroking the sweat from his brow she had ample opportunity also to admire his masculine beauty and reminisce over the kiss they had shared under the dripping canopy of trees in the semi dark. She had never experienced such a burning fire from a kiss before, and the memory of it seemed to be seared into her bones. She knew enough to recognise that it was mutual. She had been able to feel his arousal pressed into her belly, both the length and hardness of it and the heat. Just thinking of it brought back the wave of aching need his kiss had aroused in her, and she found herself touching him.

She caressed his sweat slicked skin, admiring the contours of his chest and the tangle of dark hair that covered it. For he had, the peculiarity of flame red hair on his head but dark eyebrows, lashes, and beard. The colour of the hairs on his chest darkened by moisture had red highlights among the darker strands. His chest was muscular and his stomach washboard ribbed and flat. He was as fine a specimen as Connor, whose masculine beauty had until now been her benchmark for handsome.

While she mooned over his body in between worrying herself sick about his welfare, she acquired a familiarity with his form, scent, and sense of his nearness, and she found it strangely attractive, addictive even. The time passed in a blur of moments strung together by stretches of disturbed sleep.

Three days of nursing him through the fever took their toll on her. She was exhausted by the time the fever broke, and she finally knew he would recover. It was a combination of relief and exhaustion that brought tears to her eyes and caused her to collapse on the bed beside him and sob into the pillow.

Fortunately, he was sleeping and didn't see this lapse.

Now that he was through the worst of it, she should slip away, before he regained consciousness and strength enough to chase after her. If he would even bother?

She glanced at the window, it was just before dawn. She could slip out of the Inn, saddle Sugar and be on the road to London before anyone knew she was gone. It was her best option. In good conscience, she hadn't been able to leave him while he hovered between life and death in the grip of that wretched fever, but now he was on the mend. She could go. She should. She must. Before he woke and decided to give her up to the magistrate.

She turned back to look at him, visible in the flickering light of the candles on the bedside table. His face was relaxed and younger than it appeared when he was awake. She wondered fleetingly how old he was, over thirty she'd warrant. The perpetual sardonic look was smoothed away and for the first time in three days his skin was cool to touch, not red and slicked with sweat from the fever. The bandage on his shoulder where the doctor had removed the bullet and stitched the wound closed, was clean. It was showing no signs of further break-out bleeding, and the sickly-sweet smell of infection had evaporated too.

He had called her his angel and begged her not to leave him when the fever was at its worst. It was just the fever of course. It didn't mean anything, but it had been strangely seductive to be needed like that.

It made her chest feel warm as she clasped his hand tightly and said softly, "I shan't leave you."

But now she *was* contemplating leaving him. Fleeing into the dawn. Into the new life she had planned for herself, which the money she would get from the sale of her mother's brooch, would make possible. She would vanish and no one would find her, not Uncle Garmon, or Connor Mor or the Duke of Mowbray.

Not that she thought her uncle would bother to look for her anyway, she was a burden he hadn't asked for and didn't want, he'd made that clear on numerous occasions. She grimaced, she didn't pretend to understand her uncle. He was a hard man, his upbringing in St Giles had squeezed the humanity out of him.

She didn't think Connor would bother either.

His attempts to seduce her had always been half-hearted. He pretended to be her friend, when in truth he just wanted to tup her. But not enough to go looking for her. *He didn't care. No one did.*

Not since her father died, and even *his* affection had been haphazard and mostly (she suspected), born out of guilt and obligation. He'd cared enough for his base-born daughter to offer her a place in his house after he learned of the death of her mother. Enough to educate her and clothe and feed her. Enough to defy his family's disapproval, but not enough to pay attention to her. She remembered her five-year-old self trailing after him wanting nothing more than to crawl into his lap and be hugged. But once he brought her home he seemed to want little to do with her. He consigned her to the care of the servants, installed a governess when she was old enough to learn her letters and left her to her own devices.

He didn't really love her. Not enough to remember her in his will and protect her after his death. She wiped away a tear impatiently. No use crying about it now. What was done, was done.

She played idly with the Duke's good hand and traced the contours of his handsome face with her eyes. He was quite a subject for a sculptor, his nose well-formed and straight. His cheeks, jaw and chin showed the strength in his personality; masculine, and perfectly proportioned to be pleasing to the eye. But it was his lips where the sculptor would have their challenge, capturing the full, sensuous, and yet clean lines of his mouth. His jaw was covered in stubble, the dark shadow of whiskers, a stark contrast to the deep red of the hair on his head. And no sculptor could capture the fire that burned in his eyes, the transfixing blue gaze that skewered her and turned her bones to water.

If his eyes invited her to danger, it was his lips that sealed the deal. His kisses had burned their way into her body and wouldn't let go. She craved to feel the pressure of his mouth again, the tingling sweet explosion of pleasure and the seductive delight his lips and tongue wrought in her body. How could one kiss have such an indelible effect?

The yearning to lean forward and press her lips to his mouth now... *This was madness. She needed to leave. Now!* She swallowed the sudden lump in her throat and shook her head to dispel the feelings threatening to overwhelm her.

There was no room in her life for this kind of self-indulgent folly. Just as there was no room for sentimental nonsense over the brooch. It might be the only thing she now had connecting her to her mother, but it was a means to an end not a keepsake. It was too valuable for that, and she was too pragmatic to entertain such sensibility. It was her ticket to freedom, and she was taking it no matter the cost.

Letting go of his hand gently she rose from the bed and quietly pulled on her jacket and boots, bundled her hair up and pinned it in place, jamming the hat down over the top. She picked up her saddlebag and crept over to the door. He hadn't moved. With one last look, she opened the door quietly, slipped through and closed it gently, behind her.

Creeping to the stairs, she made it to the bottom without encountering anyone. Slipping out the rear door to the stables, she ran lightly across the muddy courtyard. The rain had been persistent these last few days and showed no signs of lifting. The stables were warmer than the outside air, with a fug of horse dung and hay that was strangely comforting. She found Sugar and saddled and bridled her in quick order, strapping on the saddlebag and stowing the pistols she had stolen from her uncle's armoury.

The stable hands would be emerging at any moment, and she wanted to get away unseen. Leading Sugar out into the yard she mounted and clopped around to the front of the hostelry. The horizon was a bright pink, orange and purple, presaging the imminent rising of the sun. A gust of cold wind set the Bull's Head sign swinging above the arched doubled doors of the entrance and a spatter of rain drops made her pull her cloak closer round her shoulders. She urged Sugar onto the road with her heels and set her course for London.

CHAPTER 9

Anthony woke to the dull ache in his shoulder, and the rumble of his empty stomach. His head was clear and his body free of the fever. This was good news.

He looked around the room and made a discovery. There was no sign of Miss Lovell.

He reached for the bellpull beside the bed, banked up the pillows and leaned back against them. A maid appeared in mob cap and apron.

"Yes, your Grace?"

"Where is my cousin?" he asked, finding his voice hoarse from lack of use. He cleared his throat.

"I don't know, your Grace." she twisted her hands in her apron nervously.

"Well find him and tell him I'm awake, will you?"

She nodded and bobbed a curtsy.

"And fetch me something to eat and drink I'm parched and famished!"

"At once, your Grace!" she said and scuttled from the room.

Why did he always have that effect on servants? He closed his eyes, swallowing. His mouth was sticky, and his tongue felt swollen with thirst. His chin itched too. He scratched the bristles. How long had he been in the fever dream?

He recalled holding her hand tightly, and of her offering him drinks and wiping his brow. *Quite the nurse Miss Lovell. Where was she now? Getting some air or something to eat? What time was it?* He squinted across the room to the clock on the mantelpiece above the fireplace but couldn't make it out as it was too dim in here. The candles had all but guttered, and the light through the window was poor. It was still raining he concluded, listening to the intermittent lash of water against the panes.

He dozed a bit and woke when the door opened and two maids appeared. One had hot water and the other bore a tray, which she brought straight to the bed and set across his knees.

He seized the tankard of porter and drank deeply.

"Thank you," he said with a nod to the servants. "Where is my cousin? Did you find him?"

"No, your Grace. No one's seen him this morning."

He suppressed the curse that rose to his lips, an unwelcome suspicion forming in his mind. "Check if his horse is still in the stable."

"Yes, your Grace." she bobbed another curtsy and scuttled out followed by the other girl.

He surveyed the tray and picked up the knife and fork with relish, he was famished indeed. Once he had eaten, he could see if his legs would bear him. He very much feared that Miss Lovell had given him the slip while he slept. He tried to recall the last time he had seen her, but his memories of the past few days were hazy at best. There were whole blocks of time he had no memory of at all. But what he did remember, the fleeting snatches of clarity, all contained her.

He clung to a faint hope that she was in the stables seeing to her mare and would reappear at any moment. But the next visitor was the landlord with the news that his cousin was indeed gone, as was his mare.

Disappointment made his stomach swoop, or perhaps it was just hunger. He cursed beneath his breath at this news. *The little wretch thought to escape him, did she? Well, she would soon learn her mistake!*

Having eaten as much of the generous breakfast provided as he thought wise, the Duke ordered a bath. He stank so badly he could smell himself. He bathed and dressed noting that his clothes had been cleaned while he lay hostage to the fever. He thanked the landlord, paid his shot and mounted Midnight to give chase to Miss Lovell.

He knew it was madness. He was weakened by the fever, loss of blood and three days without food, and if the wound reopened, he would be in serious trouble. But none of that mattered. For some reason that escaped him, finding Diana Lovell was more important than anything else. He would find her or die trying.

One of the maids had helped him fashion a sling for his arm from a ruined neck cloth, and that, he hoped, would prevent the wound from suffering any damage. The wound itself had been expertly bandaged, he suspected by the doctor, of whom he had only the haziest of memories.

He already knew that his powers of recovery were excellent, having recovered from the wound dealt him by Viviana in only a sennight.

He stopped in the next town, Groby, and asked if a slender young gentleman on a dapple-grey mare had passed this way. His first few inquiries drew a blank, but then he was gratified to finally find someone who had seen her. Confident that she was heading back to London he pressed on, only pausing to drink and eat when he got the opportunity. Midnight was fresh and fully capable of taking him all the way to London if need be. It was his own stamina he feared would slow him down. She had several hours start on him, and he was afraid that either the trail would go cold or she would continue to draw further ahead of him. Or that he was wrong about her destination. He needed to catch her before she reached London, lest she vanish in the vast metropolis. He needed...her.

By the time mid-afternoon came, he was swaying with exhaustion in the saddle and facing the very real possibility that he wouldn't be able to catch up to her. He knew that he had made up some time, Midnight was a faster horse than her mare. He'd pushed himself and his gelding hard for the last twenty miles in hopes of catching her, but there was still no sign of her, the further he travelled. And each time he stopped to ask if there had been a sighting of her, he lost time. For that reason, he had decided to just press on, grimly convinced that he was on her tail. He must be.

What possessed him to embark on this crazy chase he didn't fully understand, but he knew that solving the mystery of Miss Diana Lovell was something he was determined to accomplish. There was something about her...half-forgotten memories, ephemeral as fragments of dreams plagued him of her presence, the feel of her, her touch, her scent, her lips... He wanted her with a raging hunger. He was going to bloody well find her if it killed him. Which it was likely to do, his shoulder throbbed and his body ached with fatigue, but he pressed on regardless. Nothing and no one was going to stop him from finding her.

Reaching the turnpike of Riseley High Street in Bedfordshire, he approached the toll booth operator, who merged from his cottage at Anthony's hail.

"Miserable day, Sir!" the operator was a grizzled man, wiry of build and walked with a limp.

"Ex-soldier?" asked Anthony with a nod to his leg.

"Aye. Got this at Badajoz. Shrapnel from a cannon blast. Lucky not to lose the leg. This weather reminds me of those days. Mud for miles! And the rain!"

Anthony nodded wearily. "Has a slender young gentleman on a grey mare passed this way today?"

"Aye, about an hour ago, maybe less."

"Thank you," Anthony perked up. "How much is the toll?"

"Five pence Sir, but as I told the young gentleman, the Rivers up and has cut the road ahead. You'll have to go to The Boot for the night until the water recedes."

Anthony smiled, *at last, got you!* He paid the toll and passed through.

He found The Boot, a small double-storied building in the shape surprisingly enough, of a boot, with a steep roof and whitewashed walls. He dismounted, handed his horse into the care of the stable hand who came forward to take him and strolled into the Inn. There he spied her seated at a table in the tap room, drinking beer from a pewter tankard. He watched her for a few moments, enjoying his victory and contemplating her courage.

As if she sensed his presence, she turned her head and saw him. Her eyes widened, and she flushed, an expression of chagrin, with a tinge of fear, overtaking her. He grinned and strolled towards her. Pulling out a chair, he sat.

She leaned forward and said, softly, "Are you mad? You should be in bed!"

"I agree, preferably with you," he said equally softly. He remembered vividly how it felt to kiss her, and he wanted to do it again, soon.

She flushed scarlet and rose abruptly to her feet. He reached out, grabbed her arm, and pulled her back down. She glanced around and sat reluctantly. No one was looking at them.

"It will serve you right if your wound breaks open or becomes reinfected!" She hissed through clenched teeth.

"I was willing to take the risk."

"In heaven's name why?"

"For you," he said softly, holding her gaze with his. For the first time, he was able to fully appreciate her eyes. A clear violet-grey with long, dark lashes set under elegantly arched brows. The flush, which had barely subsided, rose again.

She took refuge in her pot of beer, which he eyed thirstily.

Signalling to the waitress he ordered one for himself.

"Have you eaten?" he asked her.

She shook her head, and he ordered food as well. He was famished and slightly light-headed. His shoulder pulsed with a dull ache.

His beer arrived, and he quickly drained the pot before ordering a jug. While he was waiting for the jug, he leaned across the table and spoke quietly. "Now you will tell me why you felt it necessary to hold me up and shoot me."

She sighed, avoiding his eyes, and he waited for her next fabrication. She was so good at them. He had come to learn in this short time of their acquaintance that she was very good at making up stories. It amused him to hear her tales, and he wondered how long it would take before he got the truth. She surprised him, again with her retort.

Raising her eyes and looking directly at him, she said, "Because you had something I wanted."

He raised an eyebrow and waited. *So, she had taken whatever it was from him while he was unconscious.*

She appeared to struggle with herself for a moment, and then she blurted, "My mother's brooch. Your grandfather took it from my father. It was the only thing I had of my mother's, my father gave it to her as a present, when I was born." She looked down but not before he caught the tell-tale signs of tears forming in her eyes.

"Took it or won it?" he asked, ignoring the tears. Feminine tears had long failed to move him since he learned how well his mother used them to manipulate her many lovers and even on occasion his father.

She wiped her nose with her sleeve and sniffed. "Took it! When he killed him, he took it off his body. Papa always kept it in his breast pocket, after she died. It wasn't there when his body was returned to the house, so I knew your grandfather had it." She threw him a venomous look and added. "And I was right, because you had it in your saddlebag."

He frowned. "The emerald and diamond brooch in the design of a four leafed clover, set in gold? Is that the one?"

She nodded.

The food arrived then, and they ate in silence for some minutes. The stew and fresh bread were excellent, or perhaps it was just his hunger that made it taste so good. Diana finished her bowl and topped up her beer pot from the jug.

"Quite the hard head, haven't you?" he remarked watching her sipping the beer absently. She was frowning at something, and it wasn't, he thought, something she was looking at. She transferred her gaze back to him and said bluntly. "The brooch is mine by right. Will you let me keep it?" The challenge in her voice was unmistakable.

She must be mad. That brooch was worth something in the order of five thousand pounds, each emerald was the size of his thumbnail. It alone wouldn't solve his financial woes but every little bit helped. "Do you know what that brooch is worth?" he asked quietly.

She shook her head. "A considerable amount I should imagine."

"Five thousand pounds."

She changed colour. "That much?"

He nodded.

"The other jewels you have in that bag must be worth considerably more." she pointed out.

"You weren't tempted to take them?" he asked, finishing his pot, and refilling it.

She stiffened, offended, and hissed back at him. "I'm not a thief! Your grandfather was the thief. I was simply repossessing what is mine!"

"Yes, that is something that has me in a puzzle," he frowned at her. "My grandsire was a bad man, no doubt about it, but I cannot credit that he would rifle his dead opponent's person and take a piece of jewellery, like a common thief. No gentleman would do such a thing, and if he did, it would have been witnessed by the seconds of both parties and surely gossiped about. I never heard of any such tale and believe me I have heard many unsavoury stories about him. But not this one."

He sipped his beer. "Which brings me to another question. How did you come by this information?"

"I told you, he always kept it on him, and it wasn't there when his body was returned to the house."

"Yes, but what made you conclude that my grandsire had it?"

Her lips compressed into a thin line, and for a moment he thought she wouldn't answer. She let out a breath with a huff and said with asperity, "Because the subject of the duel was my mother!"

He held up his hand. "Wait a minute, none of this makes sense. Refresh my memory, when did you father die?"

"Eight years ago."

He frowned. "How old are you?"

"Two and twenty."

"Lovell's first wife died over twenty-five years ago. I never heard that he married again. And I never heard that he had a daughter either."

She flushed, biting her lip.

"So, this tale is a tarradiddle, is it? Made up out of whole cloth? I must compliment you on your inventiveness. You had me going there for a while. Now tell me the damned truth before I lose my temper!"

"It *is* the truth!" she swallowed and the tears threatened to spill again. She was a good actress he'd give her that. "My parents were never married!"

He hadn't expected that. Feeling slightly winded he sat back in his seat, contemplating her flushed face and sparkling eyes. "Why not?" he asked bluntly.

She swallowed again and dropped her eyes but not before he saw the shame in them. She whispered, "Because my mother was already married."

His heart skipped and he suddenly believed her. "Who was she?"

"Lady Letitia Barrington."

"Good God!" he rubbed his chin in an effort of recall. "Barrington was my father's cousin. My grandfather's nephew through his sister. I was thirteen at the time but if I recall correctly, he shot her and then himself. They did their best to cover up the scandal. I seem to remember that the daughter disappeared. That was you?"

She nodded, her lips visibly trembling, two tears spilled over and ran down her cheeks.

"How old were you?"

"Five." She wiped her nose with her sleeve again. She closed her eyes and took a breath. He reached out a hand and clasped hers briefly. During the time they had been sitting there, the tap room had started to fill up and had become quite noisy with conversation. He hoped theirs was going unnoticed.

"Come on," he said roughly, pulling her to her feet and walking her out of the room. A door to a parlour stood ajar. He poked his head around it and discovered the room to be empty. Pulling her inside, he shut the door and guided her to a settee before the lit fire. Sitting beside her, he took her hand again and rested it on his knee. Her head was bowed, and he watched as drops of moisture fell onto the cloth of her breeches. But she made no sound.

"What happened to you?" His voice was rough. He cleared his throat, which felt strangely thickened, perhaps it was the wood smoke, the chimney must need a clean.

She wiped her nose again on her sleeve and exasperated, he

let go her hand to reach into his pocket and shove a handkerchief at her before taking back possession of her hand.

"Thank you," she said her voice husky, and blew her nose.

"I saw it. I was behind the books. I don't remember how I came to be there, I must have been in the library. I only remember them arguing, he was shouting at her, and she was crying. She screamed, and I remember the shot and the blood. He stood over her body and howled," she shuddered. "I ran then, but he didn't see me. Looking back, I think, that if he had, he would have shot me too, but at the time I didn't understand any of it. I heard the second shot as I left the house, so I ran and ran until I reached the tree house. I climbed the tree and stayed there; I don't know for how long. It seemed like a long time; I know I wet myself because I was too afraid to move." She took another shuddering breath. "Papa found me and took me away to live with him." She licked her lips. "When he died his family threw me out. They knew who I was and wouldn't have anything to do with me."

"You were fourteen."

She nodded.

He swallowed an unaccountable lump in his throat. "What did you do?"

"I found my Uncle Garmon. He is papa's natural brother. He owns a gambling hell called Lovells. He took me in, put me to work." She scrunched the handkerchief in her hand on her knee. "So now you know everything."

"My God, what a tale!" he said softly.

"Do you believe me?"

"Yes." He squeezed her hand and let it go.

She looked up at him. "Thank you."

"For what?"

"Believing me."

"How did your father find you?"

She sighed and wiped her face. "He told me later, when I was older, what actually happened. He was there, at the gates waiting. He'd come to take mama and me away, but Barrington caught us leaving the house. Mama confessed the truth, and he must have dragged us into the library. I must have hidden behind the shelves. I don't know the sequence of events then, my memory is very hazy. But Papa told me he heard the shots and came running. He then spent hours looking for me. He found me and took me away."

He frowned thinking through the implications. "Technically, you're Barrington's daughter under the law you know, and therefore my second cousin."

She shrugged. "What odd's does that make? His family would never acknowledge me."

"They could be forced to." He said grimly.

"No! That is the last thing I want."

"What *do* you want?"

"To disappear, make my own way." She straightened her shoulders.

"That's what you wanted the brooch for? To finance your venture?"

She nodded.

"So, what was your plan?"

She shook her head.

He lifted her chin with a finger, forcing her to look at him. "You must have had some plan, what is it?"

"To travel," she admitted with a slight smile. It was the first smile he had seen from her in a while, and it spread a warmth through his chest. He had a fancy to see her smile more often.

"That could be arranged, he said quietly. *Was he mad? He had a Dukedom to look after. Yet her smile could make him think of leaving it all behind just to be with her.*

"WHAT?" She stared at him confused.

"I may have to disappear myself, if I can't settle the mound of debt my grandsire has left me," he said with a rueful smile. Her heart thudded, that smile was sinful. *He shouldn't be allowed to smile* she thought wildly. Her emotions were all over the place, she felt raw and off balance.

Before she could formulate a response, he bent his head and kissed her, and the touch of his lips was every bit as intoxicating as the first time.

Instinctively she pressed into the kiss, the tingling pleasure of his lips sending tendrils of delight through her body. She parted her lips for the invasion of his tongue, her heart thudding, and her breathing accelerating. Her hand came up to clasp his good shoulder, and her hat collided with his, knocking it off her head onto the floor. His good hand tangled in her hair, sending pins cascading after the hat and bringing her hair tumbling round her shoulders. His hand cupped the base of her skull and tipped her head for better access to her mouth. He devoured her with a passionate kiss that sent fire rolling through her body, tightening her nipples, and sending a rush of aching, wet heat between her legs.

His arm that had been tied in the sling across his chest, prevented her from getting any closer, but didn't stop her kissing him back with all the fervour she possessed. No stranger to the rush and release of passion, though it were self-administered, she had never known such a flood of desire for a man before. Her forays into kisses and more in the past had been tame compared to this.

He broke the kiss, breathing as hard as she, his eyes blazing with that irresistible blue fire. "Fuck, I want you!" he muttered sitting back, his eyes closed. He put a hand to his shoulder as if it pained him.

She didn't blink at the obscenity. She'd heard this and much worse at the hell, surrounded as she was by drunken, debauched men for hours at a time. In the years since Uncle Garmon had made her start working in the hell she had seen it all, she thought. She doubted if she had any innocence left to lose.

"You've hurt yourself!" She said unable to keep the concern from her voice.

He opened his eyes and his lips twisted in a half smile that made something inside her melt. *God this man was so dangerous to her. She needed to get away from him before she completely lost her mind.*

"Aye, it's an effective chaperone. No matter how much I want to ravish you, it will have to wait until I'm sufficiently healed that I won't bleed all over you or pass out."

She subsided back onto the settee beside him, suddenly realising how exhausted she was. She had nursed him for three days, getting almost no sleep and spent over eight hours in the saddle today. The beer she had drunk was also making her muzzy headed. "I need some sleep," she confessed staring at him, her vision starting to blur.

He nodded. "A good idea. Have you bespoken a room?"

She shook her head.

"I'll do that, go fetch my saddlebags. They're tied to Midnight in the stable"

She nodded, and rose from the settee, picking up the pins which she dropped into her pocket before twisting her hair up into a knot and stuffing the hat back over the top of it. "Two rooms!" she said heading towards the door.

"Oh no!" he said just behind her. "You're not escaping me again, coz!"

She looked back at him over her shoulder, and he grinned that wicked grin and her stomach dropped, heat making her pelvic muscles contract. She licked her lower lip, and he caught her jaw and kissed her again.

She made a noise in her throat as he let her go, and she gasped. "What makes you trust me to fetch the bags and not run?"

"You're more tired than I am. I don't think you'll flee before you've had some sleep, but I don't trust you not to try to escape me again at dawn."

She sighed. "You're right. I'm out on my feet."

"Good girl. I'll see you upstairs."

DIANA EXITED the parlour and took the side entrance out to the stables. She didn't see the man watching her from the tap room.

CHAPTER 10

Anthony sank down on the bed in the room he'd been given with a groan. His whole body ached. This one was the twin in layout of the red monstrosity from the previous inn, except it was done out in puce taffeta instead of brocade and had apple green walls. The furniture was walnut. He sighed and closed his eyes, while he waited for Miss Lovell to return and help him out of his boots and jacket.

Had he made a mistake letting her out of his sight? He didn't think so. *She was not only physically tired, she was also emotionally drained. Telling that story about her parents had cost her a great deal. Yet she hadn't cried hysterically.*

Yes there had been a sprinkling of tears, but they fell silently. She had been through hell, and it had made her strong. He admired her strength and her courage, and by God, he wanted her, fiercely. Fortunately, it seemed to be mutual. This damned wound was going to slow things down. His lips twisted at the irony.

He glanced at the clock on the mantle and frowned. *What was taking her so long?* He was about to heave himself to his feet and go to investigate when the door opened, and she appeared, lugging the saddlebags. He smiled with relief.

"What kept you?" he asked as she dumped the saddlebags on the floor.

"I wanted to make sure the horses were fed and watered properly and had been rubbed down sufficiently," she said removing her cloak and hat. He watched her hair tumble down round her shoulders and his hand itched to feel those heavy silky tresses again. Her hair was, as he had surmised, brown, but not unremarkable brown, a rich deep brown that glowed red in the candlelight.

"Of course, thank you." He watched her pull her fingers through her hair, separating the strands. She encountered knots and gave up, coming towards him instead. He held out a foot, and she knelt to take off his boots. With her kneeling at his feet, images he shouldn't entertain came unbidden to his mind. Yes, he craved her, but he would have her properly, when he was whole and could ensure the encounter was everything they both wanted.

She rose and helped him out of his jacket.

"The pocket is heavy," she remarked. "Oh, of course, the jewels, you wouldn't leave them in the saddlebags." It occurred to him to wonder where she had stowed the brooch, but he wouldn't ask. That was a topic best left alone for the nonce.

She hung the jacket over the back of the chair and returned to help him with his neck cloth, waistcoat, and shirt, revealing the sling beneath and the neat bandage, which showed no bloody tell-tales. "You're lucky no damage seems to have been done."

"I've been careful to keep the arm as still as I can."

"Does it hurt?"

"Yes, but not unbearably."

She stood between his legs and traced a finger over his bare chest, tangling with the hairs there. His skin prickled and the muscles twitched, his cock lengthening inside his breeches as he swallowed a groan.

"Injured or not, you're a fine specimen," she murmured,

bending her head, she kissed him and her hair falling forward, caressed his skin. He did groan then, his fingers plunging into her hair to hold her head and angle it correctly for his return kiss.

When she lifted her head, she was breathing quickly and her eyes had dilated. She was as attracted to him as he was to her, this was no pretence to gull him. A warmth he couldn't name bloomed in his chest and he smiled, caressing her smooth cheek.

"You're quite beautiful, even in boys' clothes. I'd give something to see you in petticoats, your assets set off to advantage," he murmured, his eyes narrowing as he tried to imagine what she would look like.

She laughed, turning away, and ducked behind the screen to undress, jacket, waistcoat, and neck cloth appearing over the top of the screen. He wanted to see her naked, *what would she wear to bed and could he keep his hands off her when she did? She hadn't protested about sharing a room with him. Was she used to sleeping with a man?* The thought was unpleasant and made his muscles clench with a nameless urge to—what? Remove every damned male from the earth who had looked at her, let alone touched her. The stab of possessive jealousy took him by surprise.

She emerged wearing only her shirt, which came to mid-thigh, giving him an excellent view of her bare legs, and the knowledge that she wore nothing beneath the fine lawn fabric set his pulses racing. He swallowed another groan, his cock already painfully hard, somehow got harder and more painful.

What did she mean by this casual intimacy? He lay down, his head propped up by his arm against the pillows and watched her wash her face and fetch a brush to disentangle her wild hair. Finally satisfied that she had all the tangles out, she plaited the mass of it. It was too long to be fashionable, but he didn't give a fig for fashion, it was a glorious mane, and he longed to bury his face in it. His body, tense with desire, ached.

She blew out the candles on the mantel and dresser, leaving

only the bedside candle and the glow of the fire to illuminate the room. She turned back to the bed and caught him looking at her. Something in his gaze pierced her armour and she blushed, which made his desire burn hotter. She looked adorable in the oversized shirt, the long plait over one shoulder and her legs bare, her eyes large and luminous, her mouth a luscious pink, ripe and kissable.

He still wore his breeches and the tent of his arousal showed clearly as he lay looking at her. Her eyes travelled down his body, over his bare chest to the bulge in his trousers and snagged there. She swallowed visibly and her eyes jerked to his.

He noted the fatigue in her face and the slump of her shoulders, remembering how little sleep she had probably had while nursing him and then an eight-hour ride on top of it today.

"It's alright. Come to bed," he said gently. "I promise not to ravish you. I can't, I'm hors de combat, remember? And you're exhausted." *And so am I.*

She nodded and came towards the bed. He shifted to pull the coverlet over himself, and she slid under it on the other side of the bed. This mattress was harder than the previous one and a bit lumpy. She blew out the bedside candle and curled up on her side, facing away from him.

"Good night," she murmured out of the dark, only the fire's glow gave them light.

"Good night, Diana." He lay listening to her breathing as it evened out, and she fell asleep. And very soon, in spite of his priapic condition, drowsiness overcame him too, and he slipped over into sleep, his last coherent thought that Diana Lovell was unique among women.

∽

CONNOR MOR CLUNG to the trellis below the window of the room at the back of the inn where his quarry lay, asleep he hoped. It had taken him three days to find the Duke; having lost him somewhere between Leicestershire and Bedfordshire. He'd overshot and got almost all the way to London before he realised, he must have missed him and was forced to double back. *All in the sodding rain!* His temper was close to breaking point when he spotted the Duke talking to a youth with a face that looked eerily familiar.

What the hell was Diana doing out here with the Duke? He moved casually across the tap room and took a seat behind them, and *low what an interesting conversation that proved to be!*

Now here he was, clinging to the trellis and praying the window sash would open quietly. His prayers were answered. This was a well-maintained inn and the sash went up silently. The room was cloaked in darkness, but a sliver of moonlight peeking through the cloud cover gave him just enough light to see the layout of the room and spot the saddlebags on the floor. *Was that where the jewels were?* He looked to the bed but couldn't see anything in the dark, the soft sibilant breathing told him his quarry was asleep. *Where was Diana?*

His jaw tightened. *Likely in the bed with him, the whore.*

He slid silently in through the window and crept across to the saddlebags. He checked all three and found nothing but clothing. Frowning he stared round for another possible hiding place and spied two jackets hung over the backs for the chairs. The first one yielded a brooch and a wallet from the inner pocket. The second one, a heavy pouch from the outside pocket of the greatcoat and a purse and silver flask from the jacket beneath. He took a quick swig from that and slipped it into his vest pocket. He then stowed his other finds. Smiling, he crept back to the window, slipped through, closed the sash quietly and descended the trellis. *Fortune had smiled on him at last. He would take the jewels to Garmon as promised. The flask, purse, and wallet he might keep for himself, a little payment for his trouble.*

CHAPTER 11

Diana woke to the unaccustomed sensation of another warm body beside her. Rolling over carefully so as not to disturb him, she sat up and contemplated her bed companion. The man was temptation personified. She had kissed him like a wanton last night, and agreed to share a bed with him, too tired to protest and trusting that his injury would keep her safe. Which had proved correct, but for how much longer?

She should take the brooch and flee, she knew she should, but oh how tempted she was to stay and see where this fiery connection might lead. Because for her, it was more than a physical connection. She knew his reputation, he was well known for being unscrupulous, violent, selfish, and brutal. And yet he hadn't been any of those things with her. Or only a little, and then only because he was angry and justifiably so. She had put a bullet in him.

She swallowed, her heart skipping. She could have killed him. And while he hovered between life and death fighting that fever, she'd had plenty of time to think and regret her actions. And to fall under the spell of his physical attraction.

And when she thought she had escaped him, he followed her.

Got up from his sick bed, followed her and forced the truth from her and in the process. Then listened to her story without condemning and without - she groped for the words she wanted to describe the connection they had. It was a silent almost unconscious understanding. They just 'knew' each other in a way she couldn't describe. She could feel it, and she was pretty sure he felt it too. They were kindred spirits of a kind she had never thought was possible.

Her heart turned over in her chest and began to thump hard. She had to leave, before this yearning for something she couldn't have consumed her. He was a load stone, pulling her into destruction. She could dash herself to pieces on the rocks of his passion and die happily doing so. Nothing, nothing had pulled at her like he did, and nothing had ever terrified her more.

She moved to slide out of bed, and his eyes opened and blinked at her. Eyes as blue as a summer sky roamed over her, and a lazy smile curved his beautiful mouth. He was sinfully handsome when he smiled.

"Good morning, Diana."

"Good morning your Grace." She blushed like a ninny and her eyes skipped away suddenly shy and uncomfortable under his knowing stare.

"Good morning sweetheart." His voice reminded her of a big, lazy tiger. She swallowed and tried to edge away, but he shot out his good hand and grasped her arm. "An attack of maidenly shyness Diana? I didn't think having the vapours was your style?"

Her chin came up, and she fought to get a grip on herself. "It's not, I just -"

"I'm only teasing my angel, come here," he coaxed, tugging at her arm gently. His use of the term angel made her heart stutter. He'd likened her to an angel during the fever. *So, he remembered that much? What else did he remember? Her curling up next to him on the bed, her caressing his chest, mooning over his beauty?*

It was then his eyes lighted on the bruises on her arms, they were fading now to faint greenish purple but still visible. He pushed the sleeves up to see the full extent of the damage.

"My God where did you get those?" he asked, his face reflecting horror.

She swallowed and shrugged. "You, when we first met..."

He closed his eyes a moment and then opened them, the blue was fierce and bright. "I'm sorry. I'm a brute."

"It doesn't matter, I deserved it after all. I shot you and left you in the middle of the road."

He stroked his hand down her arm, caressing, gentle. "I'm still sorry." he gave a rueful smile. "My damned temper."

He tugged her closer, "Let me make it up to you."

"We should be going!" She blurted and pulling out of his hold, slid off the bed and darted behind the screen, her heart thudding uncomfortably hard.

ANTHONY STARED at the screen conscious of a stab of disappointment. Her attack of shyness and evident desire to get away from him–again– suggested that last night's intimacy engendered by the kisses and confidences that they had exchanged, had evaporated with the dawn. And that was disappointing, disconcertingly so. She was like a will-o-the-wisp, every time he thought he had her, she eluded him. And those bruises were reason enough for her to be wary of him. He cursed his temper and brutality.

He threw back the coverlet and stood up, just as she emerged from behind the screen wearing her breeches. Her eyes landed on him, and her cheeks coloured. He smiled letting her look her fill at the cockstand tenting his falls. She bit her lip and dragged her eyes away, reaching for the hairbrush. *Well, she was still interested, that was something.*

He took his turn behind the screen and emerged to find her fully clothed. She seemed highly anxious to be on their way. He had hoped to delay a little, perhaps explore a few more heated kisses, see where they might lead. His cock certainly wanted that. The thought made him irritable.

He was doing his best to wash one handed at the bowl on the dresser with his back to her when he heard her curse. Turning he found her feeling all the pockets in her jacket.

Her face was pale, and she looked at him shocked. "The brooch! It's gone."

He frowned. "Could it have fallen out of your pocket?"

She shook her head. "I had it in the breast pocket of my jacket."

"Did you take your jacket off at any point yesterday before we retired?"

"No."

"It's unlikely that it was rifled by a pick pocket then. How long were you in the tap room yesterday before I arrived?"

"About half an hour." she said checking under the bed.

"Did you go to the bar to be served or did the waitress come to you?"

"Waitress." She rose, looking around for anywhere else it might have fallen.

"Was there anything else in that pocket?"

"Yes, my purse. It's gone too."

"Damn! It would seem you have been robbed, but when?" He dropped the washcloth in the basin and reached for his shirt. Popping his head through the collar he said, "Did anyone brush up against you, in the tap room or the stables?"

"Not that I recall."

She sank down on the bed, her shoulders drooping.

He picked up his waistcoat and stood holding it. "Can you help me with this?"

She looked up with a start and sprang to her feet taking it from him and helping him get it over his arm and then pinning it in place over the sling. She then took up his neckcloth and folded and wrapped it round his neck, stuck it with the cravat pin from the bedside table, and then she picked up his jacket.

"The jewels, did you move them?" she asked hefting the jacket, it was obvious the heavy bag of jewels wasn't in the pocket of his jacket.

"No!" He reached for the jacket, clutching the empty pocket. "Damn and blast!" He stared at her in consternation. "Check the key is still in the lock," he said grimly with a nod at the door, as he turned towards the windows. There were two, both sashes, and both he would have sworn were shut tight last night against the weather. But this morning one was slightly open, a gap of about an inch at the bottom. He shoved it up, it went easily and more to the point, soundlessly.

"The key is still in the lock," she said coming up behind him as he closed the window again.

"The thief, came through the window, while we were asleep. A risky move. He is either courageous or stupid, I'm not sure which." He spoke grimly, his mind turning over scenarios and questions at a rapid rate. He turned back to his jacket and checked all the pockets. His silver flask and his purse were also gone. Everything except the cravat pin which had been on the bedside table, and his signet which was still on his finger, was gone.

Was this just a thief getting lucky? Or did the thief know what he'd carried and targeted him deliberately? Which brought to his mind the thing that had been nagging at him yesterday but had gone unquestioned because–because he was so damned distracted by Diana!

He turned to her and snapped, "How did you know where to find me on the road and how did you know I had the brooch on me?"

She backed up at his ferocity until she ran into the chair, her eyes wide and face pale. She wet her lips nervously and if he hadn't been so furious and consumed with suspicion it would have been erotic. Her mouth would be the death of him.

"Well?" he pressed, advancing on her, crowding her, grabbing her arm, and shaking it. "Answer me, damn it! How did you know?"

"Garmon knew!" she panted. "He has eyes and ears everywhere. He knew you were coming to London to sell them-the jewels-and that you were riding alone. I heard him telling his manager, Connor Mor and instructing him to take them from you, as payment for your grandfathers' debts. I left as soon as I heard. I had to beat Connor to you to get the brooch. Which I did."

"So, you're in league with them. A plot to rob me, was it part of the plot to kill me too?"

"No! I told you I didn't intend-"

"Last night- it was all a distraction to ensure I never suspected. This Connor, did you let him in the window? If you did, why didn't you just flee with him? Why stay?"

"I didn't know he was here!" she cried.

He continued as if she hadn't spoken, too furious to listen to her denials. His chest ached and it wasn't the wound. It was the ache of betrayal. Bitter betrayal.

"You knew he was on my tail, and you never mentioned one word of it to me. So, you were in league with him. You were sent to trap me, distract me while he robbed me. This story about the brooch belonging to your mother, is it even true?"

"Yes! Yes, it's true, everything I told you last night was true!" he noted with detachment that there were tears streaming down her face, but as he had thought last night, she was an excellent actress. She was wasted in a gaming hell, she belonged on the stage!

He went back over the events of the previous evening in his mind, looking for evidence to corroborate what he now perceived must be the truth. Her subterfuge. But why stay this morning? Why not flee with her compatriot? They could have gotten clean away, and he wouldn't have been able to do anything about it. But perhaps she feared he would track her again, and she stayed in hopes of putting him off the scent? After all, if she could convince him that a random thief had stolen everything... That she was as much a victim as he... then she could have ditched him at some point after they left the Inn. After she wounded him again, to prevent him following her a third time.

"God, I'm a damned fool!" He stared at her. "A curst *idiot* for believing one word out of your lying mouth! You scheming, deceitful, *bitch*!" he turned away shaking with fury. His throat was tight. His chest ached. Every woman was a lying whore, hadn't his mother's example taught him that?

"Fuck, you'll pay for this!" he rounded on her. "You'll help me retrieve what's mine, all of it, including the damned brooch, and then I'll hand you over to a magistrate for theft and attempted murder! You'll fucking hang!"

She stood stock still staring at him, such an expression of glazed horror in her pale face. She was white as a sheet, that he wondered if she had lost her reason. Then as he watched, her eyes rolled back in her head, and she crumpled at his feet.

If it was a counterfeit faint, it was a good one. Some of his fury drained away as some vestige of humanity crept into the stone thing in his chest and made him bend over her to check her pulse. It fluttered under his fingers, where he held her delicate wrist and then her eyelids twitched, and she blinked at him, dazedly. As sense returned to her eyes, she tried to scramble away from him, but he reached out and seized her arm.

"Oh no! You'll not escape me again my little witch." He gripped her jaw and made her look at him. "You will tell me where my jewels have gone, then you will take me there and help me get them back. Do I make myself clear?"

She swallowed but said nothing.

"Do. You. Understand?" he said as if to a simpleton. God had her wits deserted her? He transferred his grip to the back of her skull. He could feel her body vibrating.

"Yes," her voice was husky. "If I do that, will you let me go?"

He stared at her. Was she trying to bargain with him?

"If not, you may as well take me to the magistrate now, because I will not help you." Her voice was low and surprisingly steady given that her body was quivering like a leaf in a thunderstorm.

He laughed. There was no mirth in it, but it relieved the tightness in his chest somewhat. "I could force you to tell me."

She licked her lips and he suppressed a groan, remembering with sudden visceral clarity what her mouth felt like to kiss.

"You could," she said. Her voice sounded far away as his mind was filled with sense memories, the feel of her lips. He forced his attention back to the present with an effort as she added, "But you won't."

"Why won't I?" he asked, curious.

A little smile curved her luscious mouth and a glint of moisture appeared in the corner of her eyes. She didn't answer, just continued to look at him, slowly he sat back on his heels, until his back hit the foot of the bed, and he tugged her forward into his lap and kissed her. Hard, deep, savagely. And she kissed him back with the same passionate desire that was tearing him apart. When he broke the kiss, minutes later, he was breathing furiously, and she was panting and flushed, her lips red and swollen, her eyes blown.

"That's why," she said softly.

He stared into her clear grey eyes, that resembled storm clouds this morning and whispered, "You will help me get my fucking jewels back!"

"And my brooch," she confirmed. "You'll never find them without me. I know what Connor looks like, and I know his horse and how he thinks."

"Can I trust you?"

"You'll just have to, won't you?" she said rising to her feet and offering him a hand up.

He took it and held on to it. His cock was stiff and hard, he wanted to bend her over the bloody chair and fuck her. He turned away instead. She was under his skin, in his blood. And she knew it.

Diana looked at his back and stiffened her trembling knees. He terrified her, and she ached with wanting him. *When he was in a temper, he was capable of anything.* She had seen sheer murderous fury in his eyes, but she had seen pain as well. The pain of betrayal. He felt betrayed by her and although what he accused her of wasn't true, it was true that she had concealed from him fact that Connor had been sent by Garmon to take the jewels. She had done so, not from malice, but because it didn't seem relevant. *She could see now that that was to be her undoing, for how could she regain his trust when she had lost it so devastatingly?*

But she had brought him to heel with her challenge. If she could be brave enough to stand up to him, as she had today, despite her faint... She could lead him to the jewels, retrieve her brooch and escape with her dubious virtue and her treacherous heart intact.

It would be a miracle if she achieved one of those things let alone all three, but she had to try. Anything else was suicide. He had meant the threat about the magistrate, but she doubted he'd go through with it, unless his temper got the better of him again. But then perhaps she miscalculated the extent of his hurt. The cause of that pain eluded her, but she could feel it in him. *If she could discover the heart of it, perhaps she could do something to ease it?*

What was she thinking? The man was beyond redemption, too damaged for that, she'd seen the brutality in his eyes. And yet... she ached to soothe that pain. She shook her head to clear it and reached for the saddlebags.

CHAPTER 12

The Duke had left a note with the landlord with his seal as proof that the room would be paid for when he was in possession of his funds. The man was sceptical but cowed by the Duke's ferocity.

As the road was cut by the flood they were forced to detour via Keysoe and Thurleigh.

But as she pointed out, Connor would be forced to do the same. "With any luck he stopped to rest, and we will catch him before he reaches London," she said with rather more optimism than she was feeling.

"And if not?" asked the Duke grimly.

She shrugged. "We will need to plan how to get the jewels from Uncle Garmon. He has men, who protect him and the club, and there's Connor."

"Who is this Connor to you?"

She glanced sideways at him and noted the tightness of his jaw and the clenching of his fist on the reins of his horse. *Was he jealous of Connor?*

"Nothing to me. But he'd like to be more."

"Would he?"

She hid a smile. "Aye, he's worked for Uncle Garmon for years, so I've known him for a long time. We're friends of a sort, but lately he has become a bit persistent with his attentions."

"Hmm." The grunt was expressive in its contempt.

THREE HOURS later they had re-joined the London road, and the rain, which had held off so far, returned with a vengeance. In a short time, Diana was, cold, and miserable. The road, a muddy river, made it treacherous to proceed at more than a walking pace, and they could do nothing but slog on in silence. As they had left without breakfast, she was starving and thirsty, so they stopped for bite at an hostelry where the Duke was forced to use his credit again. Resuming their ride, he seemed disinclined for conversation and the longer the silence persisted between them, the more reluctant she became to break it.

Her hopes of catching Connor on the road seemed unlikely to materialise. They had asked at a number of Inns on the way for any sign of a man answering his description and received only negative responses.

By mutual consent they concentrated on covering as much ground as a fast as possible, their objective to reach London, by nightfall. But they discovered the road was flooded and impassable at St Albans. Forcing them off the road into a detour that found them in a field with a barn, as darkness began to descend at around four o'clock. Tired, cold, wet, and concerned for him, he was swaying in the saddle dangerously, she suggested tentatively, "Perhaps we should take shelter here for the night, I'm not even quite sure where we are right now."

He regarded the barn and nodded. "Good idea."

The barn was dim inside, she used her flint to light a lamp they found with some oil still in it and then make a fire to try to warm themselves and dry out some of their clothes. Their cloaks steamed in the heat, both were damp but not wet through being oiled to repel the rain. They had brought some bread and cheese, leftovers from lunch and a bottle of wine to wash it down. Camped round the fire, sharing the bread, cheese, and wine, she glanced at him, his face was pale but at least he showed no signs of the return of the fever.

"How is your shoulder?" she asked.

"Sore," he replied shortly. He was still angry with her and who could blame him. Unconsciously she sighed.

He turned his head to look at her. "That is the third sigh in the past hour, what is it?"

She shook her head, "Nothing."

"Except that you are tired, cold, wet, and hungry. And your companion is a grumpy bastard."

Her lips twitched. "Well yes."

"Have we lost Mor do you think?"

"I fear so. He will have gone back to Lovells." She gave a convulsive shudder, despite the fire she was still wet and cold as he had noted.

He held out a hand to her. "You're frozen." His tone was almost scolding. She edged closer, and he wrapped an arm round her shoulders. "We had best keep each other warm tonight," he murmured against her hair. Her heart thudded.

"You're arm-"

"My arm will stay in its sling," he said mildly. "There is a clean dry shirt in my saddlebag, you wear that. Your clothes are wet through."

She smiled tiredly and nodded. "Thank you."

He rose and nodded towards the scattered bales of hay. "We should fashion a bed out of that with our cloaks." She moved to help him pull the bails together and used her dagger to cut the strings and spread the hay into a bed. With his cloak spread over the rustling straw they had a serviceable bed.

She helped him off with his boots and jacket. "I'll keep my shirt on, but my breeches are too wet to sleep in," he said.

There was no modesty screen tonight, so she moved away from the light of the fire and the lamp into the shadows. Where she quickly stripped off her damp clothes, donning his shirt, which was much bigger than the one she had appropriated for her own disguise. It came to her knees and gaped somewhat at the throat until she tied it closed for modesty. The sleeves were too long, so she rolled them up. Emerging into the light once more, she saw that he had already got under her cloak.

"It's remarkably comfortable," he said, holding the cloak up for her to join him. She swallowed and slid in beside him, the straw rustling beneath her. He wrapped an arm around her and tugged her towards him. "We will need to keep each other warm."

She dropped her head to his shoulder, allowing herself to be pulled against his side. But she couldn't relax, her body was trembling, and it wasn't with the cold. She was so aware of his body, warm and hard lying beside her, strong with his scent. His shirt under her check couldn't disguise the thud of his heartbeat. Nor could she ignore the fact that they were both naked beneath their shirts. Her feet were lumps of ice, and she rubbed them together to try to warm them, her damp thighs rubbing also. She longed for the opportunity to relieve the ache between her legs; it was getting unbearable.

"Comfortable?" he asked.

"Yes, thank you," she lied, settling her face into his chest, and putting a tentative hand on his stomach. She felt his muscles contract under her touch and she withdrew her hand quickly. *He was suffering from the same problem as she was. Lord where would this end?*

"It's alright, you can touch me," he murmured.

"I-"

"Hush, go to sleep." His voice was low and husky. *So, he was going to be good, she needed to be too.* She rolled over, still using his arm as a pillow, curled up and closed her eyes. Heat from his body along her back began to thaw her out and in a few minutes she felt herself relaxing as he just lay there, not doing anything alarming. *He must be tired and sore, too tired for dalliance.* She squashed the flicker of disappointment and insensibly her body relaxed, drugged by heat and fatigue.

Anthony lay listening to her breathe and trying to ignore the nagging ache in his groin. He was hard despite the chill and, the discomfort in his shoulder, as the heat of her rump pressed against his hip, gave him fantasies he needed to suppress. His fury with her from this morning had dissipated as the day wore on. Such that the sight of her sitting forlorn and bedraggled by the fire had got under this skin and made him feel like a bastard for treating her so roughly earlier. He swallowed his usual irritability and braved the notion of another night with her in his bed when he couldn't touch her. *Who knew he was capable of this kind of restraint?*

An owl's hoot woke Anthony, at what time he didn't know, it was still pitch-black outside, the fire had died down and the lamp gone out. He discovered that Diana had rolled over in her sleep and was curled up against him, her head pillowed on his good shoulder, her arm across his waist and her leg thrown over his.

His breath caught in his throat as he hardened and resisted mightily the urge to thrust his hips upwards to relieve the pressure. He clenched his teeth and held still but couldn't prevent the tremor that passed through his body, or the wave of pounding desire that engulfed him. His good arm was trapped under her warm body, and he lay a moment or two just breathing, trying to decide what to do.

She stirred, her head nuzzling his shoulder, her hand flexing on his waist. Her leg moved higher, the hem of the shirt she was wearing riding up, and her hips rolled, pushing her damp mound against his bare thigh. It was too much and he groaned.

"Diana!"

She lifted her head, her eyes glittered a moment, and he found her mouth in the dark and kissed her. He managed to extricate his pinned arm from beneath her body and wrapped it round her, his hand finding the smooth round globe of her buttock and squeezing hard, pressing her closer onto his thigh.

She made a noise between a mewl, and a moan and moved her hips in a sinuous roll that made him break the kiss and curse with lust.

"Diana," he panted, "I'm not made of stone." He swallowed. "I think a little mutual release is in order. Or I'll be forced to take myself in hand. Do you take my meaning?"

"Yes," her voice was hoarse and low. Her hand moved lower where the shirt covered his groin, and she gripped him tightly through the fabric, making him groan again.

"God, Diana!"

She huffed a laugh and raised the hem of his shirt. Her hand found his length and caressed it making him buck under her with another curse, the pleasure of her touch, sharp and sweet. Despite the chill night air, sweat beaded his skin and his breathing accelerated, chasing his heartbeat.

"You've done this before..." it wasn't a question.

"I've had a few encounters."

"Are you a virgin?" he asked directly. Wanting and not wanting to know the answer.

"Not physically, no."

"What does that mean?"

"It means I've used a dildo on myself, my maidenhead is gone." Her bluntness should shock him, but it was more arousing than shocking, as his imagination conjured images of her pleasuring herself–with a dildo! He stifled another groan.

"But you've not been with a man in the fullest sense?" he

asked his chest expanding with hope of being her first, all evidence to the contrary.

"Some kisses and fondling is all. Given my history, I've had enough sense to keep my legs together… until I met you," she confessed. "Not that there haven't been attempts to take what I wouldn't offer freely. I've a technique or two for preventing that."

"I'm flattered," he murmured. His fingers traced her cheek in the dark. Somehow the darkness made it easier to give up secrets.

"There was a woman I thought my perfect match and I did everything I could to make her surrender to me. But she chose another. I never thought I'd feel the level of desire I had for her again. But you -" he sighed. "The way I want you, exceeds it tenfold."

"I've not felt desire for a man like this before," she said softly. "The passion in your eyes undid me, set fire to me. I-" her breath hitched. "It was beyond me to resist you. But I'll not pretend I'm not afraid. I know better than most the consequences of unchecked desire."

"That's one of the things I admire about you most. Your courage," he admitted. "But you needn't be afraid right now. I've no intention of taking this further than a little mutual relief, tonight. Relief we both sorely need. You agree?" He reached for her, bringing her head down so that he could kiss her, latent desire sending fiery tendrils out from his taught groin. During their conversation his cock had remained rigid and demanding of his attention, but he'd ignored it.

"Yes," she breathed, surrendering her mouth to his and returning his fervid kisses with fire of her own.

"Straddle me so that I can touch you properly," he said softly. She obeyed him shifting her leg over and settling her knees by his hips, the straw shifting and rustling beneath him. Her hand stroked him gently root to tip, and he shuddered with the sharp pleasure.

"It feels like hot iron encased in velvet," she murmured.

He huffed a laugh. In the dark he couldn't see much more than her outline. He longed to strip off her shirt and devour all of her, but that would wait until they could do this properly, until he could have her fully. Right now, was about solving a problem of inconvenient desire that plagued them both.

His hand slid up her inner thigh, under her shirt and found the apex of her legs. He groaned again as his fingers encountered sticky curls and lushly wet flesh. His finger parted her velvety lips and her hips jerked as she uttered a moan that made his cock twitch, and throb.

"And you feel like slippery satin," he whispered, extracting his fingers he put them to his mouth. "Sweet and salty, the perfect combination."

She made a noise that caused him to leak and leaning forward, she found his mouth again in an open assault with her tongue. He surged up into her kiss, wishing he could hold her, appreciate her curves and skin, lose himself in the scent and heat of her body. His shoulder throbbed, reminding him of his limitations.

A growl of frustration surged in his throat as his hand ran down her front, seized a breast through the shirt and then dropped to her bare thigh. Running his hand back up her body under the shirt he caressed the curve from waist to hip and grabbed a handful of curved buttock. Caressing, he slid along the crease of her hip and down her inner thigh to squeeze her soft flesh and seek again her wet, velvet channel.

His fingers traced the full length of her from bud to centre and back. Her hips flexed and bucked, and she broke the kiss with a groan.

"Anthony!" his heart thudded harder at the needy desire in her voice, his pelvis cramped with sudden sharp demanding, lust. *Fuck!*

"Yes, Diana, you want more?" he panted, his fingers continuing to trace a path along her flesh, back and forth, back, and forth.

She gasped. "Please!"

He slid his finger down to her centre and plunged inside. She clenched on him, and his cock surged in her grip. He pushed a second and third finger inside, a little rougher than he meant to, seeking, thrusting, in and out, working her up. To his delight, she took them, sitting into his hand with greedy, needy lust. Her head flung back as his thumb found her nub and swirled, his fingers deep, his hand wet with her juices. Pushing, pulling, rubbing. He panted, "Glorious, Diana, come for me. Come, Diana!"

Her grip on his cock loosened as her hips moved more frantically. Her breathing became erratic, she stiffened with a deep groan and her body clenched and pulsed on his fingers. He gasped with her, his cock twitching and leaking, a throbbing ache washing outwards from his groin.

She slumped forward but was careful not to fall on his folded arm, holding herself up with her shaking arms. He listened to her panting breath and felt the dying throbs of her ebbing release. His hand stilled and he slowly withdrew his fingers, cupping her with a gentle squeeze.

She raised her head as he deliberately licked his hand clean of her juices. Could she see what he was doing in the dark? Her eyes glittered and he fancied that she could. He wanted to lick her to another peak of pleasure, use his tongue to make her groan and cry out, make her come again. His hips jerked with frustrated aching desire, and he wanted desperately to plunge his cock inside her, take her, possess her, make her his.

"Diana?" his voice, hoarse and raw with desire, reached her through the fog of blissful release, and she nodded and whispered, "Yes, I know."

Shuffling down their makeshift bed a bit, she bent over his

deliciously hard member and took him in her mouth. He tasted salty and musky, her flesh pulsed in response, his gasp and groan as she engulfed him made her smile in satisfaction. She'd seen this done a time or two, peeking through curtains or the cracks of doors, while she touched herself. He was large and filled her mouth to stretching point, yet the heft of him was satisfying in a way she couldn't describe.

She experimented with her tongue, swirling it around the head as she pulled his foreskin clear of the crown and sucked and licked him. Her hand grasped him firmly, rubbing up and down the solid shaft, as his hand came down on her head, showing her the right rhythm. His hips moved in time with her strokes, causing the straw to rustle, and his breathing became hoarse and ragged, as he gasped and groaned and cursed colourfully. She doubted he was aware of what he was saying, so caught up in lust was he. But his language was filthy and descriptive, telling her in no uncertain terms what he wanted to do to her.

Her body responded with a kindling fire. She moved her other hand down between her legs and swirled her fingers, driving herself towards a second release, as her hand and mouth drove him over the precipice. His member jerked and his groans hit a new deep note as hot, bitter, salty-sweet fluid filled her mouth in several gushing jets. She swallowed it down and licked him, before finally letting him go, while the hand between her legs brought her to the edge and over. She fell into another sweet, convulsive explosion of pleasure that made her gasp and rub her face into his groin like a cat. His hand found the top of her head, and he murmured, "Again, greedy girl?"

She lifted her head with an effort and murmured, "Was that satisfactory?"

"It will suffice for the moment, but I doubt it will hold me long if you insist on pleasuring yourself with such abandon. Come up here, I want to hold you." His voice was rough with ill-concealed emotion, and it made her melt inside. She was in a world of trouble here. But right now, she just didn't care.

She crawled up and collapsed beside him, wrapping herself round him like an octopus. His arm held her close against him, and he kissed the top of her head. She nuzzled into him and sighed, her body going boneless as sleep overtook her again.

Anthony lay awake a few minutes more, savouring the peace that washed through him in the wake of a thunderously pleasurable release. Her body pressed against his was a promise of what was to come. He chafed at the wound that held him back from taking her fully, devouring every delicious inch of her. Her mouth might have been untutored, but its effect had been devastating, his explosive release flooding his whole body with sharp, exquisitely satisfying pleasure. And the peace that came in its wake, melted his bones.

More. He wanted more, much more, of Miss Diana Lovell.

CHAPTER 13

*D*iana woke to a sense of peace and contentment that was foreign. She was warm and nestled close to another body, an arm round her made her feel safe. It was an unaccustomed sensation, and she rubbed her face against the cloth covered chest under her cheek, almost purring like a cat. She opened her eyes reluctantly and raised her head.

The early morning light, streaming through the window above the barn door, dim as it was, gave her an excellent view of his face and upper body. He slept, heavily, lying on his back, the slinged arm nestled across his chest, the fingers curled, relaxed. His jaw was dark with stubble again. She sighed and just watched him for a few breaths, her mind roving back over the pleasure they had given one another in the dark. Her cheeks heated and her body throbbed. She had been wanton and lust ridden, and it felt wonderful. No words of love had been exchanged; last night was a physical transaction, she understood that. She also understood that last night wasn't the end of things, it was the beginning. He certainly intended it to go further. He had made it clear last night that he would not be satisfied until he'd had all of her in the very visceral sense. What she couldn't afford, she realised with a pang, was to give him all of herself, visceral or otherwise.

She had lived her life to date, careful not to repeat the errors of her parents. She had no wish to love a man she couldn't have and risk birthing a bastard child, and yet, here she was flirting with going down the same path as her mother. Only in her case, she didn't have the dubious protection of a husband to hide her folly. She had no illusions that Anthony would marry her, no matter how much he wanted her body. He was a Duke and she was a bastard. Never mind that she could claim a fraudulent legitimacy as the daughter of Lord Barrington, Anthony's cousin no less! She knew the truth and so did both the Lovells and the Barringtons.

She resisted the urge to nuzzle into him, thinking to rise, but he must have sensed something for his arm tightened round her, and he murmured, "You're not going anywhere."

She sighed and subsided, giving into that nuzzling urge. He kissed her hair, and she raised her face, which led to him kissing her. Sometime later he broke the kiss, breathing hard, and growled, "I wish I was whole and fit, what I wouldn't give to have you under me now."

She swallowed, feeling the pull of his blue eyes dragging her into self-immolation. She needed to get away from him before he ruined her completely. She moved, "I need to-" she scrambled out of the hay bed and sped to the door which she pulled open and dashed outside.

HE SLUMPED BACK into the hay and watched her flee from him, an unreasonable amount of disappointment surging through his chest. The fear in her eyes as she drew away from him, pierced his armour. *Had his abominable temper made her afraid of him?* The thought cut up his peace and made him irritable. All his disgruntlement from yesterday came surging back, along with doubts. *Was she stringing him along? What was between her and Mor, really? Were they lovers? She had denied it yesterday, but then she would, wouldn't she. She certainly knew what she was doing and by her own admission she was technically no longer a virgin. Did she tell him that story to make him think-*

A shriek from outside had him up in moments, grabbing his pistol and pushing the barn door wide to be confronted by the sight of man in shirt, overcoat and homespun breeches struggling with Diana.

He aimed the pistol at the man, cocked it and said with deadly calm.

"Unhand her or you die."

Distracted by Anthony's command, the man turned his head, and Diana kneed him hard and bit him, the double assault had him coughing, backing away, doubled over.

"Get out of here before I shoot you dead!" growled Anthony training the pistol on him with real menace.

"No need for that guv!" the man wheezed red-faced. "Thought she was a fancy piece ripe for the pickin'." He turned disapproving eyes on Diana. "You didn't ought to go around undressed like that! Gives a man ideas!"

"That is my wife!" bellowed Anthony advancing on him. He passed the pistol to Diana who took it aiming it at the cowering man. He whimpered, trying to flee as Anthony reached out, caught him by the coat, swung him round and punched him in the stomach. The man doubled over with a howl of pain, and Anthony forced him to his knees. "Now apologise to my wife you filthy cur!"

The man blubbered an apology and Anthony picked him up by his coat with disgust and flung him into a prickly bush. The man howled, tore himself free and ran.

Anthony watched him go and then turned to look at Diana who was standing with the pistol pointed to the ground staring after him, her face pale.

"Was that degree of violence necessary?"

"He had his filthy hands on you!"

"I could handle him," she said contemptuously. "I've had worse."

"Well, you will not be subjected to that kind of insult again!" Anthony's irritability rose. "I won't tolerate it! What the hell were you thinking to run out here half naked anyway?"

"I-" she stopped and shook her head.

"Are you accustomed to running around half dressed?"

"Of course not!"

"Well then?"

She shrugged and stomped towards the barn. "I don't want to talk about it."

He grabbed her arm and swung her around to face him. "Oh no you don't! What were you running from?"

She stared up at him, and he shook her arm, willing her to say something, anything. Tell him the truth.

"Are you afraid of me?"

"No!"

"What then?"

Her gaze dropped and she said softly, "I'm afraid of myself. This it's too much!"

He stared down at her bent head helplessly. He knew what she meant. It *was* too much. Everything had happened so quickly. But seeing that man attack her had unhinged him. He would have killed him if she hadn't been standing there. Only her presence stopped him from being a complete barbarian.

"Why did you say I was your wife?"

"What else could I say with us both standing there in shirts and nothing else?"

She shrugged and stomped towards the barn. He followed her pulling the door to behind him. She reached for her breeches pulling them on and tucking the too big shirt into the waist band.

He reached for his own trousers and tried to pull them on one handed, which didn't improve his temper.

Seeing his struggle, she abandoned her own dressing to help him with a tsk of her tongue.

"Why are we fighting?" he asked.

"Because you're irritable and I feel guilty!" she snapped, pulling up his trousers with a jerk.

"For what?"

"Shooting you of course! I should never have done it!"

He tucked his cock inside his breeches and let her button up his falls, while he took her head in his one good hand and said, "Well, stop it! What's done is done. No sense in regretting. Anything."

Her hands stilled, and he kissed her, hard. "I don't regret it and if I was whole, I'd show you just how much!"

She panted backing away from him. "Anthony, no!"

"No, what?" he asked, advancing on her.

"We need to get to London and get the jewels back!" she said backing away further towards where they had stabled the horses.

He stopped several paces from her, the cold thread of doubt invading his chest again. *She was in league with Mor. It was some plot to defraud him of the jewels. She was playing with him. She knew she had power over him, and she was very cleverly using it to tear him apart. And it was working! She'd got under his skin. She had him so confused he couldn't tell when she was lying and when she was telling the truth. If she ever told him anything that was true? Yes. He was sure the story about her parents was true. He couldn't say why, except that he felt it. He felt it in his soul.*

Uncertainty made him furious, but he controlled the urge to give into his temper with an outburst of rage. Instead, he nodded curtly. "You're right. Let us be on our way."

They packed up in silence and mounted their horses in silence. Heading out of the field they made their way back to the road and having ascertained their location with a modicum of conversation,, silence descended between them again. Only by not talking, could he keep a tight rein on his temper.

DIANA aware that she had made him angry but not really sure exactly how or why, still thought it might be for the best. She needed desperately to get away from him before he destroyed all her plans for her future, and the more time she spent with him the harder it became to remember that. The silence offered her ample opportunity to review the events of the past twenty-four hours. She dwelt longer than she should have on that little hiatus of peace she had experienced tucked up against him this morning before he woke and everything was ruined.

She sighed and shifted her focus forcibly away from the seductive notion of waking beside the Duke every morning, to the practical problems of how to help him get the jewels away from Uncle Garmon. Once that was done, she could–hopefully persuade him to give her the brooch, and they could part ways.

IT WAS LATE AFTERNOON, and they were on the outskirts of London, the light, never good all day, was very dim and the rain that had dogged their steps for the duration was still coming down. More of a sodden drizzle than a downpour now. She was frozen, her teeth brazenly chattering.

"I had b-best head to L-lovells," she said wiping water off her face and trying to control the chattering.

"No."

"B-but–"

"No. You'll come with me, to my house."

"W-why?"

"You know why. I told you, I'll not let you out of my sight until I get the jewels back." His voice sounded weary. He must have been in a deal of pain and discomfort. She was miserable enough herself, and she didn't have a hole in her shoulder.

An hour later they arrived at a four-story mansion in Cavendish Square. Flambeaux lit the Square and the steps up to the house. He dismounted stiffly, and she lifted her leg over and stepped down from the stirrup with a jolt, hanging onto the saddle strap to stop her knees from buckling. Everything ached, and she was so wet she squelched when she walked.

Following him up the steps to the front door, she waited miserably while his grace knocked for admittance.

"Your Grace! We wasn't expecting you 'til at earliest, tomorrow!" a middle-aged, dapper looking butler stood in the doorway, his expression shocked at the sight before him.

"Has Shorten arrived with my luggage?"

"No, your Grace," said the butler, moving aside so that the Duke could step over the threshold.

"Damn! Never mind, send someone to escort the horses to the stables and ensure they are thoroughly rubbed down and fed. I want two rooms with hot baths, one for myself and one for my cousin, Miss Barrington."

Diana started at this introduction, her heart thudding madly. *What was he about to announce her thus? The scandal...*

The poor butler gaped at this series of instructions his eyes starting out of his head as he took in Diana, bedraggled, and smothered in wet cloak and dripping hat.

"Is there a problem Kilham?" snarled the Duke.

"No, your Grace! At once, your Grace!" the butler sprang into action summoning and directing a footman, as he deftly removed the Duke's cloak and took his hat. Seeing the state of the Duke's arm he exclaimed, "Your Grace, what happened to your arm?"

"A bullet, nothing to be too concerned about."

"N-nothing -? Does your Grace wish me to fetch the doctor?"

"Not tonight, in the morning." He looked around the hall, which was vast and tiled with marble, and spied a woman in black bombazine and a white apron. "Mrs Penstone, the green room for my cousin, a hot bath and–damn!" he turned back to look at Diana and said, "Find a gown for her."

The butler was made visibly speechless by this and Mrs Penstone turned her gaze on Diana with a gimlet glare. Diana, still garbed in wet cloak and hat, tried to shrink into her sodden garments and wished the floor would open and swallow her up. A convulsive shiver shook her whole body, and with an impatient growl, the Duke stepped forward, and stripped off her hat and cloak himself and flung them at the butler.

Rounding on the housekeeper he barked, "And dinner in the dining room for two in an hour."

Mrs Penstone dipped a curtsy. "Yes, your Grace." She turned her gaze back to Diana and said in arctic accents, "If you will follow me Miss…"

"Barrington," snapped the Duke, preceding them up two flights of stairs. At the top he peeled off to the right, and Mrs Penstone lead her to the left.

Diana followed her in a kind of daze, shivering so much she was having trouble putting one foot in front of the other. The woman used a key on the large chatelaine at her belt to open a door and moved into the room where she began lighting candles from the wall sconce in the hallway.

Diana stood in the doorway staring at the room. It was huge with an enormous bed, and the whole thing was done in dark green brocade. The furniture was heavy and old-fashioned and the room smelt faintly dusty and stale as if it hadn't been aired in a while.

"Come in!" Mrs Penstone waved at her impatiently, and she stepped over the threshold. "Try not drip on the carpet!" she said sharply. "The maids and footmen will be here shortly with your bath and to make up the fire." And with that she left Diana alone, shutting the door behind her. For an insane minute, Diana thought of fleeing, out the door, down the stairs and out into the Square.

The Duke had run mad. What was he thinking, introducing her to his servants like that? The scandal would be all over London by morning. She stood just inside the door, her limbs locked in an of ague of cold for an interminable time until the door was suddenly flung open and the room was full of maids and footmen.

A fire was laid and lit, and as she seemed to have lost the ability to move of her own volition, she was moved bodily by the maids to stand in front of it. Where she steamed gently. She watched bemused, while a bath was brought in and filled with steaming hot water, buckets, and buckets of it. The footmen departed, and the maids began undressing her; they said nothing during this process, although their eyes spoke volumes.

When she was naked, the older of the two maids said, "Do you wish me to wash your hair miss?"

"N-no, th-thank you. I'll do it myself."

"Very well, there's soap and towels. Dinner will be at six in the dining room. His Grace doesn't like to be kept waiting." On this the maids bobbed and left her.

She put a tentative foot into the scalding hot water and squeaked at the pain. Gradually she worked her feet into the tub and then, even more slowly, the rest of her, until she was immersed to her chin in soothing hot water. The sensation was so blissful she just lay there, her head propped on the side of the tub for an age and drifted in a semi daze. Finally, she roused herself to wash her body and her hair and stepped out of the rapidly cooling water to dry herself. And was confronted with the fact that she had nothing to wear. Even if she could have born to put them back on, her sodden clothes had been taken away, and the promised dress had not materialised.

She sat in one of the chairs wrapped in a dry towel in front of the fire and stared at the clock as it counted down to six o'clock and passed it. At just after a quarter past six, the door was flung open by the Duke, who stood in the doorframe. He wore a black velvet jacket, silver satin waistcoat, buff-coloured pantaloons, and black shoes. His arm was still in its sling under his shirt, waistcoat, and jacket, but otherwise, he looked none the worse for their adventure. Unless you counted the shadows under his eyes and his grim expression.

He took one look at her and shut the door with a snap, waving a white garment. "I thought as much! Stand up." she rose slowly from her seat and blinked at him. She was light-headed from a lack of food and the cumulative effects of the last twenty-four hours.

She stared at him bemused as he came towards her and reached for the towel.

"Your Grace!" she squawked as he pulled the towel free of her grip and dropped it over the chair.

"Here," he snapped, flinging the white garment over her head. She put up her arms instinctively to pull on the sleeves. Turning her roughly, he pulled the laces tight in the back and tied them off awkwardly using his teeth and his one hand. Turning her round, he looked her up and down. "It will do until morning."

She looked down at the plain cream worsted gown. The weave of the cloth was coarse and uneven, but it was warm, and she was more than grateful for that. She had become chilled again while sitting in the towel.

"Thank you," she managed. Her tongue felt swollen and sticky from thirst. "Where did you get it?"

"One of the maids. Come, dinner is getting cold."

"Wait! My hair. Can I have my comb and brush?"

He turned back and frowned. Putting up a hand, he pulled his fingers through the tangle of damp curls, snagging and tugging. She winced as he got the worst of the tangles free. "There that will do. You can brush it properly later." He grabbed her arm and towed her to the door. Her bare feet slapped on the floorboards.

He looked down and muttered, "I'll have to make a damned list. Come on, I'm starving."

She let him lead her down one flight of stairs and into a room on the right. At one end of the large table, which would comfortably seat twenty she thought, settings for two were laid out. He led her there and waited until she was seated before sitting himself. The footmen served them some kind of vegetable soup. It was hot and salty and she devoured it, along with a generous glass of water and mouthful of wine.

Both of them seemed too hungry to speak and in any case she was at a loss for what to say. His behaviour today had been erratic, and she wasn't quite sure what he would do or say next. He gave off an air of suppressed fury or perhaps tightly reined in tension, she wasn't sure which. She was tired and her confidence at its lowest ebb.

The soup was followed by fowl and fish dishes with sides of mushrooms and artichoke hearts, peas, and carrots. The final course included an apple pudding and custard. It seemed like the best meal she had ever eaten. At the end of it, she was full and drowsy from the warmth of the fire and the wine.

When the servants finally left them with wine, cheese, and fruit, she sat back in her chair with a sigh and sipped the delicious red wine. "Why?" she finally asked.

"Why, what?" he cut another slice of cheese, and pairing it with a date, took a bite.

"Bring me here. Introduce me to your servants as your cousin, the scandal will be all over London by morning."

He shook his head. "No, my servants know better than to gossip about me."

"I find that hard to believe, but in any case, why?"

"Your boy's disguise wasn't sustainable, given how soaking wet you were. The servants would have discovered your gender in short order. Introducing you as my cousin seemed the best I could do on short notice."

"If you had allowed me to return to Lovells none of this would have been necessary."

"You're not going back there."

She spluttered her mouthful of wine and choked for a moment. When she could breathe, she said, "You can't control where I go and what I do."

"Yes, I can. You're not returning to a damned gambling hell to be ogled and groped by every libertine in London!" His eyes flashed blue fire at her, and she gaped at him stunned.

"Why do you care?" The hunger in her for someone to care, reared its head like a slavering beast. Her heart quaked, and she tried to push the need away. If she let him see how much she craved his care he would take it away. They always did.

He leaned across the corner of the table between them, seized her arm and dragged her close, "Because, damn it, you're mine!"

And before she could do more than gasp, he wrapped an arm round her and kissed her. It was a savagely searing kiss that reduced her to a puddle of panting need in a few moments. He had her dragged half across the corner of the table before he pushed his chair back and pulled her all the way onto his lap and went on kissing her.

When he broke the kiss, he was breathing harshly.

"That is why," his words an echo of hers yesterday. It seemed an eon since then. He broke down all her carefully erected barriers. His possessive need of her fed the starving orphan in her soul and the fiery ache in her body, pushing logic out of her head. The tugging ache between her legs made her pivot, lift her skirts, and straddle him, kissing him, her hands pushing through his still damp hair. His one functional hand grasped and kneaded her buttock, pressing her closer against the hard heat behind falls.

Her hips rolled, and she panted, rubbing herself on him shamelessly, anything to assuage the aching need in her flesh.

"Diana, you witch!" he groaned and pushed the plates away from the edge of the table with a heedless clatter. Lifting her up, he deposited her bottom on the edge of the table and fell to his knees. Pushing her gown up out of the way, he buried his face between her legs and his tongue seared her from nub to centre and back. Her hips jerked at the delicious sensation, and she lay back on her arms, surrendering to the bliss of her his tongue licking furiously on her softest flesh. His fingers worked inside her, and she clenched on them hard with a moan, her head falling back as his tongue thrashed her with rising pleasure.

"Anthony!" she whimpered helpless in the throes of the pulsing waves of pleasure engulfing her body. He pushed his fingers in and out rapidly, curling them slightly as he dragged them back, and she convulsed and cried out as the pleasure peaked, held, and exploded outwards from his fingers and tongue.

He felt her release not only in his fingers and mouth but through his body like a shockwave of sizzling, sparking heat. He dragged his fingers from her centre, his mouth still suckling her through the pleasure and scrabbled at his falls. The buttons flew off, popping and rolling under the table, as he grasped his throbbing aching cock and reefed it again and again.

His hips thrust at the air beneath the table, driving him to release the sharp pleasure that had been plaguing him all day. He groaned as the wave hit. Fountaining up in jets of searing, gut-wrenching pleasure, that made him grunt and groan like a beast. Spraying hot streams of his seed onto the carpet and splashing his pantaloons, hand, and waistcoat.

He collapsed forward on her belly, breathing hard as the wave ebbed, little aftershocks making him tremble and shudder as he fought to breathe, his nostrils full of her delicious scent.

Eventually he moved, lifting his head, he looked up at her along the curve of her belly above the bunched-up cloth of the worsted gown. He looked down at the pink glistening flesh he had just ravaged with his mouth and groaned.

She fought to prop herself up on her elbows, and he drank in the sight of her flushed face with eyes gone huge and hazy with satiation. "You make me behave like a beast," he said hoarsely.

"No less than you make me behave like a wanton," she admitted with a twisted smile.

He rose to his feet, looking down at the mess he'd made of his pants, waistcoat and shirt and reached for a napkin to tidy himself. She sat up and did it for him, wiping sploshes of seed from the back of his hand and his clothing.

"You've lost several buttons," she said examining his falls. He nodded and sat down abruptly in his chair. His now softening cock still visible through the flap, along with a quantity of coarse dark hair, with those tell-tale red highlights.

He closed his eyes and rested his head against the high back of the chair. "Tomorrow we will deal with the matter of my jewels. For now, we are going to bed. To sleep." he opened his eyes and looked at her. Her hair was a tangled mess, her gown rumpled and still half up over her knees, her cheeks pink, her lips full. Her breasts outlined by the high-waisted bodice of her gown and showed her nipples poking through the fabric because she had no chemise or corset under the simple gown. She was deliciously indecent.

He remembered the brief glimpse he had got of her when he ripped the towel off her and wondered how he hadn't ravished her there and then. Hunger had driven him to ignore that base urge and instead bring her downstairs to eat. But once his hunger for food was satiated, the carnal hunger that had been driving him mad all day resurged. And when she returned his kisses with such fervour, when she straddled him and rubbed herself on him, it had been too much to resist.

He rose and pulled her down off the table. Her gown settled

round her ankles. He cupped her bottom with a proprietorial squeeze and kissed her forehead.

He pushed niggles of her possible duplicity out of his mind. If she was playing him false he almost didn't care, *he wanted her too much to let her go.* He'd keep her here and when he was whole, he'd have her in every way possible and then, well then, he would decide what to do with her. Decide if he could grow tired of her, discover if having her would assuage this ravening desire, quench the never-ending thirst for her that seemed to have him in its grip. And discover if she was as false as all women were, or if she was the exception he desperately hoped she was. The thought made him flinch internally, he was mad to even contemplate that possibility. That way lay hurt and the kind of passionate insanity that destroyed his father. *He would not repeat that mistake!*

He'd have the doctor to look at his wound tomorrow, and perhaps it would be healed enough for him to do away with the sling. He couldn't wait to get both hands on her.

SHE STOOD quiescent in his embrace, and he moved his hand from her bottom to her waist.

"Come on, upstairs."

She let him lead her up the stairs, turning right at the top. She entered his room in the crook of his arm with her heart thudding hard in her chest and her stomach fluttering. He had indicated they would just sleep, but she wondered what would happen if they woke in the night as last night, or what might happen in the morning. It was clear they couldn't keep their hands off each other. *How was she to avoid the inevitable when she couldn't resist him, and he wouldn't leave her alone?*

His room was bigger than the one she had bathed in, with an even bigger bed. The room was warm from the fire, and the russet-coloured velvet drapes matched the coverlet. The bed had been turned down and the clean white sheets looked inviting.

She realised suddenly how very tired she was, her body ached all over.

He unlaced her gown at the back, and then she helped him off with his coat, waistcoat, shirt, and breeches. When he was moving towards the bed, she finally shed the gown and moved to join him. A pleasurable anticipation of experiencing the same comfort she had felt that morning washed through her, and she struggled with herself. If she slept in his arms, it was inevitable that more would happen. But that, she reasoned was inevitable anyway. *So why deny herself the comfort she craved in a vain attempt to stave off something that was going to happen anyway?*

She crawled in beside him and curled up with her back to him. She should at least start out trying to resist.

"Come here," his voice was low and rough.

She swallowed. *So much for good intentions.* She rolled over into the shelter of his arm and nestled her head on his chest. *It felt so good.* This taste of something like affection. *It wasn't of course. It was lust. The man was mad with lust for her. But he didn't love her. Was he even capable of love?* She suppressed a shiver. She could enjoy this counterfeit affection, as long as she remembered that was what it was, and not something deeper.

"That's better," he murmured. She closed her eyes and let the weariness she had been fighting for the last hour engulf her. The warm comfort of his arm and the steady beat of his heart under her ear soothed her, and she slept.

ANTHONY TOOK a little longer to go to sleep, the disturbing comfort of her proximity was a source of pleasure and pain. One thing he knew, he thought muzzily as sleep claimed him, he wasn't going to let her go until...

CHAPTER 14

Dawn came and Diana kept her eyes shut in an attempt to prolong the sensation of warmth and comfort. She had spent the night curled into him, and she wanted desperately to stay there. Stay comfortable, warm, and safe.

When he had said last night "Because, you're mine!" something inside her had melted. Unwanted by two families, the Barringtons, and the Lovells, she had never really felt that she belonged anywhere, even with her father. Yet she felt that sense of belonging with him. His possessive obsession with her, was addictive, irresistible. Even if it was borne of a physical desire that would burn itself out once satisfied, the voice of reason inside her head pointed out. She stomped on the voice, desperate to hang onto peace for just a few more minutes.

But the peace was broken. Unable to lie still, she opened her eyes reluctantly and sat up slowly. This was her last chance to escape, if she didn't run now she would inevitably follow in her mother's footsteps, a path she had sworn all her life she wouldn't follow. How had a week in this man's company so undermined her resolve that she was even capable of contemplating giving into her own desires and his? It was because he seemed to need her, crave her, want her, she could feel it in the way he touched her, held her. Not in the things he said, although those were frequently seductive too. It was the soul connection she felt that was unravelling her resolve. She had to get away from him now. *If she didn't...she was lost. She knew it.*

She stole from the bed, and washed hastily, glancing over at him frequently. But he slept soundly. Her heart quaked, he was exhausted. She hoped he had taken no lasting hurt. *Perhaps his wound was worse?*

She shook her head to ward off her concerns. Threw the gown over her head, crept out of his room, and scuttled along the corridor to the room they had put her in last night. The tub was gone and, in its place, a neatly folded pile of her cleaned and dried clothes, complete with her boots, cloak, hat and saddlebag containing her brush and comb. The candles and fire had gone out hours ago and the room was dim. She scrambled into her clothes and spent some considerable time getting the tangles out of her hair. She was just preparing to bundle it up into a bun and pin it in place when the door opened and Anthony stood there, dressed in a banyan, his hair tousled and his expression murderous.

She dropped the pins and backed away from him as he advanced on her slamming the door behind him.

"This is getting tedious, Diana!" he growled, corralling her against the chair she had inadvertently backed into.

"What part of, you *belong to me*, do you not understand?"

She closed her eyes at his proximity and swallowed. If she helped him get the jewels back she would have done something to assuage her guilt overshooting him and then perhaps she could find an opportunity to flee after that.

"The best way to get your jewels back is to let me go back to Lovells. I can get them for you. I promise."

She opened her eyes when this elicited no response and found him regarding her with an expression part way between fury and exasperation.

"No. I will get the jewels back, they are mine, and they were stolen. I'm a Duke, it has some advantages you know. This matter will be settled by lunchtime. Before that I am going have the doctor examine my wound so that I can get rid of this damned sling and function, I hope, with two hands. You will stay here, safe and hidden until I can obtain some clothes for you."

She shook her head, a sense of panic rising in her chest. "Anthony, no! Have you ever been to Lovells?"

He shook his head. "I've heard of it, but it's not a hell I've patronised."

"You don't know my Uncle Garmon, he's ruthless and powerful, and he believes he has a right to those jewels because of the debt your grandfather owes him. He won't give them up without a fight. A fight you will lose with only one arm, please believe me."

His mouth tightened. "You underestimate me."

"I don't! I told you my uncle has men who protect him. You can't take on a dozen men, even if you were fully fit!"

"I don't plan to take him on in a fist fight."

"Then what do you plan to do?"

"I plan to have him arrested."

She shook her head. "That won't work. He is protected."

"Nonsense, you expect me to believe he has Sir Nathaniel Conant in his pocket?"

"He has everyone in his pocket!" She scanned his face for a sign that he believed her. "Look, I know where he will have put the jewels, he has a safe and I know how to open it. I have a skeleton key, I stole it as I thought I might need it. I *can* get your jewels back if you will just trust me!" She put a hand on his arm. "Please Anthony, trust me!"

. . .

ANTHONY STARED into her eyes and felt himself torn between his instinct to trust no one, especially a woman, and his desire to believe her. *No, not a desire, a burning need. Something in his gut told him to trust her, despite all the evidence to the contrary and his own bitter experience that had taught him women were faithless and unreliable at best.*

He broke the lock of her gaze, turning away and pacing towards the window. He couldn't think with her gazing at him with those luminous grey-violet eyes. He just wanted to drown in them, in her, and the time for drowning was not now. *Later perhaps, later definitely. He had not suffered all this discomfort to forfeit his reward at the last. He would have her, just not yet.* Forcing his mind away from the fantasies that had been plaguing him for days now, he stared out the window at the mews and tried to think.

What she said made sense, but everything in him rebelled at the idea of putting her in danger. If Lovell was as dangerous and ruthless as she said he was, he doubted that the man would stay his hand through any compassion or affection for his niece. As far as Anthony could tell from the little, she had let fall, Lovell had used her and quite pitilessly. *What kind of monster exposed his innocent fourteen-year-old niece to the debaucheries of a gaming hell?*

He needed another plan, one that utilised her knowledge without exposing her to undue risk. *He needed to protect her. The last thing he was going to do was send her in there alone.*

He turned back towards her. "Alright, I will take a different approach. But I'm not sending you back to Lovells alone. When we go, it will be together."

Her shoulders relaxed and she smiled. His body reacted with a flood of heat and warmth in his chest.

"When?" she asked coming towards him.

He reached for her, half unconsciously, *he couldn't keep his hands off her. When he woke this morning, and she wasn't there, he felt bereft.* He drew her into a half embrace. Her hair was tumbled round her shoulders and she wore her boy's outfit, that loose, shirt and the breeches that showed off her bum to perfection. She hadn't tied a cravat round her neck, so the shirt gaped and reminded him that he had yet to explore her lovely pert breasts. He'd been saving them for when he had both hands. That didn't stop him looking down the front of her shirt now and appreciating the glimpse of nipple and breast. *He really shouldn't be distracted by...*

He lowered his head and nibbled on the side of her neck, the skin was soft and warm, and she still smelt of roses from her bath last night. She uttered a little sound, half gasp, half moan as he licked her skin and bit her earlobe gently. So far, their encounters had been base and direct, designed to achieve release and nothing more. But he longed to do it properly, cover her in kisses and caresses, make her feel wanted and desired.

God, he was losing his mind. He lifted his head and took a breath to steady himself, *she had asked him a question, what was it? Oh yes, when?*

"Tonight, I think. We will need to plan it carefully, use your knowledge. One thing we haven't considered. We have been assuming Mor made it back with the jewels, what if he hasn't? Would he betray Lovell, make off with jewels for himself?"

"No, he wouldn't. Garmon owns him, like he does everyone. He's loyal." she chewed her lip, and he swallowed, *God he was a mess for her. She just had to breathe and he got hard.* "But you're right, we are assuming he was ahead of us and made it back yesterday. He may still be somewhere on the road. But I think we have to assume that he is back or will be by tonight."

He nodded. "Agreed." He ran an absent hand over her back and down to her bottom, squeezing, pressing her against him. "You need to change back into your gown. I will organise some suitable clothes for you, but they won't arrive until tonight I should think."

She looked up at him, resting a hand on his chest. "Where will you get female attire from?"

"A modiste I patronise." When she looked surprised, he smiled sardonically. "When one has a mistress, one tends to foot the bills."

She changed colour and said sharply, "You have a mistress?"

"Not currently, the post is vacant."

She looked away visibly troubled, and he stroked her back in instinctive comfort. Drawing her back into his arm, he kissed her hair. She remained stiff a moment, and then she leaned her head against his chest and he swallowed a groan. *She was a witch, and she had cast a spell on him, he couldn't think when she was in his orbit. Or rather he could think, but only of one thing, having her.*

She sighed. "My clothes are at Lovells."

"Yes, and you don't have access to them. I'll take you with me tonight, but you'll go dressed as a lady and wearing a mask. Will that look out of place?"

"No, many ladies of the ton visit the hell and wear masks to protect their reputations."

"I thought as much." His hand roamed over her bottom, squeezing, and pressing. His cock ached. He ought to leave her to get changed, but it was beyond him to do so. He wanted a taste of her again. His head lowered and he kissed her, but this time he did it gently, not the savage feasting he had indulged in before.

She responded as she always did when he kissed her, melting against him, giving him back kiss for kiss, using her tongue and lips until he was delirious with wanting her. He pressed his bare thigh between her legs and she rolled her hips wantonly on it, her breath catching, breasts pressed against his chest.

He swung her around with his one functional arm and laid her down on the bed, her legs dangling over the end. He shrugged off his banyan so that he stood naked, his cock jutting up, red and hot and quivering. She lay looking up at him, her eyes wide, her lips full, her breath rapid. Her nipples jutted hard through the thin fabric of her shirt, a blatant invitation; he couldn't wait any longer to sample them. He pulled the cloth up with his hand, and she raised her arms to let him take it off over her head, exposing all of her upper body to his gaze.

"You are so beautiful," he murmured, hardly aware that he spoke aloud. Her breasts were round, white globes, finished with small, tight, rose-coloured nipples. Her smooth milky skin, goose-bumped in the cold air of the room. He bent and kissed her neck, her collarbone, her shoulder, working lower over her right breast until his lips reached her nipple. His hand cupped and caressed her left breast, his fingers teasing the nipple as his tongue circled the other one. He sucked the tight little nub into his mouth and pulled, eliciting a moan from her as she arched her back, pressing up into his touch. He swapped hand and mouth to give the other breast the same treatment, breathing in her scent and taste with each suckle.

Her hands came up, and she ran them over his bare chest, shoulders, and arms, careful of the bandage and sling. Her small hands were cold, but he welcomed her touch as it left a tingling burn in its wake, making his cock jump and leak. He ached to press himself flat all along her length, but the arm across his chest prevented that. The wound throbbed, reminding him it wasn't yet healed.

He kissed between her breasts and down the sweet curve of her belly, feeling the pulse of her heartbeat, rapid and fragile, like a trapped bird, under his lips. She quivered, her hips rolling.

"An-thony..." her voice hitched, his name almost a prayer.

"Yes, my angel, it's alright," he soothed, his fingers working the buttons on the waistband of her breeches. She put a hand on his to stay him.

"Anthony-" her eyes wide.

"It's alright, angel, I won't–not till I'm whole, I promised you that. I just want to taste you. Let me?"

She swallowed visibly and nodded, moving her hand away.

He tugged at the cloth, and she raised her hips to help him pull them down and off her legs. She was gloriously naked to his eyes, the brown curls at the apex of her thighs, visibly damp.

It would be a simple matter to pull her to the edge of the bed and plunge inside her and for a moment the temptation to do so, despite his promise, was overwhelming, his mouth filled with saliva thinking of it and his cock leaked. A drop fell on her belly and the muscles contracted. He bent and licked it off her skin and she arched her back thrusting her hips up into him. His cock grazed her lips and he groaned, shivering with desire.

"Diana! Oh God, Diana..." He swallowed and ran his hand down her belly, trailed his fingers through her damp curls and rubbed between her engorged lips. Her hips jerked and she moaned.

His hand seized his cock and he traced the head between her lips, the sharp edge of pleasure that the smooth glide of her on the head elicited, made him groan with helpless longing. His breath came in pants as he slid up and down the crevasse of her lips, teasing himself and her, his knees felt as if they would collapse. He kept rubbing his cock between her lips, unable to stop the roll of his hips, the pleasure sucking him in, swallowing him whole.

"Anthony!" her voice cracked, her hips moved.

Heat and agonising pleasure spiked and his member jerked and quivered in warning, forcing a loud groan from his throat. His grip tightened on his aching cock as his knees gave way, dropping him to the carpet. He buried his mouth in her cunny and moaned, his tongue spearing her as his cock jerked and spilled his seed in an explosively heated rushed.

He gasped with the sharp intensity of it, his hand wringing the final waves of pleasure from his member. His nose nuzzled at her nub, his tongue thrust deep inside her, and his mouth sucked hard round her entrance as he felt her body convulse. She cried out and her thighs squeezed his head so tight he saw stars. He closed his eyes, breathing her, breathing only her. He let go of his cock, using his hand to grip her hip as he licked and suckled her, milking every last drop of pleasure from her body. He felt her ride a series of palpable aftershocks, her moans, jerks, and quivers slowly winding down until her legs subsided, and she lay limp on the bed, her breathing audible in the silence of the room.

DIANA STARED at the canopy of the bed and felt the little rills of pleasure settle gradually through her body, as she listened to her heartbeat, thud heavy and slow in her chest. Sensed the heat of his breath between her legs, the last ebbing tendrils of pleasure elicited by his tongue.

She could hardly believe he hadn't thrust inside her this time, despite her entreaty. He had come so close, and she couldn't have stopped him. Yet he kept his promise. The pleasure of his cock parting her lips and thrusting over her nub had sent her almost immediately into an intense release, one that matched his own. She wasn't sure which of them peaked first. She was already pulsing when his tongue speared her, pushed deep inside her and his mouth suckled, his nose nuzzled, and drove her into a series of rolling peaks of pleasure.

She was wrung out, spent, her limbs weak with satiated desire. Yet if he touched her again, she feared she would explode once more with very little encouragement. His forehead and hand rested on her thigh and she could hear his breathing, steady now. He had groaned so loudly at the apex of his pleasure, she feared the servants would know what they were doing. *But then, it was likely they knew already, after the passage of debauchery between them on the dining table last night.*

He sat up and kissed her belly, which made her stomach muscles contract and her swollen lips throb. He smiled, that delicious, sensuous, wicked smile, and she smiled back, unable to resist. He had kept his promise. Not until he was whole. But for how much longer could they skirt temptation?

His hand ran up and down the inside of her thigh and she swallowed an involuntary moan. *They must stop this. She must stop this.* She was edging closer and closer to disaster, she would help him get the jewels back, and then she would flee. Get away before he ruined her. *She would not bear his bastard. She would not repeat her mother's mistakes. But oh, when he came so close to plunging inside her, so close to giving them both what they so desperately craved...*

Why hadn't he? What was holding him back? Did his promise to her mean so much? He did his best to tell her what a beast he was, yet he was a gentleman at base, he wouldn't break his word to her.

He got to his feet and went over to the basin on the dresser. Poured some water into the bowl and wet a cloth, he brought it back to her and gently wiped her clean. She watched in silence as he returned to the bowl, rinsed the cloth, and cleaned himself. He bent, picked up his banyan and pulled it on, tying it round his waist awkwardly one handed, hiding his magnificent body from her gaze.

He nodded towards her. "You need to get dressed." he picked up the gown as she sat up and then stood, letting him dress her as he had last night. But this time he was gentle, pulling the laces firmly but not too tight. He pushed her hair over one shoulder and kissed her neck, squeezing one breast with his good hand.

"When I have the use of both my hands," he murmured, "I will make you mine at last. Soon, my darling, I cannot wait much longer."

She gasped as his hand tightened on her breast and his finger and thumb squeezed her nipple. He soothed it with a stroke, but that didn't stop the tingle in her breast and the hot throb of pleasure between her legs.

He picked up her hairbrush and pulled it through her hair until all the new tangles were removed.

He turned her to face him and inspected her. "Come on, I'd better feed you before I eat you again."

She gasped on a laugh. "Not again, surely."

He glanced back at her. "If you could see your face, you would know I mean it. You look thoroughly debauched and delectable." He touched her chin, his thumb stroking her lower lip. "Your lips are swollen, her cheeks flushed and your eyes still have that hazy, satiated expression."

He turned away to open the door and lead her back to the first floor. But this time he took her to a parlour at the front of the house, where a generous breakfast awaited them. The presence of the servants prevented any salacious comments or touches and gave her time to regain her equilibrium. They were almost finished when the butler announced the arrival of the doctor.

"At last!" he threw down his napkin and rose, striding from the room. Not quite sure what to do, she stayed seated and finished her toast and coffee. Assuring the footman that she'd had sufficient breakfast, she rose and went to the window to look out at the Square. For the first time in days, it didn't appear to be raining. She turned away and headed back up to her room, suddenly weary again.

ONCE THE DOCTOR LEFT, he rang for his valet, who had arrived with his luggage an hour ago, and got dressed, well pleased to have the use of his arm again. His shoulder was still sore, but the doctor had assured him he was unlikely to break the wound open again, provided he did not place undue strain on that arm or shoulder. He took himself off to the library where he sent a note to Madame Therese with a detailed list of requirements and the request that she come at once to outfit a young lady. He was specific that she was to come herself and be discreet. Therese arrived promptly with a coach full of bandboxes, needle, thread, and pins.

He directed her to Diana's room where he was relieved to learn she had retired, with a strong reminder that he depended on Therese's discretion.

Madame Therese, whose real name was Tilly Barstow, assured him with dignity she could keep her bouche shut and sailed upstairs to see Mademoiselle.

He saw her leave with some amusement and considerable relief. Diana would be closeted all day with Therese. He would not, could not allow himself to be alone with Diana again, until this evening, when they would go to Lovells and retrieve the jewels. He did not trust himself with her, especially now that he had the use of both hands. He had been promising himself that he would have her once that occurred. But now he hesitated. He had been thinking about what was to become of her. She had declared her intention of using the money from the brooch, assuming he let her keep it, to start a new life for herself. She had rejected out of hand his suggestion that her lawful father's family, the Barrington's be made to take her back and acknowledge her.

As an Earl's daughter she could lay claim to the title of Lady Diana... He smiled at the thought of that. She had an air of confidence and dignity at times that could translate well into just the right haughtiness suitable to a Lady Diana Barrington. She had the speech and manners of a lady–most of the time. It would seem her natural father had seen to her education and provided her with a governess, but she lacked the polish of a debutante. She had spent too many years in a damned gambling den, exposed to all the rougher elements of society. It was a miracle her virtue was still more or less intact.

And then she met him, and he tore it to shreds in a matter of hours of her acquaintance. Well not technically–yet. But if he took her, made her his as he wanted to with every fibre of his being, he would be forced to take her under his protection or marry her. Not that either prospect was distasteful. If he hadn't been saddled with a mountain of debt.

He sighed and poured himself a brandy. The other alternative was to run away to the continent with her; leave his debts, his title and all the responsibilities that came with it behind. He had flirted with that idea yesterday.

No, something in his bones shied away from that. He wasn't born to be the Duke of Mowbray, but having inherited the title, he couldn't forsake that, for a chit he might grow tired of in a year or two.

He tossed off the brandy. Not that he could see himself growing tired of her, but he knew himself, and he hadn't truly had her yet. *When he did, would he feel differently? Would this nagging ache of desire be satisfied? Would it dissipate? And then what was to become of her? Was he truly that selfish?* For the first time in his life, he realised that he actually cared what happened to another person. *He cared whether she was happy or not.*

This morning's passage of intimacy had changed something, or perhaps it was the comfort he derived from sharing his bed with her. He knew that he wanted desperately to make love to her properly, thoroughly. The solution was to make her his mistress, yet he knew she deserved better than that. She was a lady by birth, however unorthodox that birth might be. She was a lord's get by blood on the daughter of a lord, and she was simultaneously Barrington's daughter under the law and deserved to be recognised and treated as such. For all there was no actual blood connection, she was lawfully his second cousin. As head of the family, he owed her his protection, quite apart from the medieval feelings he had on the subject of protecting her from harm. He growled in frustration.

The honourable thing to do, was to give her up before he ruined her. It was what his insufferable brother-in-law would do. But he wasn't an honourable man, he had never been a good man. He was base and selfish, and capable of both brutality, and cruelty on occasion. He had learned as a youth, that it was the best defence against the pain that the world could inflict on those that didn't protect themselves. And he had a duty to his name and title, which he found suddenly mattered more than he had thought it would. He had debts he couldn't ignore. He had to do something to retrieve the family fortunes and marriage to an heiress was the only feasible solution.

And if he had any shred of decency, he would refrain from ruining her, he would see her established creditably and safely. She would be better off without him. He most definitely did not deserve her. And yet they had tonight to get through, a night he had promised himself the pleasure he had been delaying. He didn't trust himself in her vicinity. Tonight, was going to be torture if he maintained this position.

Or they could have tonight. Just tonight. He'd be careful, the risk was low, she was already as she admitted herself, no longer technically a virgin, so he wouldn't be taking that away from her, she'd done that herself. They could have tonight and then, then he would give her up, ensure she had the best possible opportunity to find happiness, and he would do his duty and save his inheritance. The prospect made him feel sick. But it was the best he could do.

He turned away from the window and sat down at his desk, pulling towards him a pile of papers he'd had sent with the coach which had arrived this morning.

CHAPTER 15

Diana had barely drifted off to sleep when a knock at her door heralded the arrival of a whirlwind. A diminutive lady with improbably red ringlets, dressed in the height of fashion, swept into her room followed by a troop of foot men carrying a dozen bandboxes.

"I am Madame Therese, Mademoiselle, and I am here to dress you at the command of Le Duc!" she announced as the last footman left and closed the door behind him.

Sitting up in bed, the sheets drawn up to her chin, Diana blinked at her.

"Come!" commanded the little French General, "I must measure you and make these dresses fit. But first we will assay the size of your foot!"

Diana slid out of bed, the cream worsted gown falling round her feet.

Madame Therese gave a scandalised shriek at the sight of the worsted gown, her hands going to her cheeks. "That abomination must go at once!" she spun Diana and ripped the laces free hauling the gown off over her head so that Diana stood naked on the carpet. Madame Therese knelt at her feet and proceeded to try on several different pairs of slippers until she found a pair that fit. "Excellent!" she clapped her hands and rose to rummage through another box and produced a quantity of white cambric. "And now we will replace that monstrosity!" she held up a morning gown with a high waist, and long sleeves. It was plain except for blue embroidery round the hem and a pale blue ribbon threaded through the band under the breast line. "You like?" she asked with an enquiring smile.

Diana nodded, dazed. Therese then proceeded to garb her in chemise and corset, over which she threw the gown, lacing it firmly in the back.

"It is very fine fabric," said Diana fingering the high-quality muslin, so fine it was almost transparent.

"Of course! For le Duc, nothing but the best!" Madame then pinned the bodice, sleeves and hem which all need to be taken up or in. She peeled this off carefully and set it aside.

"Now," she announced, "The pièce de résistance!" She produced a violet silk creation finished with amethyst beads and ribbons and set about pinning that also.

Diana glanced at herself in the mirror and was conscious of a little thrill. The gown was exquisite and the colour became her so admirably, she couldn't help but be glad Anthony would see her in it. Violet brought out the same colour in her eyes and gave her hair a lustre. She would have to leave the gown behind when she left him, but at least he would see her in it this once.

"It is a lovely gown," she remarked.

"Naturellement!" Said Madame with a sniff. "All my gowns are lovely!"

Therese prepared to leave after pinning the evening gown, with the promise that the gowns would be returned before the day was out. She had left a plethora of items for a lady's toilet, including pins, combs, ribbons, a necklace to match the evening gown along with, matching satin gloves and slippers, fan, reticule, a black velvet cloak and loo mask. "And you shall have a shawl, spencer and slippers in navy blue for the morning ensemble, oh, and I shall send a night gown and robe." she nodded at a third bandbox that she had left. "You will find a toothbrush, tooth powder, soap, powder and scent in that one and things for your courses when you need them." Diana flushed with gratitude.

"Thank you." She swallowed.

Therese squeezed her hand, "Le Duc thinks of everything. He is generous, no? A good lover?"

Diana's blush deepened.

Therese laughed. "You may rely on my discretion ma petite, I have dressed many of his women."

She turned towards the door, but Diana grabbed her arm, blurting out, "What were they like?"

Therese turned back and assessed her. "Beauties all. But not like you."

Diana cocked her head. "How do you mean, not like me?"

Theresa pursed her lips. "You are a lady by your speech Mademoiselle. But that isn't it. There is a something about you. A quality, I cannot name it. But it is there. You are special. You will lead him a dance, yes?"

Diana swallowed.

"Farewell petite, I shall return your dresses swiftly. Good luck!"

She left and Diana sat down on the bed and stared at the slippers on her feet. *Was she special? Truly?* She sighed, she did not think so. *She was an illegitimate child, a mistake that should never have happened. An embarrassment. Unwanted and unneeded.* She wiped her cheeks and shook herself. *She would not cry. There was no point, she had learned long ago that it changed nothing. She needed to get her brooch back and then resume her plans for a new life. After tonight...*

Her nuncheon arrived on a tray to her room shortly after, and she slept most of the afternoon, exhausted by the events of the last few days. An invitation, or rather a command to present herself downstairs for dinner, was accompanied by the arrival of the gowns as promised.

She entered the dining room with some trepidation, not sure what reception she would receive after his avoidance of her all day. He was waiting for her by the fire, dressed in a blue swallow-tailed jacket, cream waistcoat and white skin-tight pantaloons with black shoes. As usual he looked delicious and formidable, and her heart thumped at the sight. He had the use of both hands, the sling was gone. Excitement and apprehension danced along her nerve endings at the implications.

All her usual courage seemed to have deserted her. She'd had too long to think about all the women who had come before her. The fact that she was just another diversion for him, another applicant for the role of mistress to the Duke of Mowbray. She felt fragile, shaky, and cheap. She had been a wanton for him, and that was not his fault but hers. The truth was he needed only to touch her, and she melted. She had to get away from him, or she was doomed to follow in her mother's footsteps and be the mother of bastards. *She would not, she absolutely would not subject her children to that shame.*

But oh, how hard it was to remember that when he touched her, kissed her, held her, as if she was precious and desirable. She had never felt so wanted as she did in his arms. It fed a hunger in her, she had never known existed until he awakened it. Or perhaps it had always been there, but she had not understood what it was. A whimpering thing deep inside her, that desperately wanted to belong, to matter to someone.

His eyes scanned her as she came towards him. The table was set at the end nearest the fire, for two. Her cheeks flushed, remembering what they had done in that spot last night, *was he thinking of that too? How could he not?*

His eyes glittered blue as a summer sky, but his expression remained closed. *Was he angry with her? If so, why? What had changed since this morning?* The footman stepped forward to seat her and Anthony sat also. Silence reigned while the soup was served and cleared and the main course laid out. The Duke dismissed the servants with a wave of his hand, and they were alone with the food and the crackle of the fire.

"Is- is my dress suitable?" she asked unable to bear the silence a moment longer.

"Very," his short response made her heart sink.

"Are you angry with me?"

He put down his fork. "No, I'm angry with myself."

"Why?"

He picked up his wine glass and drank. Setting it down with a snap, he said, "Because I have realised in the course of the day, that I want something I can't have."

"What?" she asked, her heart thumping unaccountably fast.

"You," he said and cleared his throat when the word came out husky.

"Oh!" she flushed, her heart turning over in her chest. She put down her cutlery and seized her glass of wine and swallowed two large mouthfuls. Setting down the glass carefully she looked at the salt cellar and said quietly,

"Why have you changed your mind?"

"I need money, a lot of it. Even if I get the jewels back, it will not be enough to pay off my debts. My only recourse is to marry it. A wealthy wife will solve my financial problems."

She hadn't ever really thought he would marry her, but hearing him say it, say he would marry someone else–she thought for a moment the pain in her chest was her heart failing. But it was merely breaking. She had been right to be cautious. She needed to get away from him and soon. If not, she would become his mistress and the very thing she had sworn to herself she would not do would become a reality.

She blinked back the tears that stung her eyes and swallowed the hard lump in her throat. She straightened her shoulders and forced herself to look at him, forced a smile to her lips and said,

"Of course. I understand that did you think I was nursing girlish fantasies? I'm not a beggar maid, and you are not King Cophetua. We are not living between the pages of a silly romance." She picked up her wine glass and took a large swallow.

"I'm sorry-" he began, and she cut him off.

"Don't be ridiculous, you owe me nothing. On the contrary, it is I that has wronged you. You would still be within your rights to give me up to the magistrate. But I hope you will not?"

He shook his head, watching her over the rim of his wine glass. His gaze was intense enough to make her shiver and force a flood of heat through her traitorous body. Her cheeks flushed, and she couldn't sustain his regard, her eyes skittering sideways to the fire behind him. She bit her lip hard to stop its trembling, her eyes tearing despite her best attempts to stop them.

"Diana, sweetheart-" he reached out a hand to cover hers squeezing it tightly. She swallowed again and withdrew her hand with a little shake of her head.

"We should discuss the logistics for tonight," she said in an attempt to divert the conversation into less dangerous channels. If he was nice to her, she would melt, and they would both be in trouble.

She heard him take a breath and let it out slowly.

"Where is the safe?" he asked and his voice was steady if a little hoarse. He cleared his throat and took a swallow of wine.

"In the office, it's at the back of the main gaming room, the entrance will be hidden by curtains, but there is a second door at the back. I can enter it from there." She took another sip of wine, her nerves steadying.

"How would you propose to do that?" She noted that he had made no attempt to resume eating, and she hadn't either. She didn't think she could stomach any food now.

"If I make an excuse to use the facilities I can slip away, perhaps you can distract Garmon?" He nodded and refilled both their glasses from the carafe that stood on the table.

"I expect my presence will be distraction enough, but yes I can do that." he frowned.

He glanced at the clock behind them on the mantelpiece. "We should get ready to depart. Did Therese supply a cloak and mask?"

"She did." She rose with him.

"Will it be a sufficient disguise?"

"If I'm careful, I think it will, as long as I'm not too close I don't think any of the staff will recognise me, especially if I keep my voice low and do not speak much."

He nodded and appeared to hesitate as if to say something, but then he cupped her face and kissed her lips softly. It was a gentle, tender kiss, and it melted her heart. He broke it before she could respond, and he said huskily, "Go!"

She turned and fled upstairs to collect her cloak and mask. Descending the stairs again to the ground floor, she found him waiting for her and her heart turned over at the sight of him, his blue swallow-tailed coat made his eyes even bluer. This would be their last night together and everything felt heightened. She needed to allow herself to feel every moment of this night, to imprint it on her memory, so that those remembrances could sustain her in the future.

She reached the bottom of the stairs, and he took the cloak from her arm and settled it round her shoulders. His hands lingered a moment, and then he offered her his arm to conduct her out to the waiting carriage.

She stepped up into it and took her seat. He entered, sitting opposite, and shut the door. The equipage started with a jerk and for a moment the sound of the horses' clopping hooves was the only thing she could hear.

HE WATCHED her sitting opposite him, fidgeting with the mask and drank in the sight of her. The gown became her well, the colour enhanced the violet in her eyes and reddish highlights in her hair. Twisted into a confection on the top of her head, held in place with pins and combs. Therese had provided an amethyst pendant to go with the gown, and it nestled on her white bosom, just above her cleavage. The bodice was fashionably low cut and the silk skirt so skilfully designed that it clung to her shape and made his blood rise just looking at her.

He had been honest with her at dinner, and she had taken it on the chin as she took everything, but his heart wrenched in his chest seeing the tears in her eyes. *He had never met a braver or more admirable woman in his life and he most assuredly did not deserve her. Or more to the point, she deserved a much better man than him.*

And none of these thoughts did anything to dispel the raging desire he had for her. He had see-sawed back and forth all day on what he would do tonight. Convinced at one moment that he must give her up and at another that he could not. That he must not have her and that he could not deny himself the pleasure he had promised them both. He was still in a hopeless state of indecision on the matter, despite the conversation over dinner. At least he had told her the truth, she had no illusions now about what he could give her.

She turned her head to stare out at the darkened street passing by the window. His eyes snagged on the white column of her neck, the rise and fall of her bosom above the bodice of her gown, the delicate lobe of her ear.

It was too much! He rose and sat down on the seat beside her. She turned, startled, and then she was in his arms and he was kissing her luscious lips, the soft skin of her neck, nibbling that sweet earlobe. Her gloved hands clasped round his neck and her breasts pressed against his chest, their thighs pressed close. Raging heat and desire washed through his body and one arm held her close while his other hand cupped and caressed her breast. Such a joy to have both hands to touch her, hold her, love her with.

"Diana..." he whispered.

"I know..." she whispered back. He closed his eyes and held her tight. She hugged him back, and for the first time he felt something like acceptance, affection, love? *Had he ever felt loved? He couldn't remember this feeling. Yet it felt both strange and familiar. As it were something he had waited his whole life for and all but given up hope of experiencing* His throat was clogged and his eyes damp. *Hell, what was wrong with him? Was he sickening for something?*

The carriage began to slow. They were nearing their destination and this interlude must end. He loosened his hold on her reluctantly and sat back. She blinked at him and smiled a watery smile that made his heart crack. He cleared his throat.

"You should put your mask on."

She obeyed, and he helped her tie it in place. Then he lifted the hood of her cloak over her head and tried to view her as another would, not knowing her identity. *Would Lovell recognise her? His own niece?*

The carriage came to a stop, and he kissed her lips swiftly and squeezed her hand. "Ready?"

She nodded, and he moved to descend from the carriage as the door was opened and the steps let down. He helped her out and tucked her hand in his arm, turning towards the steps leading up to the discreet front door of Lovells.

CHAPTER 16

*D*iana's heart hammered hard in her chest as she ascended the steps of the building that had been her home for eight years. She was still recovering from that hug in the carriage. Never had anyone held her like that, as if his very life depended on her touch. She swallowed and tried to breathe through the maelstrom of emotions coursing through her body. She didn't have time to dwell on that now, but the residual warmth of it sang in her blood and buoyed her steps as she pushed back her shoulders and drew in a stabilising breath.

She could do this.

The door was opened by Carlos, the porter, whose eyes widened at sight of the Duke. She pressed her fingers into Anthony's arm in warning.

"Welcome, sir," Carlos said smoothly, taking the Duke's hat, coat, and cane. "Your cloak, my lady?" Behind him the staircase rose to the upper levels and a corridor reached into the depths of the building.

She shook her head and clasped the Duke's arm tighter, pressing her cheek shyly against his bicep.

"Certainly, my lady, discretion is assured here." Carlos murmured. "Enjoy your evening y- sir."

They moved to the stairs and as they left Carlos below them, she leaned in and murmured, "I think he recognised you."

"Undoubtedly. My cursed hair and eyebrows. At least he didn't recognise you."

The hubbub of noise from the first of a suite of saloons met them at the top of the stairs. Entering the room, they found tables given over to hazard, rouge et noir and Bassett. In the second saloon towards the front of the house, they encountered a noisy game of roulette and a rather more serious game of faro in full swing, with a dozen patrons gathered round each table.

"What was your game?" he asked quietly, his eyes scanning the room.

"Faro or hazard mostly, although I can turn my hand to most games at a pinch." she murmured. "Garmon and Connor are not here." she added. "Which means he may not have yet returned with the jewels."

"Damn! Morton and Wroxton!" the Duke muttered, turning aside. "My cursed brother-in-law's best friend, with Stanton's sister's husband. I didn't expect to see them here."

"Did you not? Morton is a regular, I've not met Wroxton." she said quietly.

"Harcourt!" the Honourable Ashley Morton, a tall, lanky gentlemen, considerably cast away she judged, waylaid them with an outstretched arm, his glass of burgundy sloshing dangerously. "Wroxton, dear chap it's Harcourt. Haven't seen you in an age!" he said listing slightly in the Duke's direction.

"He's Mowbray now," said Wroxton, who was rather less intoxicated than his companion. Wroxton was a stockily built man with black hair, showing a touch of grey at the temples.

"Eh? Oh yes, did hear something to that effect. Congratulations Harcourt," said Morton patting him on the shoulder, which made the Duke wince.

"Our condolences on your loss," intervened the more sober Wroxton.

"That's a point," said Morton, swaying gently. "Shouldn't you be in mourning Harcourt?"

She felt Anthony stiffen and dug her fingers into his arm in warning.

The Duke smiled urbanely and said, "You're foxed Morton, so I'll ignore that insult. Take him home Wroxton, there's a good chap."

"No, no night's young!" protested Morton. "Come and play Harcourt, ah Mowbray, keep forgetting." He took another mouthful of his wine and waved at the faro table. "Faro's the thing don' you think?" He flung an affectionate arm round the Duke and tugged him towards the faro table. She feared for a moment that Anthony would explode, but he contained himself and allowed the drunken Morton to tow him to the faro table. Wroxton followed amiably, and they took the three vacant seats at the table. The croupier was Rooke, one of her Uncles' more trusted men.

Morton blinked owlishly at him and said, "Eh, where's the gel? Pretty one with brown hair?"

Diana stiffened and dropped her head, to hide her face further. The Duke dragged her onto his lap and put an arm round her waist, cinching it tight. The heat and strength of him wrapped round her was reassuring, comforting. He signalled to a waiter for wine.

Rooke glanced at Morton as he placed the shuffled deck in the shoe for another round. "Not here tonight, sir." Rooke was a swarthy man of solid, muscular build and taciturn disposition. "Place your bets gentlemen?"

Bets were placed and Rooke turned the first card which was discarded and then the banker's card and the player's card. Sighs, groans, and shouts of triumph from the winners and losers resounded. The Duke who won, said nothing, simply sipped his wine and moved his winnings to another card. Morton, who lost, replaced his with a new rouleau. Wroxton wasn't betting. Three more draws ensued, in which the Duke lost one and won two. She murmured in his ear. "Stay here, I will slip away and meet you back here in ten minutes."

He nodded keeping his eyes on the play as she put down her wine glass and rose. Edging out through the press of spectators, she slipped across the room and out to the landing, only to spy Garmon coming up the stairs. She shrunk back behind the curtain that hung beside the door frame and waited until he had gone into the gaming room.

With a thudding heart, she walked rapidly down the corridor to the servant's door at the end of the short passage. This gave into a service corridor that ran along the side of the saloons. To her relief there was no one in sight. She scuttled to the last door before the stairs, it was locked. Removing the skeleton key from her coiffure, she used it to open the door and slipped within, closing it behind her swiftly and silently. The fire was banked and gave a faint glow to the room. She rapidly lit a candle and moved to the large, ornately framed picture on the wall behind the desk. It was a portrait of Garmon himself, in hunting attire with a dog at his feet and a whip in his hand. He'd had it commissioned a year ago.

She lifted it off the wall with an effort, as it was heavy; laying it down on the desk she turned to the safe set into the wall. Using the skeleton key again, she opened it easily and pulling back the door, held up the candle, her heart thudding with hope and apprehension. The bag with the jewels was there, which meant Connor must be somewhere around. *Why wasn't he in the rooms?*

Dismissing the thought as irrelevant, she seized the bag and stuffed its contents into her reticule. She then snatched the paper knife off the desk and stuffed it back into the bag to give it weight. She closed, and was in the act of relocking the safe, when she heard the door open behind her. A cold rush of panic washed down her back as Connor's voice cracked sharply across the room.

"What the hell are you doing?"

She dropped her left hand into the folds of her skirt to hide the reticule beneath her cloak and seized the candle stick, flicking out the candle and turning slowly to face Connor.

"Who -"

Connor crossed the room towards her and tried to seize her hand, she brought her knee up and at the same time she slammed the candlestick into his jaw. His head flicked back and with a grunt he went down.

"I'm sorry Connor!" she said softly, bending over him and checking his pulse. It beat steadily under her fingers. She fled to the door, pulled it shut behind her and scuttled back to the servant's door and to the gaming rooms. She slipped quietly back into the room and found the Duke still seated at the faro table, but Rooke's place had been taken by Garmon. She came up behind Anthony, keeping her head down and squeezed his shoulder gently. The Duke turned his head and covered her hand with his, she bent and kissed him whispering, "I have the jewels, we need to leave, now!"

The Duke squeezed her hand and turned back to the table.

A small pile of winnings sat at his elbow and his latest bet was doubled as she watched. "On that note," said the Duke lazily, "I think I will retire for the night." He reached for his winnings and Garmon put out a hand to stop him.

"Your Grace, I must protest, you have been with us a mere moment in time. If faro doesn't interest you perhaps, I can offer you greater entertainment?"

"Another night, Lovell," the Duke said rising and putting his arm round Diana. "I have sufficient entertainment for tonight."

"I believe, your Grace, you consider yourself a competent piquet player?"

"I do," responded the Duke, glancing back at Garmon as if bored. "Do you think you can beat me, Lovell?"

Garmon smiled showing a quantity of even white teeth. The man was forty, but still handsome. He reminded her strongly of her father at that moment, as she remembered him from her childhood.

"I do," he said in blatant imitation of the Duke's earlier words. "I challenge you to play me now."

The Duke shook his head. "Not tonight Garmon, I'm spoken for," he cinched Diana closer, and she nuzzled her face in his shoulder.

"Seems I can't compete with the charms of the lady. Tomorrow night then?"

"I'll see you at eleven, Lovell," conceded the Duke and turned away. Diana, her pulse skipping and jumping, walked slowly with him out of the room and down the stairs. Carlos was there and produced the Duke's coat, hat and cane and helped him don the coat. The whole process seemed agonisingly slow to Diana, but finally they were out in the street and walking to the corner where the carriage waited.

Only when they were seated in the carriage and the horses were moving did she let out her breath and hand him her reticule.

"Here, I didn't check it, but I hope all the pieces are there."

He took it from her but instead of checking the contents, he put it aside and gathered her in his arms. "I am never going to let you do anything like that again," he said against her hair. The hood of her cloak had fallen back but she was still wearing the mask. He reached up and pulled the strings, letting it fall. Then he kissed her hard. The kiss softened and then he broke it.

"Never again!" he said softly. "What happened?"

She collapsed against his shoulder, her head lolling back on his arm, reaction from the tension of the past hours setting in. "Connor caught me in the act, I had to knock him out."

"What?" he stared at her aghast.

She giggled from reaction. "It's alright he's not dead. I clocked him with the candle stick. And I kneed him in the cods. He will be a bit sore when he comes round."

"Did he recognise you?"

"I don't think so."

"My beautiful virago, remind me not to make you angry," he said cupping her face in his hand and kissing her. The kiss went on and on, a delicious, drugging delight, that made her blood sing and ignited a heat deep inside that clawed at her to be satisfied. She was drowning and she didn't care. So much for getting away before he ruined her.

He broke the kiss, his eyes blazing blue-fire that threatened to consume her, his breathing as ragged as her own. His hand caressed her cheek, his expression so tender and raw her heart turned over in her chest. "Diana, sweetheart, tell me you don't want this, and I'll stop." She curled her fingers in his hair, anchoring herself to him, as if she might float away if she did not.

"Anthony, you make me *want* to do the one thing I swore I would never do." *One night. Just one night. Surely she could have that?*

"What is that my darling?" he murmured kissing her hair, her forehead her nose, as if he couldn't stop.

She turned her head and captured his mouth with hers, kissed him with everything in her soul.

"I understand my mother's folly now," she whispered, tracing kisses along his jaw.

CHAPTER 17

He groaned, his body was on fire for her, and her lips were the sweetest torture he had ever endured. He hauled her against his chest, pulling her into his lap, kissing her deep and ravenously. Her legs straddled him, and he pressed her close, revelling in having both arms and hands to love her and hold her and squeeze her with.

"Diana, love..." he murmured, his lips finding her neck and her bosom, his hands sliding up her body to capture and massage her lovely breasts through the fabric of her gown. She arched into his touch, her hands, she had ripped off her gloves, plunging into his hair and holding his skull as he traced his tongue over her bosom.

He couldn't wait to get her dress off, so that he could suckle her fully. Touch her all over, squash her flat to bed and *have* her. The die was cast on this, they would have tonight and if there were consequences he would protect her, keep her. In any case, she was his to have, to hold, protect.

His cock, stiff, hot, and hard, pushed at the fabric of his trousers and nudged her mound through the layers between them. She rolled her hips in wanton need, every bit as lost to desire as himself.

The carriage slowed, and he gave her neck one last lave of his tongue before he pulled back, his breathing rapid. "We're home." he set her back on the seat and helped her pull the cloak back over her head and gather up reticule, mask, and gloves. He left his hat and cane.

The carriage door opened and he leaped out, turning to lift her bodily from the carriage. Sweeping her up into his arms he carried her up the steps and into the house. Ignoring whoever had opened the door, his focus all on her, he moved swiftly up the stairs to his room. Shutting the door with his shoulder, he set her gently on her feet and cast off her cloak, as she dropped reticule, mask, and gloves to the floor. He cast off his overcoat and pulling her into his arms, he said, husky with emotion, "Diana, you do understand that after tonight you are mine, don't you?"

"Anthony," her voice broke, and her eyes glinted in the candlelight.

"Don't cry love, you're mine to protect, always. Whatever happens." He kissed her gently, and she wrapped her arms round his neck, leaning into his kiss. He reached up to pull the pins from her hair and rake out the braids with his fingers, cupping her skull and deepening the kiss. The delight of having her in his arms, both of his arms, of holding her fully against him, was more intoxicating than wine. He buried his face in her hair and her neck, taking in great drafts of her scent, her skin was silky smooth and her perfume made him drunk.

He found the laces at the back of her gown and loosened them. Then, he spun her gently so that he could pull her back against his stomach and push the sleeves of her gown off her shoulders. He kissed her neck and shoulder with nips and licks of his tongue, tasting her with every sip of her skin. He moved his hands from her shoulders to reach down into the bodice and cup her breasts, feeling their weight and warmth, their soft heft. He captured each nipple between his thumbs and the side of his fingers and rolled them gently, listening to her moans with satisfaction. Her head rolled on his shoulder as her back arched, pushing her breasts more firmly into his grip. He squeezed them, playing with her nipples which had gone deliciously tight and hard under this treatment.

He ran one hand down her stomach splaying it over the curve of her belly and pushing her lovely bottom back against his aching cock. He could feel the heat and pressure of her soft buttocks even through the layers of fabric that separated them, and he rubbed himself against her. "Can you feel that my darling? It's all for you. I've been hard as iron all day for you."

Her whimper and reciprocal movement of her hips, rubbing back on him, made him suck in a breath and tighten his hands on her. He reached down, scrabbling up her gown to get to the precious flesh beneath. Running his hand up her inner thighs he reached the apex and encountered wet curls and silky flesh on his fingers. Spearing her gently with a finger he moved his other arm to hold her up as she groaned and her knees threatened to give way.

"I have you," he whispered holding her tight, sliding his finger gently between her lips, in and out, as she gasped and put up a hand to grasp his arm and the other went to his thigh. Her head turned, and he found her mouth with his and kissed her, rubbing her gently as her hips jerked and her knees trembled.

She shuddered and gasped, "Anthony…" it was a pleading cry for release.

He continued his tortuously slow rubbing of her silky flesh and absorbed every shiver and shake of her body against his. Every moan and whimper, every incoherent cry, until she was trembling on the edge of release.

"Anthony, please…" she begged, her voice hoarse and broken.

He brought his fingers, glistening with her arousal, to his lips and licked, then he offered them to her, tracing her swollen lower lip with his fingers. She parted her lips, and he slipped his fingers into her mouth. Her tongue slid over the pads of his fingertips, he groaned at the sensation.

He returned his fingers to the place between her legs and stroked her, gently, gently, higher, tighter. He felt the tremors in her body as she ground her bottom against him, making him groan involuntarily and grind back on her. "I'm going to fuck you so hard," he whispered. She gasped for breath.

"Please An-" Her voice disintegrated into a groan.

"But you have to spend first my angel, you have to be so wet, you can take me in one hard thrust."

She moaned helplessly and her thighs clenched on his hand. He said, "Open your legs for me sweetheart."

She clenched again and panted, "Anthony..."

"I know, you're so close, spread your legs a little, and I'll give you what you want, I promise." he whispered, his voice ragged.

She moved her legs apart and he stroked her. "Good girl," his fingers caressed her sticky swollen lips teasing, winding her up again, sliding up and down her channel. With an arm clamped round her belly he walked her three paces forward and said, "Grab hold of the back of that chair and bend over."

She obeyed him looking back over her shoulder at him, her face awry with desire, her eyes almost black.

He ripped off his neck cloth and jacket and pushed her skirt up over her rump until she was bared to him. Falling to his knees he moaned at the sight of her pink swollen quim.

"So beautiful," he whispered. Reaching forward, he slid his fingers between her lips again, teasing, touching. Then he leaned over and set his mouth directly over the entrance to her body. He licked and suckled, invading her with his tongue, while his fingers teased and rubbed, pushing her to the release she craved.

She jerked and cried out at his touch, and then she bore back on him, her thighs trembling as she groaned and shattered.

He felt her release on his mouth, and his cock twitched, pulsed, and leaked in sympathy. The agony of it made him groan against her hot, wet flesh as he breathed her in, sucked, and licked the last of her tremors from her body. His hand went to his falls and pulled the buttons free on one side. He slid his hand through the gap, seized his cock and squeezed the base brutally to stave off his rising release. He sank back on his heels panting, his eyes closed a moment while he brought himself back from the edge.

Rising, he pulled her up from her slumped position over the back of the chair and turned her in his arms. Holding her close. "That was merely the first course love, a great deal more to come."

She sighed, nuzzling his shoulder, and he held her close, allowing her a few moments to gather herself. He stroked her back and kissed her neck, his hand squeezed a buttock through her gown. She pulled back and looked up at him and smiled hazily. Then she kissed him gently on the mouth.

"You wretch, I had no idea it was possible to be that close repeatedly and not spend, my legs are like jelly."

He chuckled. "It is entirely possible. I could have gone on longer, but frankly, I can't wait. I am consumed with wanting you." His hands roamed over her body, squeezing, and holding. "I want to be inside you. I want to fuck you," he muttered against her throat.

She reached for the buttons of his waistcoat and undid them. In moments, the waistcoat and shirt were on the floor, and he seized her shoulders kissing her again while his hands tugged her bodice down to her waist, freeing her arms of the sleeves. The gown slid over her hips and fell to the floor. He turned her again and unlaced her corset, casting it aside and pushed her chemise down to her waist and over her hips to pool on the floor round her feet.

"So beautiful," he whispered, running his hands over her body, cupping her breasts briefly, he wanted to touch and kiss and lick and consume all of her. His cock throbbed behind his falls urging him to the main event. Done with waiting, he picked her up and strode to the bed where he laid her down on the turned back sheets. He devoured her with his eyes while he kicked off his shoes and joined her on the bed in only his trousers.

He leaned over her and took in every inch of her hungrily. "I have you now," he said softly, "And I will make you mine in every way I can before dawn."

She shivered visibly, her eyes, already dilated, darkened further, her expression of longing deepened. His body clamoured to bring this seduction swiftly to the point. He ignored it. He was going to savour this, and if he came in his breeches he didn't care. He'd recover soon enough to claim her. Again and again before this night was over.

She reached up a hand to touch his chest, her palm caressed his skin and made him shiver in his turn. The room was warm enough from the fire, it was the latent heat between them that made them both shudder. His stomach muscles tensed with desire and his cock throbbed and leaked some more. He leaned down and kissed her again, a deep slow kiss, as her hands ran over his chest and back before she tugged at him to come closer. He surrendered to that, wanting nothing more than to have her under him. Sinking down on her full length he settled between her thighs and pressed her into the bed, his hips thrusting against her, pressing his still trousered cock against her mound. She shuddered.

"Anthony, please..."

He swallowed a groan and peeled himself off her to undo his falls fully and push his trousers down his legs and off the side of the bed. His cock was so hard it ached, his balls so tight he knew that no matter what he did, at this point he wouldn't last long.

He pushed her legs further apart and looked his fill at the pink glistening flesh bared to his sight. He touched her gently, making her jump and whimper, testing her sensitivity. Her stomach muscles tensed visibly, and he groaned at this involuntary signal of her continued arousal, that initial release had not satisfied her hunger. The tension between them was palpable and so raw his skin itched with it.

He rubbed her silky lips very gently, very lightly with his fingers making her groan again.

"Soon, my angel," he soothed, concentrating on the sight of her wet, open honeypot. He swirled his fingers around the entrance to her body and inserted a finger, she was hot, wet, and tight. He groaned, sharp and loud, unable to contain it. He reefed his aching cock with his other hand, and shifting position, he brought the head close to her entrance, withdrawing his fingers. He swallowed the rush of saliva in his mouth and leaning forward on one hand, notching the head at her entrance.

Her thighs shivered, and he moved a fraction forward, lowering himself onto her body slowly until he was full length on top of her again. The head of his cock rested at the entrance to her body.

She shifted her legs restlessly, and he lowered his head and kissed her, lips, and tongue devouring. She wrapped her arms round him, her tongue invading his mouth with greedy urgency, she pushed her hips upwards in open invitation. He could feel the trembling tension in her body, the raw insistent desire engulfing them both. With a helpless groan he surged forward, pushing inside her in one firm, smooth thrust.

The wave of sharp ecstasy that washed through him took his breath away, and for a moment, he hovered on the edge of losing all control. His body shook with the force of his desire and he battled against the brutal impetus to pound her into the bed and take his savage pleasure.

He gasped and found her eyes, locking his gaze with hers. He held still in an attempt simultaneously to control his baser self and to absorb the rush of connection, the sense of rightness and belonging. Diana! She was the one. The one who made him feel whole.

CHAPTER 18

She groaned as he plunged fully inside her, stretching her, squashing her into the bed with his delicious bulk. Surrounding her with his earthy male musk and scratching her skin with the bristles from his stubble, his blue eyes blazed down at her, and she lost herself in their heat.

"Are you alright?" he asked, his voice low and hoarse. His level of self-control was astounding, she had expected him to ravish her the moment the door shut. Instead, he'd spent an inordinate amount of time arousing her to breaking point, forcing her to beg him to finish her. She had never felt so raw, open, vulnerable, and rabidly wanton in her life. She had been wanting him to thrust inside her for what felt like an eternity. Now that he was seated firmly there, she felt a kind of pleasurable ache. She was stuffed full of him, and she definitely liked it.

"Yes," she said softly, putting her arms round him and just so that he would know she meant it, she squeezed him with her inner muscles, which made him groan and his expression splinter.

"God, Diana!" his voice came out strangled, and then he

moved, and she gasped as a whole new set of sensations made her own body move in response to his.

He found her mouth and ravaged it with his tongue and lips, moving to her neck and whispered hoarsely, 'You belong to me now.'

The push and pull of him inside her, hard and deep, thrusting with possessive ownership, made her body open up. Made her raise her legs higher and wider to take as much of him as she could. In a very few thrusts she was panting and her body tingling with a new rush of rising pleasure she hadn't expected.

"Diana!" his voice cracked on her name and his whole body jerked. He groaned, and she felt the hot rush of his seed emptying inside her.

She should be alarmed, but instead she felt a kind of primal, deep satisfaction. She truly felt like a woman for the first time.

He grunted and shuddered and collapsed on her, his body still jerking with aftershocks for some moments before he finally subsided in a dead weight on her body. She hugged him tight as he buried his face in the crook of her neck, his hot panting breath dewy on her skin, his body lax and heavy. A rush of emotion flooded through her body that brought tears to her eyes. She stroked his back and his head and held him, until his breathing steadied, and he moved his head.

Getting his weight on his elbows he looked down at her with a smile so tender her heart melted. He kissed her mouth gently and stroked a tangle of hair off her face.

"I'm sorry, that was too quick, but I couldn't hold out any longer. Did I hurt you?"

She shook her head. "No, I liked it."

"Liked -? It gets better sweetheart, I promise. Much better." He moved to disengage their bodies, and she felt the cool air on her sweat slicked skin as he rolled onto his back beside her. He put an arm round her and snuggled her into his side. She traced the sight of his wound, it was still an ugly, red, half-healed scar, but their exertions hadn't broken it open.

"Does it hurt?" she asked.

"At the moment no, I am intoxicated with something I shall call the Diana effect." he slid an arm down to her waist and squeezed.

"I'm so sorry I shot you." she said suffering an attack of remorse.

"I'm not. We wouldn't be here now if you hadn't." He kissed her hair, his hand coming up to stroke her cheek. "This," he lifted her chin and kissed her mouth. "This is what I have waited for my entire life. You." He whispered and kissed her again.

Twisting, he pushed her back into the pillows and kissed her and went on kissing her, slowly, deeply sensuously until her head spun and her body was on fire with wanting him again. Her hands ran over his magnificent body, appreciating the ripple of muscle beneath the smooth skin, the scratch of hairs from his chest on her breasts, the sheer masculinity of him, his size, bulk, scent.

And yet, despite the latent strength in him, he was gentle in his touch, stroking and kissing and licking her skin. Laving her nipples with his tongue, suckling them until the point of almost pain, that shot throbs of desire to the place between her legs. The same place where he had already ravaged her, made her crest into release, and teased her to more with the deep thrusts of his cock. She wanted that again, more, more of that. She had already crossed the Rubicon, there was no turning back now. She was committed to this course, she was his. And she didn't want to be anywhere else, with anyone else. She was dizzy with love for him.

Love. Yes, love. She loved him. She stroked his hair as he moved down her belly, leaving trails of hot kisses on her skin. She wanted to hold him, hug him. Love him. She tugged at him and he raised his head.

"What, angel?" he asked.

"Come up here, I want to hold you," she said husky voiced, her eyes tearing up.

He smiled, that sinfully handsome smile that made her melt, and moved up to take her in his arms. She wrapped her arms and legs round him and held on, squeezing him as tight as she could. They stayed like that for an age, while she fought the urge to sob. Her eyes leaked moisture onto his skin where her face was buried in his shoulder. Where she felt safe and protected.

He kissed her hair and she finally loosened her hold, letting her head drop back onto the pillow. He looked down at her and traced the wet trails on her cheeks with his thumb. "What's wrong, sweetheart?"

She shook her head and heaved a breath through her clogged throat, "Nothing, just–just too much emotion."

"My darling," he murmured, stroking her hair. "There are not words to describe how I feel about you."

Her throat locked up and a sob escaped her.

"Hush my brave girl, I didn't mean to make you cry," he said in distress. "Diana, don't cry, love. Anything but that." he kissed her forehead and rolled over gathering her against his chest. She curled into him tucking her head beneath his chin, burrowing her face into his chest. Her body shaking with silent sobs. He held her and stroked her in helpless silence, his heart aching inside his chest. He swallowed a hard lump in his throat.

The shaking dwindled and stopped, she lay damp and limp in his arms. He felt a trickle of moisture roll down his side, away from where her face lay.

"My darling," he kissed her hair. "What did I say? What did I do to make you cry?"

She sat up wiping her face and sniffing. "Nothing, it–I think it's all just caught up with me." her attempt at a smile was wry. "It has been a fraught few days."

"Yes, it has, and you have been very brave and strong." He pulled a damp strand of hair off her face.

"My Diana," he cupped her face and kissed her lips tenderly and the tip of her slightly pink nose. "My virago. My warrior woman. You are -" words failed him.

Her expression softened and she leaned forward, resting her elbows either side of his face, stroking his cheek with a slender finger. "Anthony, I-"

He cut her off, because suddenly the truth dawned on him and the words tumbled out of him. "I love you. I've never loved anyone, except perhaps my sister Anne, and I treated her abominably. I love you, and I've treated you abominably too. I'm so sorry. I'm a wretch." His heart thudded hard in his chest, terror dancing along his nerves.

"No-"

"Yes, I am. I don't deserve you, but as God is my witness, I will try to deserve you, because I want you more than I want my next breath. My darling, sweet, brave, honourable, passionate woman, you are everything I thought I could never have. I didn't believe that someone like you existed. Tell me you will stay with me Diana, I can't live without you, you have become as essential to me as breathing. Please, my darling love..."

"Oh, Anthony..." she melted against him, and he kissed her, drowning in the sheer rush of emotions he had never thought to feel. He rolled her onto her back and went on kissing her, he never wanted to stop.

"I love you," he murmured against her neck working his way down her body with an avalanche of kisses. Suckling, licking savouring every sweet, delectable inch of her. *She was his.* The surge of possessive, protective, savage desire washed through him, his hands tightening on her as he reached the juncture of her thighs.

Pushing her legs apart, he splayed her thighs with his arms and buried his face in her cunny. She smelt and tasted of him. She wore his scent, and he licked up the salty, sweet, and bitter taste of his seed. Working his tongue inside her, pressing his arms down on her thighs to keep her as wide for him as her legs would allow.

She arched up, crying out, her hips jerking under his assault on her tender flesh. He reached his fingers over to rub her furiously, urgent for her to peak, his cock rampant and demanding against the sheets.

She bucked and stiffened, groaning loudly, and releasing against his tongue in palpable spasms. Panting she moaned, "Ant-" her voice disintegrating as his tongue continued its barrage on her flesh taking her into another paroxysm.

She had barely crested the third, when he rose up on his knees and speared her hard with his rigid cock. Hooking his arms under her thighs and pushing her legs up and wide as they would go, fucking her relentlessly hard. Panting and grunting with the effort, holding her hips tightly in his hands. Watching her face as his frenzy drove her over the edge yet again.

The surge of pleasure drove higher, tightening his balls as lightening ran down his spine and exploded, forcing his seed up and out of his cock in wave on wave of engulfing pleasure. He groaned with each expulsion, his head flung back, his back arched, each ejaculation releasing something he had held tightly bound in his soul for longer than he could remember.

In its aftermath, his body collapsed forward, boneless on hers, his heart thudding heavy and slow, his panting breath winding down as he recovered slowly and returned to a state of equilibrium. His body felt heavy and light at the same time, he didn't want to move. He lay just breathing, listening to her heart rate settle under his cheek. His knees were bent under her thighs, and he was still buried to the hilt inside her.

He lifted his head slowly his eyes scanning her face. As if sensing his regard, she opened her eyes and stared at him with a hazy expression, still slightly out of focus.

"Diana?"

She licked her lower lip, her mouth curving at the corners. "Hmm. Now I know what you meant. I feel–ravaged."

He propped his head on his hand and tucked a stray curl behind her ear. "We're not done yet, my love."

He sat up slowly and eased out of her, flopping down on his side, and gathering her close. 'But," he said drowsily, "I think we deserve a break, just a short one." he kissed her hair and in a few moments he was asleep.

DIANA WATCHED him slip into sleep, his features softening and rubbed her sticky thighs together. His release had seemed to go on and on and sear his very soul. His profession of love had shaken her to her foundations. *He loved her!* She hugged the thought close and closed her eyes. *He loved her.*

A warm feeling of security curled round her heart and her body relaxed in the aftermath of three incredibly powerful releases. The pleasure had eclipsed the earlier one and his brutal thrusting has pushed her to heights of sensation she hadn't known were possible. She felt replete. The voice that had ruled her life and kept her safe was silenced in the aftermath of such bone shattering bliss. She had never experienced happiness like this, it was worth the risk. She smiled and whispered, "I forgive you, mama. I understand now." She drifted off, warm in the security and comfort of his arms.

CHAPTER 19

She woke sometime later to the realisation that they had shifted in their sleep. He was curled round her, holding her back to his front, his arm across her waist. She sighed with contentment and closed her eyes. Then she felt his lips on her shoulder and her neck.

"I was wondering when you would wake," he murmured, his hand wandering to a breast and clasping it. He shifted behind her, and she felt the hard heat of his cock pressing into her buttock.

"Again, Anthony?"

"Again, my love. I warned you I would have you multiple times did I not?"

"Hmm."

"Are you sore?"

She moved her thighs, her flesh was sticky and still a bit swollen. Yet the gentle jab of his cock, sent a pulsing throb to her flesh, he pinched a nipple sending a second shock straight south, and she moaned.

"I'll take that as a no," he said softly and repositioning himself he forced her thighs apart with his knee and angled his hips so that the head of his cock lodged at her entrance. He thrust and she gasped. The angle made her feel fuller and the position gave him easy access to play with her. His fingers speared her lips from the front, gently this time, a slow swirling motion that soon had her moaning softly as tendrils of desire flared out across her abdomen and down her thighs. He thrust in her slowly, his lips tracing patterns on her neck and shoulder, the arm under her holding her close against him.

For a long time, he just rubbed her slowly and thrust inside her with slow measured strokes, kissing the flesh he could reach, nibbling her ear, her neck her shoulder, holding her close with his arm. His touch and his thrusts built a slowly gathering conflagration in her flesh, delicious stabs of pleasure, gradually rising, tightening, demanding more. Her hips moved and he murmured, "Ah yes, ask for what you want Diana, make me give it to you."

She whimpered and gasped as his fingers moved a little faster and her hips juddered. "Please..."

"What do you want?" his voice had dropped to a low gravelly sound, dark and delicious. He nipped the nape of her neck with his teeth and a shiver raced down her spine.

"More..." she breathed.

"More what?"

She licked her lips.

"More what" he prompted. "Be dirty, be direct, tell me Diana."

"Your cock! Harder-" she gasped as he obeyed her instantly with a hard thrust.

"Like that?"

"Yes, faster, more!" She insisted, panting.

He tightened his grip on her belly and began thrusting hard and fast, his fingers speeding up to match and sending her abruptly into another sharp release. She cried out with the intensity of it, but he didn't slow or stop, neither the movement of his fingers nor his cock. The rush of pleasure washed through her and ebbed, eddied and surged again, rushing up and spreading through her body like a hot flood. She gasped, shuddering as he grunted and clamped her to him, and she felt the hot rush of his seed inside her and his body jerking behind her. His breath, hot puffs on her neck. His body relaxed and he kissed her neck, nuzzling his face into her hair and said fiercely, "You're mine."

He slipped out of her and pulled her closer. She turned, burrowing into him and their legs tangled, her arm across his body.

When she next woke it was to get a drink of water. She used a cloth to wash herself also and yelped when she felt his hands on her shoulders.

He chuckled at her squeal of fright and slapped her rump playfully, she turned and slapped him with the wet cloth. He caught it and said, "Allow me." and proceeded to wash her. She spread her legs wider for him, and he wiped her gently, returning the cloth to the bowl and taking her in his arms and kissing her.

She used the cloth on him and returned his kisses, wrapping her arms round him, pressing her naked body against his, trapping his firming cock between them.

She poured them each a goblet of water and took the drinks back to the bed. Crawling into the nest of rumpled sheets and coverlet, she sat cross-legged and drank her goblet of water, while he rebanked the fire which had almost died down. He replaced the candles that had burned down and lit them adding some light to the darkened room. Then he returned to the bed and crawled in, taking the goblet she offered him. He drank and set his aside, taking her hand. "Have you had enough of me darling?"

She shook her head setting her empty goblet down on the bedside table.

"Good, I have a notion to try something."

"What?"

"You're acquainted with dildos?

She nodded. "I have one, it's with my things back at Lovells."

"Which we should retrieve at some point," he reached across her to the bedside table and pulled out a drawer. From which he drew a wooden box. Setting it on the bed he lifted the lid and nestled in red velvet within was a perfectly carved cock made from ivory. He removed it and handed it to her to feel. It was cold to touch but very smooth. Also in the box was a small pot. He removed that also and put the box back in the drawer.

"Are you apprised of the pleasures to be obtained from penetration of the back passage?" he asked running a hand up her inner thigh.

She flushed. "I've heard of it. I understood it is the way men obtain pleasure from each other."

"True, that is one use of it. Women also find it pleasurable, in particular if it is combined with penetration of the quim.

"If the notion is distasteful to you, we need not proceed," he added, his hand massaging her inner thigh, his fingers brushing her lips. "But I assure you the sensations to be obtained are exceedingly pleasurable for the lady."

She swallowed and gasped as he pushed three fingers inside her. He pulled her towards him with his other arm so that she straddled his legs, his fingers delving inside her and kissed her roughly, his tongue thrusting between her teeth.

A rush of moisture provoked by his fingers curling within her and rubbing, made her groan in her throat.

"We can wait a little longer to sample that particular pleasure," he said hoarsely. "I've a fancy to let you fuck me." he pulled her up over his erect and quivering cock." ride me, Diana. Fuck me. Use me." His voice got rougher with each sentence.

Her body jerked and quivered with his words, and she clenched on his fingers, her heart thudding.

He bit her neck and sucked on the skin, withdrawing his fingers. He seized her hips and lined her up over his cock, "Hold me, guide me into you."

She obeyed with a trembling hand, her flesh clenching on emptiness suddenly aching to be filled up. The head engaged, and he pushed her down on him. His eyes closed, and he made a noise, half grunt, half groan. She was fully seated and, in this position, she felt very full. Each position gave her different sensations, and she supposed, hazily, it must be the same for him.

He lay back against the pillows, his hands on her hips.

"Ride me, Diana," he lifted her hips to show her what he meant. She obeyed him lifting up and down on his shaft, putting her hands on his chest for balance.

He nodded and smiled, his eyes heavy lidded.

"Fuck me," he repeated his voice low, delicious, dirty. More moisture flooded her channel and she clenched on him.

"God, yes!" He flung his head back exposing his neck.

She rolled her hips experimentally.

"Woman!" it was a prayer, an imprecation, and a curse.

His hands found her breasts and squeezed, his thumbs rubbing over her nipples. He lifted his head and suckled one and then the other. Falling back on the pillows he growled thrusting up into her.

"Spend, Diana! Use me, make yourself spend on my cock, I want to *feel* you." he panted, the cords on his neck stood out, his skin red in the candlelight, his expression fierce. His hands gripped her tight.

She rode him harder, her hand going to her nub and swirling rubbing, pushing herself towards release, panting, her heart racing.

"Fuck me!" he urged, thrusting upwards hard and fast.

Pleasure rising, rising she arched her back and cried out. The pleasure peaked and flooded her body, cascading outwards, tingling all the way to the soles of her feet and the top of her head. The tension ebbed, the thread holding her taught now broken, making her slump forward on his chest as she gasped for breath. He kept moving under her and her hips kept rolling in instinctive response. Stabs of pleasure ricocheted through her, and she continued, pushing herself to another release, clenching on him as the pleasure surged and exploded. She collapsed onto his chest panting, truly broken this time, and he clasped her close, stroking her back and kissing her hair.

HE LISTENED to his own thudding heartbeat, holding her on his body. He had felt every wrench and pulse and clench of her pleasure, he would teach her to go further and tear her pleasure from his body as he ached to tear his from her. She made him ache just by breathing. He wanted to fuck every hole she had and make her his. His filthy impulses made him wild. But they were tempered by a new warmth, a care for her well-being. She wasn't a toy to be used and cast aside. She was precious and of inestimable value. He had never known it was possible to love anyone this much. So much, it hurt.

It should be terrifying, but he was too full of the euphoria of love to care. He had laughed cynically at others when they lost their wits to love. And now here he was a fool for love and happy about it.

He gathered her close and rolled her under him. He was still deep inside her and hard. He gazed down at her and kissed her gently.

"I love you," he whispered, kissing her lips, her cheeks, her jaw, her neck, her ears, her eyes, her forehead, her nose and back to her mouth. "Your mouth is beautiful," he murmured. He moved in her slowly, but he didn't miss the slight wince in her expression. She was sore and no wonder. He withdrew slowly and lay beside her, stroking her flank. "Sleep sweetheart, you've had enough for now."

She sighed. "Anthony." He held her close, listening to her breathing even out, as he pulled the bedclothes up over her shoulder. Wrapping his arm round her, he made them comfortable, and he slept with her in his arms.

CHAPTER 20

*C*onnor had a headache from the knock to the jaw Diana had given him, and his cods were sore. Neither of which improved his temper. But those discomforts were as nothing to the fury he felt towards Diana and her blasted Duke. He had to get those fucking jewels back before Garmon realised they were missing, or he'd be suffering a lot more than sore cods and a headache.

Anthony woke to daylight and an empty bed. Sitting up in a panic he found her standing by the window, wrapped in his banyan. His heart rate settling as the alarm faded, he pushed back the covers and joined her by the window, wrapping his arms round her and pulling her back against him.

"Good morning, my angel," he said, kissing her neck. She turned her head, and he kissed her mouth.

"Look, it's stopped raining," she said, turning back to the window and settling back into his arms.

"Hmm," he said, more interested in her than the weather. He squeezed her breasts and she turned in his arms.

"You're incorrigible!" she said, with a smile, and her eyes glowed in the morning light. She was so beautiful. He cupped her face in his hands.

"I can't help it, it's you."

She laughed, a sound he realised he hadn't heard enough of. She looked down at his morning cock-stand jutting proudly between them. Reaching for the washcloth she dipped it in the water and wrung it out then wrapped his member in it. The roughness of the cloth and the cool water on his sensitive, heated flesh, made him gasp slightly, but he didn't resist her intention to wash him. He enjoyed the sensation of her grip as she pulled down the foreskin revealing the head and cleaning round the rim beneath. She plopped the cloth back in the bowl and dropped to her knees in front of him. He was rewarded with the grip of her hand running up, and down his length as she pulled down the foreskin, revealing the head for the exquisite attention of her lips and tongue.

She glanced up at him, and he watched, fascinated, as she opened that lovely mouth of hers and swallowed him. He closed his eyes the better to appreciate the sensation of her mouth and tongue sucking, licking, massaging the sensitive flesh. Her hand stroked him firmly, and he thrust his hips forward into her mouth, placing his hands on her head for balance. She kept up a steady rhythm, and he was soon panting as the pleasure rose, his balls tightening. He called a warning as the spark was struck and the rush of seed rose through the shaft and out the eye with thunderous force, foaming into her mouth. He staggered, his knees threatening to give way in the aftermath, as she swallowed down his seed and licked the last drops from him. Letting him go with a parting kiss she looked up at him and smiled with shy triumph.

"Did I do that right?"

He let out a slow breath and nodded, swallowing. "Yes, my darling, thank you." Lifting her up and he hugged her close, kissing her hair and then finding her mouth for another deep kiss of gratitude.

"A bath and breakfast?" he suggested.

"That would be lovely," she said, tracing her fingers over his chest.

"Good, after breakfast I have a couple of matters to attend to that will take me out of the house for a while, perhaps you can rest? Recuperate? I'll be all yours after that." He kissed her neck, his thoughts roaming over the tasks he had to perform on her behalf today. He had a plan to ensure the security of her future and their mutual happiness. It wouldn't solve all his problems, but it took him one step closer to achieving what he wanted. Diana.

She nodded, wrapping her arms round his body, and resting her head against his shoulder. "At least I have a dress to wear today."

"I will organise some more very shortly."

She looked up at him. "What is happening here?"

"You are mine now Diana. I will take care of you, that is all that need concern you, my sweet."

She opened her mouth to say something and shut it, looking away, blinking. "What about your debts?"

"That is my problem." His voice sounded grim.

She nodded again, and he let her go to ring for the servants.

Her fate was truly sealed now. She was his mistress. He must still marry to restore his fortune. She swallowed, how would he do that? When he said he loved her? But it was different for men. A man didn't need to love a woman to impregnate her. He would have legitimate children with his wife, whom he didn't love and bastards with her, whom he did. She shivered and her heart ached.

But then she was base born, she could never marry him in any case. She was no fit match for a Duke. She needed to be grateful for what she had. She had found her love, her soul mate, the one man who made her feel complete, and he loved her. She sighed and stretched, she was pleasurably sore. A little thrill danced along her nerves. Come what may he loved her, she couldn't ask for more.

ANTHONY HAD LEFT the house after breakfast, as he had said he would. Her contentment was somewhat disturbed by his refusal to tell her what he was about. Her attempts to enquire as to the nature of his business were met with a bland evasiveness that had her concerned. He had adopted, along with his general air of possessiveness, a kind of patronising 'I'll take care of it, don't worry your pretty head' attitude which she found both alarming and irritating. After all, it was she that had risked everything last night to get the jewels, and now he was treating her like a helpless ninny. Not that she wasn't grateful and overblown with love, but if he was going to continue to treat her like a fragile flower, they were going to come to blows.

The uncomfortable truth that she had cast to the four winds last night was that she was following in her mother's footsteps. Worse she was doing so with a man who could not and never would marry her, For all his professions of love, he could never offer her marriage he had made that clear last night.

She swallowed and sighed. The die was cast on that, she could be with child even now, after the numerous times he had joined with her last night. She had done the unthinkable because she loved him. *Oh mama, I really do understand now.*

She pushed the dark thoughts and worries into a box and shut the lid tightly. *She was happy. She would enjoy her happiness for just a little, surely she deserved that? What had he said? Never regret. Anything.* So, she wouldn't.

She smiled at the thought, a burst of love filling her chest at the thought of him and she wandered absently from the breakfast parlour to the library to find a book to read. Browsing the shelves, she found her focus wandering from book titles to memories of last night, and Anthony's words of love. Her heart filled up with reciprocating emotion.

She had been so overwhelmed by his passionate declarations she hadn't been able to articulate her own feelings, but she would do so when he returned, He deserved to know his feelings were returned tenfold. She picked a book off the shelf and sat down with it, but while her eyes traced the words on the page her mind was elsewhere.

After twenty minutes, she realised she hadn't comprehended a word and put the book aside, going to the window. The sun had come out at last, after days of unrelenting rain. The pavements were still wet, but the weak winter sun made them steam gently. Suddenly, she couldn't bear to be cooped up any longer. She ran upstairs for her cloak and bonnet and the navy-blue kid boots Madame Therese had sent.

She would just take a turn about the Square, there could be no harm in that. Anthony need never know she even went out. His instructions to stay inside until he returned were absurd, she wasn't his prisoner and if he thought she would be content to be, he would soon learn his mistake. Soulmate or not, she was no doormat to be walked all over and he would find that out soon enough.

She slipped down the back stairs to the servants' entrance and out into the mews. She stopped at the stables to check on Sugar, who was munching contentedly on hay in her manger and seemed none the worse for their adventure. Finding a stash of apples in a bag by the door, she fed her one and rubbed her nose affectionately.

Slipping out of the stables into the cobble-stoned alley, she walked swiftly to the corner, intending to circle the block, and come out in the square. She had not gone more than four paces when a hand clamped over her mouth from behind, and she felt the press of a pistol in her side.

"Don't screech or I'll shoot."

She froze. *She knew that voice. Connor.*

"Good girl. Now we are going back into the house, and you are going to fetch me the jewels. Understood?"

She stood stock still, her heart thumping painfully. *Not now! Not now she knew Anthony loved her.*

"Understand?" he pressed the muzzle of the gun harder into her side.

She nodded.

"Good." he said, forcing her to turn around and walk back to the rear entrance to the house.

"Where are the jewels?" he asked, quietly as they approached the rear door. She gestured upwards, her eyes darting about for signs of the servants, but there were none in sight, *drat it.* "Good. Up we go then, and quietly." He jabbed her with the pistol for emphasis. "Not a sound, now!"

They entered the small mud room which offered egress to the house through a door leading to the kitchens or servants' stairs on the left, that led to the rooms above. They took the stairs quickly and quietly, emerging on the second floor. The sounds of maids chattering, made him shove her into the first room they came too. It was dimly lit from the watery sunlight through the chink in the curtains, revealing a bedroom swathed in holland covers and smelling musty from disuse. "Which room?" He asked quietly, uncovering her mouth slowly.

"At the other end of the passage." she said softly. Anthony had picked up her reticule containing the jewels from the floor this morning, then dropped it in a drawer of the dresser.

When the sounds of the maids had faded, he made her open the door, and they proceeded down the corridor to Anthony's room. They entered, she found the pouch of jewels, and she held it out to him. He took it stuffed it in his great coat pocket and gestured to her to precede him out the door.

"You have what you came for!" she hissed. "You don't need me."

"I'm not leaving you to raise the alarm. Move!" He waved the pistol in her face and when she didn't move, he grabbed her arm, twisted it up her back and made her walk with the pistol pointed at the base of her neck. They moved swiftly and quietly down the corridor and the service stairs to the back entrance and out into the mews without being spotted. He frog-marched her down the alley to a waiting carriage, forced her into it and shut the door on them, signalling with a thump to the roof, the driver to start.

Seated opposite him, she shivered in her cloak and fought the urge to cry with disappointment and fury. *Connor had ruined everything!* He kept the pistol levelled at her and scowled. "You deserve that I knock you out after the trick you served me, last night." He rubbed his jaw where a sizable bruise was showing.

"I hope your cods are sore too!" she jeered.

He flushed red and compressed his lips.

"Does Garmon know where you are?"

He shook his head. "He doesn't know the jewels are missing. I intend to return them, and you, to him. You can tell him any tale you like to explain your absence, provided you keep silent about this. If you don't, I'll tell him of your plan to double-cross him by taking the jewels yourself, and your debauched behaviour with the Duke." He swallowed as if he tasted something nasty. "And to think I had a notion I might marry you. Slut!"

She flushed and snapped, "What makes you think I'd have you?"

"Clearly you'd rather be a Duke's whore than a respectable wife," he said contemptuously, and she slapped his face.

"That," he said murderously is the last time you hit me, jade!" And he launched himself across the seat and took her throat in his hand and squeezed. The pistol fell to the floor and Diana squirmed in his grip, finally getting a knee up and shoving him off her. He broke the hold on her neck with an oof of pain and fell back on the seat nursing his bruised balls with his hands. "You little shrew!" he cursed wincing. She lunged for the pistol and raised it pointing it at him.

"Stop the carriage and let me out."

He grinned which wasn't the reaction she was expecting.

"It's not loaded, darlin'." he reached into his pocket and withdrew a second pistol. "But this one is." He raised it and cocked it taking aim at her. "Now drop the pistol there's a good girl." She reluctantly lowered the pistol. "You're coming with me whether you like it or not."

CHAPTER 21

Anthony, gaining entrance to a house in Bruton St, hauled his cousin Lucas Barrington, 3rd Earl Barrington, out of his bed.

Lord Barrington gaped at him, his sleeping cap over one eye. "What in blazes are you about, Harcourt?" he protested wresting himself from his cousin's grip on his night shirt.

"Lucas, you have a niece."

"I have several nieces, what are you on about? Are you foxed?"

"Your brother's daughter, Diana."

"Dash it the girl was drowned, tragic the whole thing. What the devil do you mean by dragging me out of bed at this hour babbling about the family tragedy?"

"She's not dead and you know it!" The Duke loomed over him menacingly.

Lucas Barrington flushed and swallowed. "I know no such thing."

Anthony grabbed his shoulders and shook him. "Don't lie to me. I know the damned truth! You and your mother came to an accommodation with Lovell and hushed up the whole bloody mess!"

"Blast it, what did you expect us to do? Lovell wanted the girl, why would we stop him? He promised to keep her away from the public eye. It was a neat solution to an ugly business. He was her real father and happy to acknowledge her. Hell! I was a young, single man, what did I want with a five-year-old brat? Mother was furious with Letitia and wanted nothing to do with her mistake. She blamed Letitia for Aubrey's death. He'd never have shot himself if she hadn't betrayed him. Mother would have done anything to cover up the scandal."

"And all that might have been fine if Grandfather hadn't found out and killed Lovell. Did you know Lovell's family threw her out?"

"No, not my affair. I thought they buried her in the country somewhere. Or she might have been carried off by an inflammation of the lungs for all I knew."

"She was your niece, legally. She should never have been surrendered to Lovell in the first place."

"For Christ's sake why do you care?" burst out Lucas.

"Because I intend to marry her!"

Lucas just gaped at him. "You can't, she's your cousin by your own logic, Consanguinity laws won't *let* you marry her."

"I'll get a dispensation. I'm a bloody Duke, I can do as I damned well please."

Lucas shook his head. "You've lost your mind. Where did you meet her for God's sake? Are you sure she is who she says she is? She might be an impostor."

"She is Lady Diana Barrington and I fully intend that she be known as such. You will welcome her into the family and acknowledge her."

"What story will you put about, to account for her absence all these years?"

"She was rescued by a servant and raised in the country quietly. But she is of an age to be presented, and she will be, with all the respectability the family can muster."

"Who will present her? Mother is dead and my wife is an invalid, she never comes to town."

"My sister, the Countess of Stanton."

"What's to stop the Lovells from gossiping?"

"The same thing that has stopped their mouths all these years. Fear of scandal. Leave the Lovells to me, I'll manage them."

Lucas sat down on the bed, pushing his sleeping cap off his head, and mussed his hair.

"She'll have no dowry."

"That is where you are wrong. Your brother was a relatively wealthy man. With no male heir, his fortune went to you. You will bestow a respectable dowry on her, sufficient for her needs and those of her children, you understand me?"

"Why should I do any of this?"

"Because if you don't, I shall tell the world how you covered up her murder and that of her mother. The 'tragic accident' story that you put about to account for the deaths will be revealed as murder, which it was. I shall say you killed your brother for the money, because you had gambling debts you couldn't pay. You were his heir, you stood to gain by his death."

Lucas was white as a sheet. "It's not true."

Anthony grinned at him evilly. "Doesn't matter. It will be my word against yours, and I'm a Duke, I will be believed, and you will hang for a triple murder."

"My God, Harcourt, you're a devil!"

"I've been called worse!" He smiled, and Lucas shivered visibly. "Now, do I have your agreement? Lady Diana Barrington is your niece, and she will be presented to society by my sister. You will acknowledge her as your niece, endow her with a respectable dowry, and she will be a perfectly acceptable bride for a Duke."

Lucas swallowed and nodded.

"Good! I will send my solicitor round to hammer out the details of her dowry." He turned at the door. "You can give her away at the wedding, like a true doting uncle."

Lucas smiled weakly, and Anthony left him.

His second call was on the late Lord Peter Lovell's mother, Diana's grandmother. The woman had remained in ignorance of Diana's existence until her son's death, whereupon, according to his understanding she, her daughter and son-in-law had evicted the girl from the house. He would have liked nothing more to than to make them pay for that piece of callousness. For even more than Lucas and his mother, the Lovell's had been the architects of Diana's purgatory. But having coerced Lucas into agreeing to acknowledge Diana as his legitimate niece, all he needed from the Lovell's was the assurance of keeping their mouths shut. Since it would serve no purpose for them to gossip about Diana, he didn't anticipate any trouble from them.

Admitted into Lady Lovell's presence, he was met with a diminutive and formidable woman. She had white hair and a pair of violet eyes that reminded him so strongly of Diana, his heart did a flip in his chest.

She raised her eyes from her embroidery to regard him over her glasses and said, "Good God, Anthony Harcourt, I thought my butler must have lost his mind."

Anthony bowed. "Lady Lovell."

"You look well for a dissipated rake, what brings you to my door?" She waved him to a seat and demanded tea from the butler.

The door closed behind the servant and Anthony sat in the facing armchair opposite the lady. "I have come on behalf of your granddaughter, Diana."

The old lady stiffened, and he fancied she went a trifle pale under her old-fashioned rouge. "What of her?"

Anthony chose his words carefully, attempting to keep his temper in check, knowing it would do Diana no good to further alienate her grandmother as the woman was an influential member of society. "I was fortunate enough to make her acquaintance some days ago and to discover that she is in fact my second cousin. I have just come from an interview with Lord Barrington, who has been persuaded to recognise her as his niece."

Lady Lovell's eyes widened, and her mouth dropped open. She shut it with a snap and swallowed whatever she had been about to say as the door opened to admit the servants with the tea. Once tea was served and the servants had left, and her ladyship had sufficient time to recover her equilibrium, sipping her tea, she set the cup back in its saucer. "I am pleased to hear that Barrington has more sense than his mother. It was what I counselled eight years ago when Peter died."

Anthony swallowed a hot retort and tried for a mild tone but couldn't quite keep the edge from his voice. "And yet you let her be turned into the street."

She flushed visibly and her eyes skittered away from his glare. "That wasn't my doing. Lavinia and Paul had her evicted before I knew about it. Lavinia always disapproved of Peter taking the girl in. She was terrified of the scandal."

"And yet you did nothing to intervene."

"Not true! I contacted Garmon and asked him to care for her."

That did surprise him. "You knew about Garmon?"

She smiled cynically. "Of course, I knew! Phillip's indiscretions were well known to me." She smoothed her hands over her wide, old-fashioned skirts in an attempt to disguise their trembling. She swallowed, and he caught the glint of tears in her eyes. "I was younger and foolish then. Jealous. I knew he loved her. I was his society wife, but she was the one he loved!" Her mouth twisted in bitterness. "After he died, I made sure the allowance he had paid her was cut off."

She sniffed, searching in her pocket for a handkerchief. "After Phillip died, I told Peter, and he reached out to Garmon. His mother was dead by then. Peter, bless him, never told Garmon it was me that cut off his mother's allowance. It was knowing about Garmon, and what happened to him, that made Peter so stubborn over Diana, when Barrington shot her mother and committed suicide. He was determined Diana not suffer as Garmon had."

She took a breath and wiped her face and blew her small, pointed nose. Another feature she had bequeathed to Diana. "I should have stopped Lavinia and Paul, but I was afraid of the scandal too, afraid that people would discover what I did. It was weak of me, and I regret it."

She looked down. "I'll not ask how you have prevailed upon Lucas Barrington to acknowledge her, but I am grateful." She looked up. "I'd like to see her, if I may?"

Anthony regarded her with mixed emotions. He was angry with her for what she had done, but his self-honesty recognised that she was genuinely regretful of her actions. *What would Diana want?* She had been adamant she wanted nothing to do with either of her families, Lovells or Barringtons. "That will be up to Diana, I will advise her of your request."

She nodded.

"Will your daughter and son-in-law say anything about Diana?"

"No. I doubt they will be tempted to anyway, but I will make sure they do not."

He nodded and rose. "Then I will bid you good day Lady Lovell. I will send you word if Diana wishes to see you." He turned back. "She will be staying with my sister the Countess of Stanton."

She inclined her head, her usual regal manner restored.

HAVING DISCHARGED HIS ERRANDS SUCCESSFULLY, he returned to the house anticipating a happy reunion with Diana.

To find her gone.

The servants could tell him nothing about her whereabouts. She had, to their knowledge, left the breakfast parlour to go to the library. After that, no one had seen her. It wasn't long before he discovered the missing jewels, and he collapsed into a chair poleaxed.

He was stunned. For a few minutes his brain refused to function. *She couldn't! No.* He shook his head. *He refused to believe...*

But then it hit him. In the midst of recalling his declarations of love and devotion last night, he realised with a sinking feeling of horror, that she had not said that she loved him. A pain so sharp it took his breath away, stabbed through his chest and made him hunch over. He breathed raggedly through the pain, putting a hand to his chest as if to contain his heart which felt as if it had been torn out.

He sat bent over, gasping for several moments, holding his chest, staring at the carpet, his fevered brain ranging over his conversation with her, her actions, and reactions. *Had she played him false? Was she just a consummate actress, the cleverest liar? Had she all along just wanted the jewels?*

The voice in his head, never silent for long, rear up. *Fool! Do you never learn? Women are faithless whores. She doesn't love you, or she would have said so. And she would be here waiting for you, with the jewels where you left them. What further proof do you need that you have been duped and used?*

With a roar he rose up from his chair and dashed down the back stairs to the mews. He ran to the stables, where he was brought up short by the sight of Diana's dapple-grey mare.

If she meant to leave you, and flee with the jewels, she would have taken the mare.

He stood panting, trying to think. *If she hadn't taken the mare what did that mean? That she had not gone of her own free will? That she had gone out innocently perhaps? For a walk? For...*

He gave up. He didn't know. But the conviction that she had not left him willingly grew, lightening the darkness in his chest. Someone must have seen something, someone must know something. He went back into the house and demanded the butler assemble the staff, all the staff, in the servant's hall. An hour later, after an exhaustive interrogation of the servants, he had learned nothing more of Diana's disappearance than that she had left the house via the back door and stopped in the stables. Where she stopped to feed Sugar an apple and pet her, before proceeding out into the alley. This information was obtained from one of the stable boys, after he returned from an errand. No one else had seen her or had any idea where she might be and all denied any knowledge of the reticule in the dresser drawer of his room.

Chafing to do something, he sent the footmen and stable boys out to scour the streets and enquire if anyone had seen her. As they came back one by one with nothing, his anxiety levels and his barely contained rage grew. Two hours later, another of the stable boys came back with a street urchin who claimed to have seen something.

The enterprising urchin refused to give up his knowledge until he was paid handsomely for it. Resisting the urge to choke the information out of him, the Duke paid up and listened with a thudding heart to the lad's tale of a lady fitting Diana's description being forced into a carriage with a handsome dark-haired cove.

"'e 'ad a pistol. I saw it a sticking of in her ribs your 'onor."

The Duke's hands clenched in impotent rage, and he snarled, "When was this?"

"Bout mid mornin'?" he guessed.

"Thank you." he paid the boy another half-crown for his trouble and sent him off. Retiring to the library to think, he poured himself a drink and paced about the room.

Connor Mor. It must be. The only question was, did Lovell send him or did he come on his own? If Lovell sent him, Diana would be at the hell, perhaps being held as a hostage? If Mor was working on his own, for his own agenda, then she could be anywhere.

Now that he knew she had been coerced, the worst of his suspicions were allayed. His fears for her safety however were not. He probably had to proceed on the assumption that she was at Lovells for lack of anything else to go on. *But what could he do?* While his impulse was to hare off to Lovells and demand that Garmon Lovell hand her over to him, what leverage did he have? He was one man against, what, a dozen of Lovell's thugs? Lovell currently held all the cards, to wit the jewels and Diana. What could he possibly bring to bear against that?

If it was true that Lovell had the magistrate in his pocket, he was protected from recourse to the law. The only thing left to him was to use his position as a peer. *But how? What did Lovell want or fear?* If he had sufficient funds, he could buy Lovell off. *Damn it everything came back to money or the lack of it!* He had to solve his financial problems if he was to marry Diana and his resolve to do so was stronger than ever now. If she didn't love him yet she would, she must, because he couldn't live without her.

He sank down in the chair before the fire, his head in his hands. He had never thought it possible that he would be brought to his knees by a woman, but he was. The mere thought that she might have betrayed him had gutted him so thoroughly, he thought he might die from the pain.

This was the reality of love. An emotion he had scorned and discounted all his life. Having born witness to the dramatics of his parents' torrid love and hate for each other he had sworn such passion was not for him. He had fought all his life against his own nature, for he was a man of strong passions, he knew that, but had denied anything but anger and lust their true expression. Until Diana.

Diana! The ache to hold her in his arms again was overmastering. The idea that Connor Mor had manhandled her, threatened her, frightened her, hurt her- made him crazy with impotent rage. He would kill him if he had hurt a hair on her head. He sprang up again, pacing round the room, unable to sit still. He had to do something, but his chaotic thoughts and impulses were interfering in his ability to think clearly and form a plan of attack. She was in danger and distress while he sat here like an idiot. *Think man!*

Suddenly he remembered something he had read yesterday when going over the accounts and inventories from his solicitor. Something he had previously overlooked. The import of it hadn't sunk in yesterday and perhaps his recall was faulty...

He went to the desk and began feverishly searching through the papers. It took him some time to find it. With an exclamation of triumph, he sat back in his chair, weaving a plan that would solve all his problems in one fell swoop. With a bit of luck, and a fair dollop of risk. *If this failed, it didn't bear thinking of.* He couldn't fail.

He rose and strode out to the vestibule where he donned coat and hat. With the piece of paper tucked into his pocket he went to pay a visit to his solicitor, where he requested that a deed of title be drawn up for a certain property in Suffolk.

After that, he went to find Sir Nathaniel Conant, who was in residence at Bow Street.

Ushered into Conant's office, the Magistrate rose to greet him, holding out a hand.

"Your Grace, to what do I owe this pleasure?"

Anthony took the older man's hand and found his clasp firm and dry. Waved to a seat, both men sat down with Conant's desk between them,

"You are acquainted with Mr Garmon Lovell, proprietor of Lovells gaming hell?" he said coming straight to the point.

Conant went pale and then red. "I am," he said tightly, "Why?"

"Forgive my bluntness over a delicate matter, Sir Conant. I mean you no disrespect, but has he threatened you in any way?"

Conant swallowed and hesitated.

"I understand he has some leverage over you? You need not reveal what it is, I do not wish to know. But I wonder if you would welcome the removal of that leverage?"

Conant nodded. "How do you-?"

"I have my sources, and you need not fear the matter will be spoken of. It has come to my attention that Mr Lovell has overreached himself in certain areas and requires to be–ah, taken down a peg or two, if you follow me."

"I do," Sir Conant, leaned forward in his seat eagerly. "How might this be accomplished?"

"I have a strategy in mind, that if I am successful, will put me in a position of leverage over Mr Lovell after tonight."

"There is a paper, in his safe. I would be most grateful for its return if it could be accomplished."

Anthony nodded and smiled. "If my venture is successful I will apprise you of it tomorrow morning, and you shall have your paper forthwith. In return, I may need the services of some of your constables."

"My constabulary is at your service, your Grace." Sir Conant smiled and rose, holding out his hand. "Thank you, your Grace, a pleasure indeed to meet you."

"Likewise, Sir Conant. Good day to you."

CHAPTER 22

Diana sat in her old room on the bed and stared at the wall in frustration. Connor had locked her in and gone off to restore the jewels to the safe before Garmon noticed they were missing. She wondered what he meant to do with her. He couldn't keep her locked up forever. He would have to tell Garmon she was here.

Her mind returned to her most pressing concern, what Anthony must be thinking. Had he discovered her absence yet and that of the jewels? *What was he thinking? Did he believe her capable of playing him false after last night? Surely not?* Yet, she hadn't told him she loved him, and now she might not get the chance. It might be too late if he believed she had stolen the jewels and left him...

Tears pricked her eyes and she wiped at them impatiently. Tears wouldn't solve this problem. She had to get the jewels back and return them to him. Only then, he might believe she was faithful, that she loved him. A sob escaped her, and she clamped her hand over her mouth to contain the sound. Her shoulders shook, and she felt as if her heart was breaking. The ache to feel his arms around her, to feel safe, protected, wanted, loved, was overwhelming. She had never experienced such happiness as she had last night, and it was terrifying to discover how fragile that feeling was, how easily it could be snatched away.

She had to get out of here! Getting up she scrabbled through her dresser draw for a hairpin and went to the door, prepared to try to open the lock. Only to find the door opening inwards.

She stepped back with a gasp, as Connor stepped into the room, shutting it behind him. She discretely dropped the hairpin behind her and backed up to the dresser as he advanced on her.

"The jewels are back where they belong, and so are you!" He seized her arms. "It was obvious to me that I needed to save you from yourself!"

Anger towards him swirled in her gut. It was his fault that everything was ruined. She shook her head. "You're too late, Connor."

His face twisted. "So, you have become your mother!" He let her go, turning away with obvious distress.

She flushed with shame and anger. "What do you know about my mother?"

"I know the story, Garmon told me. Along with warning me to keep my hands off you."

"Why would he do that?" she frowned at his back, bewildered. Nothing was making sense anymore.

"Because, all evidence to the contrary, he cares about you. Enough to protect you from predatory men at all events. Pity he couldn't shield you from the Devil himself." he turned back pacing across the room and away as if he couldn't stand still.

"He's not a devil!"

Connor shook his head sadly. "You've fallen for him. He'll toss you aside as soon as he's bored with you, you know."

"He won't!" she clenched her fists in her skirts, her heart pounding. "He loves me."

"Did he tell you that?" Connor's expression took on one of disgust. "He lied, Diana! He's broken more hearts than I've had hot dinners! He's a dangerous rake and a cold-hearted murderer." He smashed a fist into his palm.

Her heart seized. "You're lying!"

"I'm not, he's killed at least two men in duels that I know of and there are rumours of others, victims of his fists. He has a dreadful temper. All the Harcourts do, and he is the worst!"

She shuddered, cold with shock. She had heard snatches of conversation, gossip, but it had not been clear which Harcourt they were speaking of, the grandfather, the father or Anthony. All three had bad reputations. She had known that, but not the full extent of it. And as she got to know him, she thought his had been exaggerated.

"If his birth didn't protect him, he would have been hanged years ago."

She shook her head trying to clear it. "He's not like that. You must be mistaken."

"I'm not."

"If you're so concerned for my welfare, why didn't you tell me earlier? Warn me off if you felt it necessary?"

"I was too angry with you. I thought it would serve you right to be destroyed by him. But I can't do it. I can't stand to see you ruin yourself!" He tried to take her hands, but she snatched them away.

"It's too late, Connor. I'm already ruined." She turned away, swallowing hard against the lump in her throat.

He put his hands on her arms again, this time gently. "Then marry me! I'll look after you."

Her heart squeezed as tears pricked her eyes. "I'm sorry, Connor. I can't."

He dropped his hands. "You love him that much?"

She nodded, closing her eyes as tears seeped out under her lashes.

She heard him let out a breath and then the sound of the door closing.

She shuddered, and the sobs grew worse. Flinging herself onto the bed, she smothered the sounds, as the pent-up years of hurt and loneliness, of betrayal and rejection, of feeling unwanted and unloved, rose up and overwhelmed her. She cried until she was almost sick with it. Eventually wrung out and limp, she slept, exhausted with her own emotions and the highs and lows of the past few days.

WHEN SHE WOKE, the daylight had gone. Rolling onto her back, she lay staring into the dark wondering what time it was. She was thirsty, there was no fire in the grate, and she couldn't see.

Anthony must know she was missing by now. He would think she had betrayed him, the despair that had overcome her earlier, threatened to creep back, but after a few hours' sleep she felt better able to tackle the problem confronting her. She would get the wretched jewels back and beg Anthony to believe she had nothing to do with their disappearance. And hang his reputation. He may have done bad things in the past, but he was clearly remorseful, he wanted to be a better person. He had said so. And towards her, he was considerate and loving.

She would go downstairs, find an opportunity to grab the jewels again and the run like hell back to Cavendish Square. It wasn't much of a plan, but it was all she had. The first thing was to wash and dress which she couldn't do in the dark.

Sitting up she groped for the flint on the bedside table and after several attempts, managed to light a candle stick. Rising, she lit several more and then set about lighting the fire. The room was icy and her feet were frozen in her kid boots. When the fire was burning, she checked the ewer and basin, but there was no water to wash with.

Going to the door she discovered that Connor hadn't locked her in a second time, and opening it cautiously, she peered out into the hallway. Her bedroom was on the fourth floor at the back of the house. Everything was quiet up here, but the sounds of patrons filtered up from the floors below. Fetching the ewer and ducking down the servant stairs, she came out in the scullery. Mary and Sarah, the housemaids, were washing dishes, and she could hear Cook barking orders to her minions in the kitchen. The maids broke off their chatter to glance at her.

"Ain't seen you for a bit, Miss, where you been?" asked Sarah.

"I was visiting a friend," she said with a perfunctory smile. "Is there hot water on the hob?" She held up her ewer.

"Aye," Mary nodded to the fireplace where the big kettle hung over the coals.

"You should a rang, Miss," said Sarah. "We would a brought it up to you. You've missed tea, would you like a bite?"

"Yes, and something to drink, that would be lovely."

Sarah smiled, "I'll fetch it up for you. Do you want me to take that?" she nodded at the ewer, that Diana was filling from the kettle.

"No, thank you, Sarah. I can manage."

She took the ewer of hot water back up to her room and was in the process of disrobing to wash when Sarah came in with a tray.

"Here let me help you, Miss," she said.

"Thank you, you are very kind," said Diana, swallowing the lump in her throat. After the latent hostility of Anthony's servants, it was nice to be home where she was treated so kindly. Really, she couldn't have stayed with him there anyway. The scandal would have been untenable. She supposed he intended to set her up in her own establishment.

She needed to find the jewels and return them to him. The best plan she could think of to do that, was to resume her life here, temporarily until the opportunity to snatch the jewels presented itself. Anthony might guess where she was, or he might conclude that she had betrayed him. Either way she needed to be able to move around the house as if she belonged here to get the jewels. As soon as she had them, she would return them to him and hope that he believed she had not played him false.

She stepped out of her chemise and shivered in the cold air. The fire had done little to take the chill off yet. Sarah left her to her ablutions, and she washed her body and her face. Folding up the gown and its accoutrements provided by Madame Therese, she put them carefully in a band box, and turning to her wardrobe, she selected one of the gowns she usually wore in the hell. It was not a suitable gown for a single young lady, being made of red silk with a low-cut bodice. It was designed to allow her to robe herself and laced at the front. She dressed her hair, put on her matching slippers, and hung a shawl round her shoulders. She drank the tea that Sarah had brought but didn't touch the food. Her stomach was still tied in knots.

Turning to the door, she took a deep breath, let it out slowly and opened the door with determination. She had to find a way to get those dratted jewels back and return them to Anthony. She wondered what Garmon would do when he saw her.

Descending the stairs to the second floor, she entered the gaming saloon and looked around. The usual selection of patrons, and both Connor and Garmon were present. Connor frowned at her and made a move towards her, but Garmon, seeing her, handed the faro table off to Rooke and came across to her while Connor stayed put. His warning expression told her he was afraid she would say something to betray him, but she wouldn't do that. She was grateful for his offer of marriage, however ill thought out it was. She'd had no idea he cared for her that much. The least she could do was not shop him to Garmon.

"Where the hell have you been?" asked Garmon quietly.

She smiled for the benefit of the patrons. "Why, were you worried, Uncle?"

"You were missed, a lot of the patrons asked after you." His tone was cold.

Connor claimed Garmon cared for her, but she still couldn't see the evidence for it.

"Did they? And what did you tell them?"

"I said you were ill. Where have you been?" He frowned at her.

"Attending to some business."

He raised his eyebrows. "I take it the business is concluded?" His sarcasm was biting.

"Not yet. Where do you want me, faro, or hazard?"

"Rooke has the faro table well in hand, take the hazard."

She nodded and moved away. He shot his hand out and grabbed her arm. "Don't think I'm accepting that explanation. I'll have the rest out of you later. Go and earn your keep."

She bobbed a curtsy. "As you please, Uncle."

She had been at the hazard table for a little over two hours when Anthony appeared in the doorway, and her heart stopped. His thunderous expression made her heart kick into high gear and her lips trembled. She looked back to the table as a main of five was called and the dice cast. She willed Anthony not to make a scene. Out of the corner of her eye she saw him turn aside and go to the faro table, with Wroxton in his wake. *Had he brought Wroxton with him? What did he intend to do? He must believe she had taken the jewels and betrayed him. What could she do?*

Her hands shook as she blindly raked in the banks winnings and set up the next play. Time slowed to a crawl as her nerves stretched to breaking point.

When she dared to look in his direction again, he was seated at the table staring straight at her. Their eyes collided, and the fire in his made her tremble and sent a hot rush through her body. She tried desperately to divine what he was thinking from his expression but all she could see was tightly reined in fury. *He must believe she had betrayed him and taken the jewels, but what was he doing here? Did he come to punish her?* She longed to go to him and explain, but of course she couldn't. She looked around for

Connor and found him glaring at Anthony across the room. *Would he give the game away to punish her? Would he say something to Anthony?* Hot agony shot through her chest at the thought.

As if conjured by her thoughts, Connor appeared at her elbow. He put a hand to the small of her back and whispered in her ear. "Surprised to see your lover here? Garmon plans to pluck him."

She stiffened but didn't respond, her eyes fixed on the dice scattering across the table. *So that was why Anthony came. Not to see her, but to play Garmon.* Connor's words came back to her. "He lied to you!" She swallowed. *Anthony didn't love her after all. It was all a lie. No, she didn't believe that. She couldn't, her heart would break if she did.* Her legs trembled and she swayed, putting a hand on the table to catch herself.

"I'll relieve you if you like," he said quietly. She glanced up at him and couldn't miss the compassion in his eyes. *He truly did care? How could she not have seen that?*

She nodded, "Thank you." She slipped away to the ladies' room, feeling Anthony's gaze boring into her back.

When she returned to the gaming room, there was no sign of Anthony or Garmon. In a panic, she glanced round frantically and caught Connor's eyes. He gestured upwards with his chin, and she nodded her thanks. Heading up the stairs to the private parlours, she found Anthony and Garmon closeted in one of the smaller rooms, about to engage in a game of piquet. Seeing her at the door, Garmon smiled and waved her in.

"Come in Diana. I don't believe you've met my niece, Mowbray? Diana, the Duke of Mowbray."

Anthony rose as she came into the room, his face under control now, and he bowed politely as she sank into an appropriately deep curtsy. "Your Grace."

"Fetch us some wine, then come sit by me and bring me luck, my dear," said Uncle Garmon with such an avuncular manner that she wondered for a moment if he knew. Anthony took his seat again as she fetched glasses and a bottle of wine, drew up a chair and sat by her uncle's side. Pouring the wine into three glasses she left hers on the table and watched the two men pick up their cards. She didn't know if she wanted to flee or stay. Connor's words kept reverberating in her head. She pushed them away, clenching her hands in her lap and attempted to concentrate on the game.

Uncle had dealt the first hand which gave Anthony an advantage in this round but a disadvantage in the sixth and last hand of the rubber. She knew both men to be excellent card players, but how they compared to each other she had no idea. She suspected Uncle would be stronger, he had played cards and won all his life. Which meant Anthony would need luck as well as skill to beat him. The other undoubted advantage that Uncle had, was a virtually bottomless purse. He, unlike Anthony, was solvent. He could afford to lose, Anthony could not. Her heart thudded uncomfortably hard in her chest as she sat, sipping her wine, and trying to look as if the outcome of this game mattered not one whit to her.

The first game, the scores were fairly even, and she guessed both men were sizing each other up. Pulled into the tension of the game she found herself forgetting her own concerns for Anthony. *What did he hope to achieve with this? Was he truly good enough to beat Uncle?* Anthony won the deal in the second game and pressed his advantage slightly to come out five hundred points up. Since they were playing for pound points that put Anthony five hundred pounds in front. At the end of the third game, he was fifteen hundred pounds the better off, and she could see the trend in the play clearly now. Uncle Garmon was chasing a big win and failing to find it. Anthony was playing more conservatively but was better able to guess the odds.

Garmon bade her fetch the brandy and smiled venomously at Anthony. "You're a better player than your Grandsire, Mowbray."

Anthony swallowed the last of his wine. "I learned to play at his knee. He could never beat me once I learned his weaknesses. Made him wild."

Hearing this she smiled at the brandy bottle as she pulled it from the shelf. Returning to the table she served them each a shot and sat down to watch, her heart in her throat. As the night wore on and the brandy depleted in the bottle, Uncle won a couple of big hands, but progressively, he went down to Anthony, game after game.

"I make that thirty-five thousand pounds." said Anthony tallying up the points. He looked up and skewered Uncle with his burning blue gaze. "That is the amount that my Grandfather owed you I believe?"

Garmon sat back in his chair. "So, you acknowledge the debt?"

"Of course. I'm a gentleman." He took a sip of brandy and waved in her direction for a refill. She obeyed and almost dropped the bottle at his next words. "I believe you have something that belongs to me. I assume you were holding it as collateral against the debt? In which case you can surrender that property to me now as the debt is cleared."

Garmon, who had been flipping a card with his fingers, dropped the card at this and stared at Anthony hard.

Anthony added carefully, "The jewels are worth more than thirty-five thousand, you know that. If you keep them, it's theft, and I'll have you arraigned and this place closed down."

Garmon's nostril's flared and he nodded slowly. "Very well. Fetch the jewels Diana," He didn't even look at her as he said that, passing her the key from his pocket. In fact, neither man was looking at her, they were staring at each other and the scent of male in the room was overwhelming. With a thudding heart, she rose and left the room.

. . .

ANTHONY TRACKED her leaving the room from the corner of his eye, but he never shifted his gaze from Lovell's. The man was furious, and there ought to be some comfort in that. He knew he should leave once she returned with the jewels, but his blood was up and his luck was in. Time to deliver the coup de grâce. Everything or nothing. Do or die.

Diana came back with the jewels still wearing that damned red dress, that was so distracting he didn't know how he had managed to block it out while he played. Except that everything depended on this, he'd dug deep to find the concentration he needed to beat Lovell, and he'd done it.

She set the pouch down on the table and Lovell opened it and shook it out to show him. They were all there, including the brooch.

He nodded. "Now I'll stake them for their real value, fifty thousand pounds. Plus, this." he drew out a paper from his vest pocket and laid it on the table.

Lovell stared at him thunderstruck, and he was aware of Diana gaping at him horrified. Lovell picked up the paper and perused it. He lowered it to look at Anthony.

"Have you run mad? This, plus the jewels, is worth over three hundred thousand pounds!"

Anthony smiled. "This, against your hell."

Lovell gaped and shook his head. "No."

Anthony leaned forward. "Best of three hands, winner takes all."

Lovell's teeth visibly gritted and his eyes glittered. Anthony watched him struggle with himself. Lovell was a gamester, and it was that Anthony was banking on to make him take the bet.

Lovell let out a breath through his nose and looked again at the paper Anthony had passed to him. It was the title deeds to a property that had belonged to his mother. How it had been overlooked in the original assessment of assets he didn't know. But it had come to light in the last sweep done by his solicitor, and it was property he could sell because it didn't form part of the entail. His heart beat a steady rhythm as he watched Lovell take the bait. His stomach fluttered with the excitement, the risk. But his luck was in, he would win. Do or die, this was it. He would walk away a winner, or he would take Diana to the continent and leave it all behind. Either way, he wasn't giving her up, no matter what happened.

"You're a madman. Yes, I'll take you. Diana, fetch Connor, I want a witness to this."

"And Wroxton," said Anthony. "You'll find he's there." He smiled at Lovell. "I want a witness too."

"And a fresh pack of cards," said Lovell as Diana reached the door.

Lovell continued to peruse the document Anthony'd had drawn up that afternoon by his solicitor, while they waited for Diana's return.

Diana returned in a few minutes with Connor, Wroxton and the requested fresh pack of cards.

"Is it true, you're staking the hell?" asked Connor, striding into the room, and coming to Lovell's side.

Lovell nodded. "The Duke has put up property to the value of more than three hundred thousand pounds. Best of three hands, winner takes all."

"Those are the conditions, Mowbray?" asked Wroxton.

"Yes. Break the pack and examine the cards, will you?" Wroxton obeyed him and Connor stood to his left to observe.

"Satisfied gentlemen?" asked Lovell.

Wroxton nodded. "I am."

"Aye," said Connor.

"Very well if you will shuffle Connor, and you cut, Wroxton. High or low, Mowbray?"

"High."

Connor and Wroxton performed the tasks assigned them and the ten of clubs was revealed, awarding the first deal to Lovell.

Anthony smiled, his luck was in. Lovell was a little pale and the gleam of sweat appeared on his brow. Wroxton stood at his elbow and Lovell was flanked by Connor and Diana.

Lovell dealt the cards, and Anthony picked up his hand and sorted it. He chose three cards from the talon and put the other two back. He discarded three and waited with his cards face down for Lovell to complete his discards.

He declared his points and Lovell responded "Good."

The game progressed rapidly from there, as the tricks fell evenly. Lovell won the hand by a slim margin. Anthony remained relaxed, but it was easy to see Lovell was buoyed by this win.

Anthony won the next game by a greater margin. But in terms of the bet, it didn't matter. It was one game each, the third would be the decider.

DIANA SAT with her hands clenched tightly in her lap and her eyes glued to the play. Anthony appeared remarkably relaxed for a man who had staked everything on the turn of a card. Lovell on the other hand was sweating and jittery, his leg vibrating under the table. It was as if he knew...

The third hand was dealt, and it was close to the last trick, the tension in the air so thick you could cut it with a knife.

Diana watched intently as each man made his discards and chose replacements from the talon. She could see Garmon's hand and quickly calculated the number of points, sequences, and sets he could earn points for. Thirty-two. What did Anthony have? She wished she could get and peer over his shoulder, but she daren't move in case she distracted him.

As they each declared their points Garmon picked up thirty-two and Anthony twenty-nine. So, he was going in three points down, which meant he had to win at least three tricks of the twelve to level up the score. Anthony lost the first three tricks, discarding low cards. Diana's heart was in her throat, how could

Anthony look so calm? He must have some high scoring cards left.

She swallowed and clenched her fingers together to stop them trembling.

Garmon led the next trick with a Queen of Diamonds. Anthony hesitated over which card to play then dropped the King of Diamonds wining the trick.

She heard Garmon curse beneath his breath, he had hoped to flush the Ace.

Anthony led then with an Ace of Spades and Garmon was forced to play his King.

Anthony played two more cards high and won the tricks. He then played a seven of clubs and let Garmon win the trick with a nine. They had four tricks each. Anthony needed to win three of the four remaining tricks to win. He won the next two tricks and lost the penultimate one. Everything depended on the final trick.

Diana's heart thudded, and she wiped her sweaty palms on her skirt as Garmon laid down his final card. The ten of Hearts. The sweat on his forehead told her how much was riding on this. Did Anthony have the Jack or was it still in the talon?

ANTHONY LAID THE JACK DOWN. Sweat trickled between her breasts and Diana's shoulders slumped with relief.

A sound came from Lovell, he was white as his shirt.

"The deed to the hell please." said Anthony calmly.

Lovell swallowed and wet his lips. "Fetch them, Connor, they're in the safe." Connor looked as if he wanted to protest, but he did as he was bid. During his absence not a word was spoken. When he returned, he put a paper on the table. Anthony picked it up, read it and put it in his pocket. He then picked up the title to his own property and the bag of jewels and pocketed them.

Anthony rose, leaned on the table, and said pleasantly. "You have until morning to remove yourself and your personal belongings. And you can take your bully boys with you." He waved at Connor, who stiffened.

"Diana, to me." He held out an arm, and she rose going to his side. He wrapped an arm round her and fixed a pale and sweating Lovell with his fierce blue gaze. "She belongs to me. The next time you see her she will be the Duchess of Mowbray, and you will address her as such. Do I make myself clear?"

Lovell and Connor stared at her.

"So, that's where you've been?" Lovell snarled. "Whoring yourself out to the Duke?"

"Take that back, Lovell, or you'll taste my sword." Anthony pushed her behind him as he spoke, advancing on Lovell who had risen from his seat.

"Mowbray, you can't fight a duel here," protested, Wroxton.

"That's up to him!" said Anthony grimly. "Take it back, Lovell!"

"Anthony, please don't do this!" she came round him to clasp his arm. "Uncle." She turned to Lovell. "You're upset, I know. But if you have any care for me at all you won't do this."

"You ungrateful chit! I took you in when you had nowhere else to go, gave you a roof over your head and this is the thanks I get?"

"You made a fourteen-year-old girl work in a damned gaming house, you cur!" snarled Anthony over her head. "For that alone I should put a bullet in you!"

"Which is it Mowbray, swords to pistols?"

"Anthony, no!" Diana shook his arm. "Stop it, or I won't marry you!"

Anthony turned to her. "Diana, love, you don't mean that!"

"I do!" she wiped the tears from her cheeks. "He may not be perfect, but he's the only family I have. And he's right, he did take me in when I had nowhere else to go. So, I can't let you kill him! Or he you. Please, stop this!" She swallowed and wiped her face again irritably.

"Uncle Garmon, I'm so sorry, but I love him, I can't let you hurt him. I already put a bullet in him a week ago, and if you open up that wound again, and he dies, I will never forgive you."

"Diana, darling," said the Duke sweeping her up in his arms. "Did you say you love me?"

"Yes," she sniffed and whacked his shoulder. "But I won't if you kill my only family." She blinked up at him and he kissed her, in front of everybody. But somehow that didn't seem to matter.

"You win, my angel," said the Duke, looking at her with a glow in his eyes that made her heart turn over in her chest. Anthony looked at Lovell over her head. "The hell is still mine. And I want you out by morning. You too." He glared at Connor who looked white and sick.

"One more thing. She is to resume her birthright, Diana will be known to the Ton as Lady Diana Barrington. Wroxton, I rely on your discretion?"

Wroxton wiped his forehead with a handkerchief and nodded.

"Anthony?" Diana tugged at his arm.

"Hush love I'll explain later." he turned back to the men. "You understand me?"

Lovell shrugged. "What makes you think I'll stay silent?"

"Because I have had a word with Sir Nathaniel Conant. The list of your transgressions is long, and I doubt you wish to be hanged or transported. There is nothing Conant would like better than to see you hang and my testimony will be sufficient to see it happen."

Garmon went white and his lips thinned in a grimace of fury, his fists clenched.

"I expect you'll keep your minions in line too." Anthony nodded towards Connor, who bared his teeth and threw Diana a look that made her move instinctively closer to Anthony, whose arm tightened round her.

"If you're not out by morning, I'll send the constables round to evict you. Good evening, gentlemen. Wroxton, can we offer you a lift?"

"Most kind, your Grace," said Wroxton.

Garmon stared at the door as it closed on the Duke and Diana, cold sweat breaking out on his skin. He turned to Connor.

"Send out the word. I want every man here within the hour. He is not going to get away with this. I want my hell back, and I'm going to get it!"

Connor nodded and headed for the door. Garmon followed him shortly after, heading for his office. There was a list of men who owed him money, and it was time to start collecting.

CHAPTER 23

Finding herself bundled into the Duke's carriage along with Wroxton, Diana subsided into the corner seat and closed her eyes, pretending to sleep. The events of the day, from last night to this, were so extraordinary she was having trouble believing it had all happened.

"Thank you for your service tonight, Wroxton, and your discretion, it is appreciated," said Anthony quietly.

"Not in my interests to gossip, your Grace, you are extended family after all. But ahem, Stanton ain't going to like it. Devilish, strait-laced Stanton."

"I'll handle Stanton, it's my sister I'm worried about. I told Barrington, Anne would present Diana to the Ton. But I haven't told her yet."

"Hm, well better you than me, old chap."

Anthony's response to this was inaudible, and it took all of Diana's will power to keep her eyes closed and not bounce up and demand that Anthony explain what he was talking about. He had already spoken of her being Lady Diana Barrington from now on and that was the last thing she desired. The Barringtons did not want her, she would not be foisted on them will nilly, no matter how good Anthony's intentions were, he couldn't interfere in her life like this.

The carriage stopped in Berkley Square to let Wroxton off, and Diana opened her eyes ready to tackle the issue of her becoming Lady Diana, but Anthony had other ideas.

"At last!" he said hauling her into his arms and raining kisses on her face and hair. "Are you hurt love? Did Mor mishandle you? I'll have his cods on a platter if he did."

"No, I am quite well Anthony, and Connor's cods have suffered quite enough damage."

"A street urchin saw him bundle you into a carriage with a pistol to your ribs. If I hadn't determined to fleece Lovell, I'd have knocked Mor flat for that alone."

She smiled and patted his chest. "No need. I wrested the pistol off him and kneed him hard enough to throw him back in the seat when he tried to strangle me."

"He what!" bellowed Anthony. "I'll whip him! I'll -"

"He didn't do any damage. See there are no bruises on my neck." she showed him her neck, and he stroked it and kissed it. She pulled back and looked him full in the eye to make her point. "Connor never could hurt me. The pistol didn't even have any bullets in it. In fact, he told me he wanted to marry me. He was jealous, that was what made him so angry."

The Duke's expression darkened. "So, there was something between you. Were you going to marry him?"

"No. I didn't love him."

His shoulders relaxed then, and he cupped her face in his hands. "But you said you loved me back there, did you mean it or was that for Lovell's benefit?"

She stroked his cheek and said softly, "I meant it." She sighed. "I'm sorry I didn't say it last night when you did. I was just overwhelmed, and you kept cutting me off every time I went to say something. You'd kiss me or touch me or..."

He kissed her again, and it was some minutes before she could say anything else. He held her close and murmured into her hair. "Thank God. You have no idea of the agonies I've suffered today wondering if I was wrong. I didn't want to believe you false, but there's this damned voice in my head–my heart broke when I thought you'd-" his voice cracked, and he held her tighter.

She hugged him back. "Anthony! My heart broke too when I imagined you thinking I'd played you false. I cried so much I was almost sick."

"Oh, my angel!" he stroked her back. "I love you so much. I can't live without you. You must marry me."

She buried her face in his jacket." I would like nothing more, but have you thought about the scandal? It will be horrendous. Too many people will recognise me as Diana Lovell, you must know that."

"Which is why you are going to be Lady Diana Barrington."

"But you can't -"

"I already have."

"But what about your sister and the Earl of Stanton, Wroxton said -"

"You heard that did you?"

"Yes." she raised her head and cupped his face to make him look at her. "Anthony, I appreciate the lengths you've gone to on my behalf, but I don't want to be foisted on the Barringtons." Her eyes filled with tears. "They don't want me, they never did!" She swallowed. "I couldn't bear being forced to live with them and pretend-"

"Oh, you won't have to do that. I'll send you to Anne, you will be presented to society in a cloud of respectability and I will marry you with all the pomp and ceremony I can muster."

"But-"

"No more buts my darling," he said silencing her with another kiss.

"When is all this going to happen?" she asked meekly enough once she could speak again.

"Tomorrow. I will take you to Anne tomorrow. We have one more night together, my love. And then we will have to behave ourselves for a while. I'm not sure how I am going to do that," he said frankly. "I can't keep my hands off you."

A LITTLE WHILE later in bed, Anthony rolled her under him, and slid inside her. She was wet and slippery and deliciously ready for him and his blood sang with a mix of elation and desire. He had hungered for her all day. He moved with deliberate slowness, deep hard strokes, that made him tremble with wanting. Wanting to move faster, to take and ravage and own her. But he was leashing the beast for a moment because there was something else, he wanted more. Meshing his fingers with hers, he held her hands either side of her head as he moved in her, holding her gaze with his. She was smiling and panting, taking each breath with him, his body was taught with tension, with tightly held desire.

Her eyes were soft and dark, like chocolate in the candlelight, and they glowed with warmth, with love, but he wanted to hear her say it.

He thrust in and her hips moved with him, she was hot and wet, tight satin and velvet, and his skin tingled, his balls ached and his cock was on fire. But that was as nothing to the feeling in his heart.

"I love you," he said softly, thrusting again.

"I love you too," she said, her face softening, her eyes glistening. Her body responding.

He groaned, suffused, and overblown with bliss, thrusting again and again.

"Diana!" the taught bowstring of his control broke, and he thrust wildly, stroking into her hard and fast, taking them both to the precipice and beyond into open space, free fall. He held her tight through it, as they trembled and shook together. And he subsided, breath ragged, heart beat hard and heavy, body sinking into hers as if they would never be parted again. "I love you," he whispered breathless against her ear.

"I love you," she said softly against his neck, her arms tight around his back, her legs clamped across his buttocks, her inner flesh squeezing him.

SHE WOKE to him stroking her, and she moved lazily to give him better access. In silence, he brought her to the edge, and then into her quiet panting breath, he said softly, "Are you too sore for me to take you again.?"

"No," she panted.

He stroked her gently, his fingers swirling, forming tendrils of pleasurable pain so exquisite they took her breath. Her body trembled and arched, aching for the release just out of reach.

"Good. I'm going to fuck you like a dog takes a bitch; on your knee's sweetheart, let me see your honeypot."

She gasped, her body clenching with desire at his words. His crudity should shock her, instead it made her flesh throb and weep. "Anthony?" she panted.

"Yes, love?" he said moving onto his knees and pulling her into place in front of him.

"My body responds when you talk like that."

He groaned. "Diana, you will destroy me with desire, you are the perfect woman." he kissed the back of her neck and bit the flesh gently. Then he sat back on his haunches, his hands resting on her buttocks and looked at her. She could feel his gaze and her flesh twitched and throbbed in anticipation.

"Anthony..." it was an entreaty.

"Patience love," he soothed. "I am looking at one of the most beautiful parts of your body." he lowered his head and, in a moment, she felt his mouth on her flesh and she moaned, it was so perfect.

His lips and tongue ravaged her flesh, his hands pulled her legs further apart, and he stuck his tongue in her as far as it would go. His lips sucked her flesh hard and her body convulsed. His fingers swirled over her sensitive bud, and she pulsed on the very edge of release.

"Diana, would you like to sample the dildo?" he asked, his voice husky and deep with longing. She looked back over her shoulder at him, her hips moving of their own accord, she was so close. His eyes had darkened and her flesh throbbed in anticipation. She licked her lips and nodded.

He reached for the box in the bedside table and extracted the dildo and the little pot of cream. His hands shook visibly as he applied some of the cream to his fingers. "We can stop if you don't like it," he said.

She stared at him, her heart racing. His darkened, eyes made it was clear to her that this idea was one that ignited his passion. He nudged her legs further apart with his knees and murmured, "Relax sweetheart. I won't hurt you I promise." The next moment she felt the cool touch of the cream between her buttocks and the soft stroke of his fingertip swirling over the rear entrance to her body. Her acutely sensitised body rippled with desire as an unaccustomed achy pleasure, mingled with the pleasure his other hand was creating on her bud..

He stroked again, softly swirling, and she moaned involuntarily as the strange achy pleasure took possession of her. Combined with his other hand working her up, the twin assault made her shiver and lower her back, thrusting her bottom higher for more of the delicious attention of his finger.

He groaned. "Love, that is so erotic."

He continued swirling, gradually increasing the pressure of his finger until he breached her, which made her gasp.

"Alright?" he asked softly.

She nodded, biting her lip. His finger penetrated further, sliding in and out, slowly. "Try to relax your muscles more." She breathed out slowly attempting to obey him and was startled when he slipped a second finger inside her. The achy pleasure increased and she arched her back, moaning softly as his other hand worked her bud, sending tendrils of heat outwards and causing her inner muscles to ripple and ache, she wanted to be filled. She gasped. "Anthony-"

"Yes, love," he kissed her buttock, continuing his slow torture. "Do you like it?"

"Y-yes," her voice caught on another wave of pleasure.

"Good, I'm going to add another finger now, which might pinch you a bit, but if you breathe and relax you should be fine. You need to be stretched enough to take the dildo."

"Hmm." She breathed out as she felt a third finger stretching her, it ached but in a good way, and she sighed. There was only a momentary pinch, drowned out quickly by the bombardment of sensations from both of his hands. The rise of pleasure made her whimper.

"Anthony-"

"Just a little more and you'll be ready love." he kissed her buttock again. "You have no idea how erotic you look, how beautiful. My cock is stiff as a poker for you."

She moaned and arched her back again, "Anthony, I want you!"

He huffed a laugh that became a groan. "Alright darling, we will try this and see how you like it. If it's too much tell me, and we will stop."

She nodded, panting and trembling with anticipation.

He extracted his fingers gently which left her rear entrance fluttering and made her shiver. Then she felt the cool blunt pressure of the dildo against her, slippery with the cream. He pushed it very gently against her entrance and she breathed again to relax as the achy pleasure built up again. Her body resisted the head of the dildo for a few heart beats, then it gave and the hard rod slid inside slowly, inch by inch. She groaned as her flesh spasmed, gripping on the inflexible, bone cock.

"Are you alright?" He asked again, his voice tight.

"Yes! It's peculiar and pleasant and achy all at once, I can't describe it."

"Ah, Diana. Do you think you can take me as well?"

She nodded, her cunny clenching on emptiness. "Please, yes, I want you. I feel empty without you."

He rose and bending over her back, she felt the blunt head of his cock at her entrance, her flesh throbbed, dancing on the edge of release. *So close...* She groaned. "Anthony, please..."

He shifted, pressing the dildo slowly deeper as he lined up his cock on her quim and notched the head to her entrance. He thrust forward and groaned as he sank into her pushing the dildo deeper.

"Diana, is this what you want?" he panted.

The angle was deep, and coupled with the dildo, fed her hunger. "God, yes!" she groaned.

Her hips jerked as he thrust into her, holding her hips, and angling the dildo with his stomach, pushing it deeper with each thrust of his hips. He fucked her with his cock and the dildo simultaneously. Then bending forward over her back, he wrapped an arm round her and reached for her most sensitive place.

His fingers swirled, the dildo and his cock thrust in unison, and she was hit with the strongest burst of pleasure. It took her breath and tore her apart. She groaned loudly, her body convulsed on his cock and the unyielding dildo, pulsing and throbbing, clenching, and aching. His fingers continued their assault, his hips applying both cocks with deep ravaging thrusts, right through the pulses of exquisite pleasure.

She gasped, shuddering, and convulsed again, with another peak of delight as wave on wave of intense, bone-aching pleasure washed through her body. Her face buried in the pillow rubbed on the cotton like a frenzied cat as she moaned and cried out, tears forming in her eyes and sobs in her throat. The intensity of it all, looking for some way out.

He could feel the hard length of the dildo along his cock as he thrust deep inside her, also sensing her flesh rippling and convulsing, as she cried out her pleasure, over and over again. Dragging a rippling shivering response from him.

"Diana!" he gasped. "Diana!" Unable to contain it further, he joined her with a loud groan as heat and pleasure suffused his senses, taking his breath, and the rush of bliss held him suspended a moment. He shuddered and braced himself on her back as the paroxysm shook him and flooded his body with pleasure. He groaned again, helpless in the grip of exquisite bliss, with the hot rush of his seed erupting and emptying into her. Hard shots of deep pleasure coursed through him, as he grunted and trembled and shuddered through a series of aftershocks, before collapsing on her back. Her knees and arms gave out under him, and she collapsed flat on the bed with him on top of her.

Slowly, he pulled back a fraction and let the dildo work itself out of her, removing it gently and wrapping it in the cloth he had set aside for that purpose. Slumping forward once more on her back he kissed her neck. "Alright?"

"Oh, yes," she murmured.

"Good." He lay there a few moments savouring the blissfully relaxed aftermath.

Then he moved back, disengaging gently and went to clean up. Returning to the bed he found her curled on her side and pulled her close.

"God in heaven, Diana," he whispered. "I love you so much!" He kissed the back of her neck and her shoulder.

"That felt-" she stopped at a loss for words. "Filthy," she finally said.

He chuckled. "I gather that means you liked it?"

"Yes," she said simply and blushed.

She rolled over to face him and propped her head on her hand, regarding him with a lazy smile. "I begin to think we are well-matched. I had no idea I could be so debauched until I met you."

"We are certainly well-matched, my love. You make debauchery new and tantalising for one of my jaded palate. I thought I had wrung all the delights from sexual congress that there were to be had. I could not have been more wrong. Making love to you is like discovering a whole new world of pleasure. Everything is heightened, everything more intense, everything more special." He kissed her. "I shall never grow tired of you." He traced her features with one finger. "Love lends a spice to pleasure that is inexhaustible." he drew her into his arms, and she settled her head on his chest where she could hear the steady thud of his heart.

"I cannot wait to claim you as my wife, my duchess." He stroked her hair and kissed it.

CHAPTER 24

"Don't be nervous angel" Anthony said, taking her hand and kissing it. "My sister is nice, you'll like her, I promise."

"Yes, but will she like me?" Diana worried at her lip and her eyes skittered nervously out the carriage window as they neared their destination.

"Oh, yes," he smiled.

"How can you know that?"

"Because I love you. She would love any woman who could tame me. She will adore you."

They were admitted to the house by the Stanton's very proper butler, whom Anthony addressed with familiarity. "Good day Porth. I hope my sister is at home?"

"I will inquire, your Grace. If you and the young lady will wait in the parlour?" He conducted them to a nicely appointed room with windows over-looking the street. The house wasn't as large or imposing as the Duke's, but everything about it screamed good taste and refinement, from the cream painted walls to the luxurious carpets and the elegant furniture. Diana was distinctly uncomfortable. She perched on the edge of the settee and fiddled with her gloves.

"Is my bonnet straight?" she asked, anxiously.

"Yes love, you look beautiful," said Anthony with a fond smile.

"To you perhaps, but the Countess-" she broke off as the door opened, and a tall woman with flaming red hair and green eyes swept into the room. She was dressed in the first style of elegance and was obviously Anthony's sister.

"Anthony, what are you about? I had no idea you were even in London-"

Anthony rose as she came into the room and held out his hands to receive her, kissing her cheek.

"You are in high bloom my dear, I see Stanton is treating you well."

"Denzil spoils me rotten as you well know," said the Countess with a fond smile for the absent Earl. Her eyes surveyed Diana who rose and dropped a curtsy.

"My dear, I wish to introduce Lady Diana Barrington, our cousin," said Anthony bringing Diana forward.

Anne gaped at him. "Anthony, you are either all about in the head or bamming me? Which is it?"

"I assure you I am not. If you will allow me a few minutes to explain-"

Anne, seeing the crimson flush suffusing the young woman's cheeks, pulled herself together and said contritely, "Where are my manners? My dear, won't you come upstairs where we can be comfortable? And Anthony will explain these extraordinary circumstances." She threw a speaking look at Anthony who gave her a grin that was so uncharacteristic she frowned in bewilderment.

Leading the way to the stairs she said, "Tea in the drawing room please, Porth and request his Lordship to join us."

"At once, my lady."

Ascending the stairs to the first floor, trailed by her guests, Anne's mind skittered about, trying to recall what she could about the Barrington scandal. It had rocked London the year of her debut, that much she remembered, but the details were hazy. To the best of her knowledge, Lady Diana Barrington, who had been a mere child at the time, was dead, along with her parents.

Comfortably ensconced in the drawing room, Anne was about to command Anthony to explain himself when the door opened, and Denzil came in.

"You wanted to see me, my dear?" Seeing Anthony, his expression changed, "Mowbray." He bowed punctiliously to his brother-in-law, his mouth setting in a grim line. Denzil still hadn't forgiven Anthony for shooting her. "What brings you to town?"

"Some extraordinary circumstances I believe," said Anne. "Come and sit down, love." she turned to the young woman perched on the edge of her chair. "Denzil, this is Lady Diana Barrington. Lady Diana, my husband, the Earl of Stanton," she said, performing the introductions.

The girl rose at once and curtsied, dropping her gaze to the carpet as Denzil, ever the gentleman bowed to her. "Delighted to make your acquaintance, my dear." He then threw Anne a bewildered look as he took his seat beside her and the girl resumed her seat, her back straight and feet together, hands clasped tightly in her lap. She was obviously terrified poor child. *What had Anthony done to her?*

"Anthony will explain, won't you?"

"I will, but firstly I need to make you aware that I intend to marry Diana as soon as can be arranged respectably." He took her hand as he said this and squeezed it, the girl blushed and threw him such a look of love that Anne's heart quite melted. She then caught the expression in Anthony's eyes and realised with a shock that her brother had at last fallen victim to cupid's arrow. Whoever this girl was Anthony was head over heels in love with her. She had never seen such a softened expression in his face.

All the bitterness and anger were gone, and she was reminded of a younger, idealistic Anthony, one she had almost forgotten had existed. So long ago had that boy's heart been torn from his chest by the atmosphere of hatred and viciousness in which they had both been raised. To his credit, her big brother had tried to shield her from the worst of it when they were young, but as they grew older, his own corrosive rage had driven even that impulse to kindness out of his heart. She had not thought to see such a transformation in him, not thought it possible.

Tears started to her eyes and she sprang up and hugged him. "Anthony that is wonderful news!" He received this effusion with more equanimity than she would have expected, rising, and patting her back.

"No need for tears, Annie." He smiled down at her, and she found her handkerchief and dabbed at her eyes.

"There is every need, I am so happy for you!" She turned then to Diana and drew her up and hugged her, kissing her cheek, which seemed to disconcert the poor girl. "My dear welcome to the family. Except if you're a Barrington, you're already family. Anyway, I am delighted, we shall be sisters. I'll warrant Mary will love you too."

"Mary?" Diana looked bewildered.

"Wroxton's wife," said Anthony. Which Diana seemed to understand.

So, she knew Wroxton? The mystery compounded.

Denzil, always the soul of politeness, had risen and offered his welcome to Diana, but she could see the questions in his eyes. When hugs and kisses had been exchanged all round, they sat again, and Anne said, "Now, Anthony please start at the beginning and tell us how you met Diana, and–well everything!"

At just that inconvenient moment, the servants appeared with the tea and conversation was halted until the tea was served, and they were alone again.

Diana had removed her bonnet, and Anthony had repossessed her hand as Anne pressed him once again for an explanation.

"We met when Diana held me up and shot me, just over a week ago was it? It seems longer."

"Shot you?" Annie's eyes went wide with shock.

"Aye, but she bandaged me up before abandoning me in the middle of road in the pouring rain." He smiled fondly at Diana, recalling the discomfort and his rage. It all seemed worthwhile now.

Annie covered her mouth with her hands. Her eyes dancing. "Well, that served you with your own sauce, but why?"

"It took me several days to discover that." He looked down into Diana's face and smiled, and she smiled back, which made him want to kiss her. He suppressed the urge, he was going to shock Stanton enough as it was, without scandalising him completely by kissing Diana in public.

"This is a shockingly scandalous tale, Stanton." He skewered his brother-in-law with a warning look.

To his surprise the Earl shrugged. "I expect nothing less from you, Mowbray, go on."

"After our own scandalous meeting, we can hardly point fingers, Denzil," said Annie with an affectionate smile that at one time Anthony would have found nauseating.

The Earl seized her hand and kissed it. "And I would do it all again in a heartbeat my dearest."

Anthony glanced at Diana who was watching this most unfashionable display of marital affection with a fascinated eye. Anthony cleared his throat and resumed the tale.

"The bullet reopened the wound Viviana gave me, and I fell into a fever for three days, through which she nursed me."

"Ah, like I nursed you, Denzil!" said Annie with a grin of glee.

"Just a moment, I thought you said she left you in the middle of road?" said Denzil, a stickler for detail.

"She did, but I got myself on my horse and chased after her. When I caught up with her, she insisted I needed medical attention. She saved my life."

"No, Anthony, the doctor saved your life, I merely -"

"Nursed me though the fever, angel. If you hadn't, I'd have died of it I'm quite certain." He kissed her fingers, unable to resist. "She left me then, and I was forced to chase after her again. I'd threatened her with the magistrate, you see, and she still had the thing she'd robbed me for."

"What was it?" Asked Annie.

"A brooch, it belonged to her mother. But I didn't know that yet. I caught up with her and finally learned the truth about the brooch and how she came to know I was on the road to London with a parcel of jewellery. I'd planned to sell it to alleviate some of my debt.

"We were robbed that night by a man who works for Garmon Lovell, the proprietor, correction, the *former* proprietor, of Lovells" Gaming Hell in St James Street. You may know it, Stanton?"

"Heard of it, never been there."

"Wroxton has, and your friend Morton is a regular, I met them both there two nights ago." Anthony threw Stanton a stern glare. "I already have Wroxton's word he'll not say anything about Diana's association with Lovells, but you'll need to ensure Morton doesn't spread the tale." And he proceeded to tell them the details of Diana's complicated parentage. "I have Barrington's agreement that he will acknowledge her and Lady Lovell's assurance that her family will say nothing. I told Barrington that you would present her, Annie, and lend her your respectable entrée to society." He stopped and waited for their reaction. He could feel Diana's tension beside him and wanted to reassure her.

"Good God, what a tale!" the Earl rose and paced to the fireplace and back. "Mowbray, how to do you expect to contain the scandal? Too many people must recognise her as Diana Lovell, surely?"

"They may well, but none can prove it. If we all stick to the story that she is Lady Diana, the scandal will fade. In any case, she will become the Duchess of Mowbray, in short order and the scandal will be forgotten quickly enough." Anthony rose and approached Stanton. "If the strait-laced Earl of Stanton maintains she is Lady Diana, who will gainsay him?"

Stanton was visibly struggling, and for a heart stopping moment, Anthony thought he might refuse, but Annie came to his rescue. Rising and going to her husband, she placed a hand on his arm and said softly, "Denzil, please?"

It was enough. The Earl's shoulders dropped and he sighed. "If you are set on it, Anne?"

"I am. Thank you," she smiled sweetly and kissed him.

Anthony turned away to afford them a modicum of privacy and returned to the couch where he sat and took Diana's hands, speaking quietly. "You see, I told you it would be alright."

She swallowed and smiled tremulously.

The Earl and Countess returned to their seats and the Earl cleared his throat. "There is the matter of your supposedly being in mourning, Mowbray. Anne can hardly be gadding about town when she supposed to be in blacks."

"The old man wouldn't have cared two hoots for us mourning him, but it should give an excuse to keep things as quiet as possible, so I wouldn't be too concerned about that," replied Anthony.

"Yes, Anthony is right," responded Anne. "Grandfather's death is the perfect excuse to keep things quiet. We will not attend any balls, we will wear lilac and grey which will become you enchantingly, my dear. I will simply make it known that Diana is staying with me, and Anthony can be seen with us in the park and perhaps at the Theatre. Your engagement will be announced forthwith and a quiet family wedding can be held in say three months?

"One, two at the outside!" said Anthony, horrified at the prospect of being separated from Diana for so long.

"Very well, two then. We will need that long just to assemble her trousseau!" said Anne. She clasped her hands together. "This will be such fun!"

Diana, quite overcome, said tearfully, "Thank you, Countess I cannot express my gratitude for your kindness."

"Nonsense, call me Anne, we are to be sisters, remember?" Anne's eyes teared up, and she gulped, groping for a handkerchief. "Oh, I am such a watering pot!" She said dabbing at her eyes.

"What is the matter Annie, it's not like you to have the vapours."

"I know. I am expecting, Anthony, and it makes me emotional."

Anthony digested the news that he was to be an uncle in silence. He reflected that given the way he and Diana had been behaving, he was as likely to be a father in short order too. His previous caution in the matter had been thrown entirely to the winds with Diana. The prospect was surprisingly uplifting. How his life had changed in a matter of just over a week.

"Congratulations, Stanton," he said with a smile and offered his hand. The Earl took it with a pleased expression.

"Thank you–Anthony." he said. "Congratulations to you too." He turned to Diana, "Lady Diana, it would seem you have done the impossible and tamed the devil."

Diana flushed pink and smiled.

"Now, I will direct the servants to prepare a room for you, and then I am going to take you shopping!" said Anne rising, which brought the gentlemen to their feet. And Anthony to the realisation that he was about to lose his intimate access to Diana for– two months!

"Denzil," said Anne moving towards the door. "I think we can give Anthony a moment to say farewell to Diana."

Denzil, with a quick bow to Diana, joined her at the door and could be heard saying, "Now, you will be careful not to overdo it, Anne," as the door shut behind them.

"I think the next two months are going to be the longest of my life," said Anthony taking her in his arms and kissing her.

She returned his kiss fervently and whispered. "I fear so. Is this really happening? I cannot quite believe it. Yesterday I was a girl in a gaming house, and today I'm a lady and about to marry a Duke. If ever there was a fairy tale, this is it."

"It's nothing less than you deserve, my darling. My only worry is that I am able to be deserving of you." he kissed her hands and let her go reluctantly. "I must leave you, or I'll ravish you on the couch and that would not do. Good day, my darling, I will contrive somehow to see you every day for I do not think I could support life if I did not. It is a great relief to me to know that you are here with Anne and Stanton, for you will be safe, and that is of paramount importance to me." Upon which speech, he fled the room and the house before he ruined all his good intentions by giving into his baser instincts.

CHAPTER 25

Diana feared she would not be able to sleep in the luxurious room the Stanton's gave her, but she was wrong. She slept like the dead, almost as soon as her head touched the crisp cotton pillowcase and did not wake until mid-morning. She had a lazy breakfast in bed and appeared downstairs in her white muslin morning gown to be greeted warmly by the Countess, who insisted on being addressed as Anne.

"Y-you're very kind, L-lady Anne," she stammered, her confidence evaporating in the face of Anne's kindness.

"Nonsense! I am so grateful to you, you have no idea!" said Anne putting an arm around her and walking her into the morning room where a fire was lit and some weak sunshine peeked between the curtains.

"Good heavens, why?" Diana took a seat on the sofa beside her hostess.

"You love Anthony and more to the point you have made him love you." Anne sat and squeezed Diana's hands where they rested in her lap. "You have made him human at last."

"I didn't intend to!"

Anne laughed. "You have no idea what a beast he was before he met you."

"I might have some idea," said Diana with a smile.

"Was he a brute to you?"

"Only a very little in the beginning, and he apologised for that." she blushed. "Since–since his feelings developed for me, he has been smotheringly protective and sweet."

"Anthony, sweet?" Anne stared at her aghast. "I don't believe it! You really have tamed the devil!"

Diana giggled. And Anne laughed. Very soon both ladies were reduced to tears of laughter in which state of hilarity they were shortly discovered by the cause of it. Anne then went away to give the betrothed couple some privacy and when Anthony had kissed her senseless for several minutes he rose and walked to fireplace to compose himself.

"Before I forget, there was something I need to tell you and ask you." He said.

"Yes?" she asked re pinning her hair which had come out of its coiled bun.

"I spoke with your grandmother a couple of days ago."

"My grandmother?" *Which grandmother? The Dowager Lady Barrington was dead, wasn't she?*

"Lady Lovell."

"Oh?" Diana stiffened. "Why?"

"I needed to inform her of the arrangement to reinstate you as Lady Diana Barrington-"

"I will never get used to that!"

He grinned. "Yes, you will. You can be quite regal on occasion, and you have a natural grace that cannot be taught. You'll make a magnificent Duchess."

She flushed with pleasure. "You think so?"

"I know so. Now don't distract me by being adorable! I've been trying to ask you this for days, and somehow I always get side tracked."

She giggled, a warmth settling round her heart as he came back to the couch and took her hands. "Your grandmother would like to meet you."

Diana blinked with shock. Her first instinct was to refuse, but then she thought about the idea of having family. More family than just Uncle Garmon, who'd looked after her physical needs, food, and clothes, but who had shown her scant overt affection. Even her father had not been overly demonstrative. She had never met Lady Lovell. Only her Aunt Lavinia and Uncle Paul when they evicted her from the house. She had always assumed the old lady felt as they did, and the little Uncle Garmon had told her about the Lovells seemed to confirm that.

"Why?" she asked bluntly.

"I believe she regrets what happened to you and would like to make amends."

Diana rose and paced to the window, suddenly agitated. "I don't see how! Does she think paying a fifteen-minute morning call will erase eight years of-" she stopped her throat closing over.

His hands clasped her upper arms pulling her back against him. "No, I don't think she thinks that. But I do think she desires the opportunity to assuage some of her guilt." He kissed her hair gently and wrapped his arms round her. She stayed stiff for a moment and then melted back against him. "If you don't wish to see her I will advise her of that. You are not obliged to see her, you owe her nothing, except I understand that she was instrumental in Garmon taking you in."

"She was?"

"So, she told me."

"Hmm." Diana stared out the window at a nursemaid with two children and a dog in tow. "Alright I'll see her."

She turned in his embrace putting her arms round his neck. "What is she like?"

"Small, white haired, formidable. You have her eyes and nose."

Diana flushed with the unaccustomed feeling of belonging and identity. "I do?"

He nodded smiling.

"Is she pretty?"

"In her heyday I believe she was a beauty, like you."

She laughed, "You're full of nonsense you know!"

"Nothing of the kind. I believe you will be every bit as terrifying as she is, you do know half the ton is scared of her?"

"No?"

"Yes. I just hope I live long enough to see you white haired and scaring young men out of their wits. You definitely get your spirit from her."

"Well." Diana sighed, leaning her head against his shoulder "I hope you do too."

THE FOLLOWING DAY, Diana sustained a visit from her grandmother, Lady Lovell, and discovered that everything Anthony had said was true.

A small finely built woman with excellent bone structure, wearing an apple green silk sacque gown in the style of her youth, entered the sitting room with all the air and unconscious grace of a queen.

Diana instinctively rose as she came towards her, hands held out.

"Diana, I would know you anywhere child, you have the Hamilton eyes. I was a Hamilton you know. And the Lovell chin." She smiled, taking Diana's hands, and kissing her on both cheeks. "Thank you for seeing me," she said simply and all Diana's prickles melted away.

"O-of course, Lady Lovell!"

Seating herself and arranging her skirts, Lady Lovell said, "You must address me thus in public child, but when we are alone

I would be delighted if you would call me grandmama. You're my only grandchild, you know."

"Yes I know, grandmama," said Diana shyly.

The old lady smiled and Diana fancied her eyes glinted. "You have something of Peter in you, but more of your mother Letitia, I think."

Diana nodded, papa had kept a miniature of her mother until Aunt Lavinia had thrown it in the fire. She swallowed at the memory of that. She had burnt her hand trying to retrieve it, Uncle Paul had hauled her away from the flames, screaming, tears of pain and grief streaming down her face.

She brought her focus back to her grandmother with an effort.

"I'm sorry, Diana, I should have done more for you. I don't expect you to forgive me, but can I explain why I did what I did?"

Diana nodded.

"You will discover my dear, if you haven't already, that jealousy can do terrible things to one's soul. My greatest sin was perpetrated against Garmon. I can hardly expect that I will ever be granted the opportunity to make amends for that." And she proceeded to tell Diana the truth of her family's history and her part in it.

They shared some tears and a hug, then Lady Lovell brought the call to a close with the words, "I shall do what I can for you socially my dear. I have some influence you know." She rose shook out her skirts, kissed Diana's cheek and left.

THE DAY AFTER THAT, Diana endured a morning call that was less pleasant. She was sitting with Lady Anne looking at bridal gowns in the Ladies Magazine when Lord and Lady Barrington were announced. Anthony had warned her to expect a call from them, but she had not expected it to come so quickly.

She had the haziest memories of her lawful father and

wondered if his younger brother bore any resemblance to him. Lucas Barrington, she found was a short, middle-aged man with a tendency to corpulence and a receding hair line. His wife was also short and plump with a perpetually sour expression. It was clear to Diana that they were tolerating her under sufferance, which put her back up and made her stiff and prickly. She kept her temper but couldn't say that she warmed to them at all, or they to her.

It was an awkward thirty minutes of stilted conversation, much of which fell to Anne, who, bless her, did not desert her during the ordeal. One thing that stunned her during the interview was the reference made to her dowry, by Lady Barrington. It was obviously a sore point with her.

When she next saw Anthony, she taxed him with it. "What did Lady Barrington, mean about my dowry?"

"I made Barrington settle ten thousand pounds a year on you for your personal upkeep and that of our daughters and younger sons should I predecease you."

"Ten thousand pounds a year!" she said faintly. "Anthony, it's fortune!"

"A small one yes, but not such a great sum if we should have several children. Most of my property is entailed to the title which will all go to our eldest son, should we be so blessed, if we should have no sons, it will go to Barrington. I wanted to ensure you were protected in the event of my death."

"Please stop talking about your death!" she begged.

"I don't intend to die, love, but one never knows."

She hugged him tight and both of them lost the power of speech for some time. Only interrupted by the Countess who came to warn them that Lady Sefton was due at any moment and shouldn't Diana go and tidy her hair?

. . .

Anthony took his hasty leave and left the house. As he climbed into his carriage, he was so absorbed in his thoughts that he failed to notice the man on the other side of the road watching him.

The carriage drew away from the curb and continued down the street and around the corner. Connor Mor smiled, and crossed the road, descending the steps to the servants' entrance. *Housemaids were so obliging.*

CHAPTER 26

Five days later, after a third session of intense shopping, Diana returned to her room, followed by a legion of footmen bearing bandboxes and parcels with the intention of having a nap. The Countess had been relentless in ensuring Diana's wardrobe was fully fitted out with all the gowns and accessories a lady could possibly need. When the footmen left, she collapsed on the bed with a sigh and kicked off her slippers.

"You've been busy darlin'."

"Connor!" she sat up with a shriek. "What are you doing in my room?" She glared at him, where he leaned casually against the wall by the fireplace. Her feelings towards Connor were mixed. On the one hand she was grateful for his care of her, on the other she was tired of his interference in her life. Whenever he popped up it spelled disaster for her.

"Wantin' to talk to you, sweet pea."

"How did you get in?"

"Easy enough when the maids are so accommodating."

"Anthony would kill you if he knew you were here."

"No doubt, but he doesn't know and won't, I'm thinkin'."

She sighed. "Stop playing games, Connor, and tell me why you're here or get out. I'm tired and my feet hurt."

"I came to warn you, love."

"Warn me about what?"

"Your Duke is in danger. Garmon means to get his hell back, by fair means or foul. He's calling in favours."

She frowned at him. "Why would you double-cross Garmon?"

"Let's say I'm tired of being his lackey? Without the hell, I'm out of a job."

"So, you'd like to offer your services to Anthony instead?"

"Something like that."

"Anthony doesn't like you. I doubt he'd employ you."

"He might if you ask him to. I got the impression he would do anything for you, my sweet. I was entirely wrong about the situation. He is clearly besotted with you to offer you marriage. You've got yourself a prize pigeon there, well done. I'd no idea you had that much guile." His voice had a bitter edge beneath the smarm. It made her skin crawl.

"Shut up, Connor, it's not like that!" she said, flushing and wishing she had a pistol to hand. She'd put a bullet through him this time, she swore she would. Her heart contracted remembering his offer of marriage. However misguided it was a noble gesture and indicated the depth of his feelings for her. It was understandable that he would be bitter at losing out to Anthony. Losing wasn't something Connor was accustomed to with regard to women. She couldn't shoot him, no matter how irritating he was.

He eyed her in silence. "You could have knocked me down with a feather when he said he'd marry you. Well done, Diana, you tamed the Devil."

She stood up and moved towards him. "Enough, Connor. Leave. Now! Or I'll scream the house down, and you'll be arrested for house breaking. The Earl would have no hesitation in giving you up."

"Not so hasty, my sweet, don't you want to know what kind of danger your lover is in?"

Diana resisted the urge to scream with frustration and said with creditable calm, "Yes, I would like to know that."

Connor smiled. "First, I want you to persuade the Duke to employ me. Once I have the contract, I'll reveal what I know of Garmon's plans."

She shook her head. "No. You'll tell me now, and I'll do my best to persuade Anthony to take you on, but I can't promise. He doesn't like you, and he doesn't trust you. Which is perfectly, understandable, given that you're here selling Garmon out. I thought you were loyal to him?"

"That was before he went mad. Taking the hell away from him has sent him round the bend. I'd rather not work for a mad man."

She frowned trying to divine if he was speaking the truth or not. Finally, she shook her head. "I think you would be better off speaking to Anthony yourself."

"But, as you pointed out, he doesn't like me or trust me. However, if you speak to him on my behalf, highlight the advantages of having me continue in my role, less disruption to the staff and operations..."

"When does Garmon mean to strike?"

"I'm not certain. Soon."

She hesitated and he leaned forward earnestly. "Diana, Garmon means to have him killed. The word is out, and Garmon has offered an attractive price for the deed to be accomplished."

She swallowed convulsively. "All right I'll speak to him, but you have to promise you'll tell me all you know about this, whether he agrees or not."

He nodded. "I will." he kissed her cheek and headed for the door.

"Wait, where can I find you?"

"Send a note to Lovells, the staff know where I am."

And he was gone, leaving her prey to panic.

"Anthony!"

He looked up from his desk, where he'd been trying to sort through papers and correspondence, to the sight of Diana in cloak and bonnet, standing in the doorway of the library. He rose coming round the desk.

"Diana, what are you doing here?"

"I had to come. It's Garmon, he's put a price on your head! He wants the hell back, and he intends to have you killed to get it. You have to be careful."

He shut the door behind her, drawing her into his arms. Her distraught expression was more alarming than her words. "Calm yourself, my darling. How did you come by this information?"

"Connor told me. He-" she gulped. "He wanted me to persuade you to reinstate him as Manager of Lovells. He was trying to use this information as a bargaining chip to get me to do it."

Anthony stiffened in rage at the mention of Connor's name. "And frightened you in the process, the vermin." he stroked her back soothingly and drew her closer. "Everything will be fine my darling, I can look after myself. Although, I appreciate the warning. What are the details of this threat?"

"That is the nub. He wouldn't tell me until I obtained your consent to reinstate him. He wants a contract. Then he will divulge the rest."

Anthony clenched his teeth. "He really is a contemptible worm, isn't he? I have a constitutional dislike of having my hand forced by anyone, most of all by the likes of Connor Mor. Where is he?"

"He wouldn't tell me. He said the staff at Lovells would know."

Anthony nodded and kissed her gently. "You need to go back to Anne's before anyone realises you are here, or all our plans are in ruins. How did you get here?"

"I walked."

"I will send you back in the carriage. Stop it a block away from the house and walk the rest. And please be careful." He hesitated a moment and then went to the cabinet against the wall and took out a small case. He handed it to her.

"What?" she opened it to reveal the small pistol, powder and shot inside.

"At least I know you already know how to use it." he said wryly. "Please be careful love, if anything were to happen to you..." he pulled her close and kissed her.

"I feel the same about you. Please take care, Anthony."

"I will, now wait here while I get the carriage sent round for you."

He came back in a moment and took her back into his arms, unable to stay away from her. She came willingly into his embrace, burying her head in his chest. He held her tight for a moment. "You must go now, before I forget myself and our good intentions. You need not worry about me love. I will be fine. Go now."

She lifted her head, and he kissed her gently, firmly, lovingly. And then, he finally let her go. She went to the door, looked back and was gone.

He breathed out slowly and turned to the cabinet where he kept his firearms. He chose two pistols, added powder and ball. In the vestibule, he donned his overcoat, slipped one of the pistols into each pocket, picked up his cane, which contained a swordstick, placed his hat upon his head and let himself out into the street.

He caught a hackney cab to Lovells and nodded to the men, Sir Nathaniel Conant had posted to guard the front entrance, before walking up the steps and knocking. The door was opened by Carlos, who bowed.

"Welcome, your Grace." He stepped over the threshold and the door was shut behind him.

"Please send for Mr Mor," he said surrendering his hat but not his coat or cane.

"Miss Lovell has already requested that I do so, your Grace."

"Anthony." She was standing at the top of the stairs.

He sighed. "I thought I told you to go home?"

She came down the stairs. "I knew you would come here. My place is at your side." she said, arriving at the bottom of the stairs.

Anthony smiled ruefully. "You make it impossible for me to be angry with you."

"Good," she said linking her arm through his. "Tell Connor we will wait for him in the office."

Carlos raised an eyebrow at the Duke, and he said, "As the lady says, and send in a bottle of burgundy and some glasses."

"At once, your Grace."

The office proved to be a square apartment with one window and two doors. A safe occupied the fourth wall. *The* safe he presumed. The marks on the wall showed where a large painting had been hung over it. The room was furnished with a large desk and three chairs.

Anthony took the chair behind the desk and Diana prowled around the room, checking the cupboards.

"What are you looking for?" he asked, laying a pistol on the desk, and propping his cane within reach.

"The ledgers," she said.

"I have them."

"How? When?"

"Sir Nathaniel Conant's men secured the place for me the morning after I won it from Garmon. They had quite specific instructions."

A servant entered with the wine, served them, and left. A few minutes later there was a knock at the door, and it opened to reveal Mr Connor Mor.

"Come in Mr Mor," said Anthony pleasantly. Mor paused in

the doorway, took note of the pistol, and came in slowly, closing the door behind him.

"Have a seat," Anthony waved him to a chair. "Wine?"

"Aye," said Mor cautiously. Diana poured him a glass and pushed it towards him. She took the other chair and sipped her wine with nonchalance. Anthony admired her sangfroid.

"I gather Diana has spoken to you?" Mor said.

"She has ah, conveyed your request for employment."

Mor drank some wine, set the glass back down on the desk and crossed his ankles. "What's it to be then?" he asked.

"That really depends on your answer to my next question." Anthony lounged in his chair and steepled his fingers.

Mor cocked an eyebrow and waited.

"Why should I trust you? It seems to me that your loyalty can be bought by the highest bidder."

"I have a well-honed instinct for survival, your Grace. I learned long ago to hitch my cart to the man with the most power. Seems to me, you fit the bill of a sudden."

"Well, you're honest at least."

"Just pragmatic."

Anthony nodded. "Diana informs me that Lovell has put a price on my head. That would argue that he still has considerable power in certain circles."

"Aye, I'm a rogue, but I don't traffic in murder. In particular murder of a peer. That's just asking for trouble."

"Sensible." Anthony sipped his wine and considered Mor over the rim. "Tell me more about Lovell's plans for me."

Mor sat forward in his chair. "Will you give me my job back?"

Anthony set down his wine and sat up. "Mr Mor you seem to be of the mistaken belief that this is a negotiation." He picked up the pistol, cocked it and took careful aim at Mor. He saw Diana stiffen in his peripheral vision, but kept his focus on Mor, who went pale and froze.

"Tell me what you know, and I might let you live, I might even employ you if you prove useful. You see, I am not so squeamish about removing my enemies. And believe me, you do not want to become my enemy."

"And you want to marry this man, Diana?" Mor asked, keeping his eyes on the Duke.

"I am going to marry him," she replied steadily. *That is my girl!* "Now tell us what you know, Connor, before he puts a hole in you."

Mor's jaw tightened and Anthony wondered for a moment if he would refuse. Then he let out a sigh. "According to my source, he plans to lure you to a rendezvous somewhere in St Giles tomorrow night and have you done away with."

"And the ruse to draw me in?"

"A note claiming Diana is in danger."

Anthony's muscles tensed, a surge of temper threatened, but he reigned it in. Breathing through his nose, he carefully uncocked the pistol and laid it down. "Thank you, Mor, you have been most helpful." He tossed off the rest of his wine and tapped his fingers on the desk reflectively. "Once I've dealt with Lovell, I will consider your application. You may go."

Mor drank the rest of his wine. Rose slowly and bowed to both of them. "I'll bid you good night then. Should you have need of my services, you can find me care of The Bucket of Blood, in Rose St, Covent Garden." Mor let himself out of the room, and Diana came to him and perched on the edge of the desk.

"What are you going to do?"

"I believe I'll keep the rendezvous with a little back up." He pulled her into his lap and kissed her. "Thank you for your support just now, you have nerves of steel my dear."

She sighed and wrapped her arms round him. "I am not happy about you going into danger."

"I will be fine, but you have to promise me something."

"Yes?"

"You will stay at home, out of danger. I am *much* more likely to find myself in jeopardy if I feel you are at risk. At best you will be a distraction, at worst-" he swallowed. "You are my Achilles heel, Diana, my weakness. And Lovell knows that. He will exploit it if he can, don't let him. You understand?"

She nodded.

"Promise me?"

"I-I promise." She kissed him. "You promise *me* you'll be careful."

"I will. I have everything to live for, do I not?"

She smiled mistily. He kissed her again. A few minutes later she said softly. "What will happen to him? Uncle Garmon?"

"That really depends on what he does and whether I can convince him to leave me alone. It will be tiresome to always be looking over my shoulder, concerned for my safety and yours. I need to put a stop to that. Permanently if necessary."

She shivered. "Would you really have put a bullet through Connor tonight?"

"Only if he forced me to, and I'd rather not do that in front of you. Not that I think you're squeamish." he grinned. "A braver woman I've never met."

He kissed her again, and again. Eventually he said, slightly breathless, "I need to get you home to Annie's before you're missed."

"Hm," she murmured offering him her neck to kiss, which he did. Her scent was intoxicating.

"Diana..."

"Soon, just kiss me, love me, we may not get another chance for a while," she murmured, swivelling on his lap to straddle him.

He groaned. "Diana, you know I can't refuse you." His hand slid up under her petticoats, up her inner thigh.

"I know," she whimpered as his fingers found her place of pleasure. She was wet, and he groaned again. His cock already firm from having her sitting on his lap, stiffened to its fullest and hardest extent, pressing painfully against his falls. His other hand found the buttons on her spencer and undid them swiftly. Then he reached under and behind to unlace her bodice and loosen it sufficiently to pop out one breast to suckle, while his other hand pleasured her between her thighs.

She rocked her hips and flung her head back as he tugged on a nipple and suckled her hard, his fingers speared her, his thumb rubbing in circles. She dropped her head and kissed him open-mouthed, wanton, needy. Little noises, that drove him mad with desire, in her throat. His tongue plundered her mouth, his breathing accelerating, his pulse racing, his cock raging in its cloth cage.

She dropped her hands between her legs and scrabbled until she found the buttons on his falls and released his stiff cock from its confines. He groaned as she stroked him root to tip. Then she knelt up and guided him towards her centre. He removed his fingers and let her engage the head and slide down his length, encasing him in tight, wet heat.

He groaned with the pleasure of it. "Diana," he murmured finding her mouth again, holding her rolling hips as she rode him. Her breathing was ragged, and she seemed quite intent on her own pleasure. He was happy to be pulled in her wake, the waves of rising pleasure in his cock, driving him towards release on an effortless tide.

Her hips rolled and jerked and shook as the wave caught and beached her hard on his body, clenching his cock with the sudden shock of her climax and triggering his own ball tearing release. He groaned, loosing his seed in a half dozen pulsating throbs of exquisite pleasure that bathed his senses in sweet ecstasy. His hands clamped her to him as he wrung the last drops of pleasure from both their bodies, and he slumped back in the chair to catch his breath.

He regarded her through slitted eyes, her face flushed and tendrils of hair falling round her cheeks and onto her forehead. Her expression was still twisted with desire, and she looked thoroughly debauched, her lips swollen and her eyes blown, her cheeks flushed. She rolled her hips and rode him a few moments more, wringing the last tendrils of desire from her body. Collapsing forward on his chest, she breathed raggedly and rubbed her face on him like a cat, her body bowed as she crunched and clenched on him, uttering one last moan of repletion. He felt thoroughly and delightfully used.

He chuckled in her ear and wrapped his arms round her. "I've been well and truly ravished I think."

"Hmm." she sat up slowly and blinked at him like a drowsy feline. "It's your own fault. You shouldn't be so–so masculine. I hunger for you." She said, her voice husky and low.

His body convulsed with an answering longing at her words, and he seized her and hugged her tight. "I feel the same about you. I want you with a bone-aching need, Diana. I cannot conceive of being without you now." His voice was thick with emotion. His eyes stung. He kissed her cheek and her hair and found her mouth, claiming her as his with tongue and lips, his hands tight on her body as if he would never let her go.

She clenched on his rehardening cock still buried deep inside her and rode him with a desperate rolling gait that in moments had her soaring again into pleasure and release, breathless and flying. He held onto her tight, his heart rate rabid against her ear, his breathing hoarse. His shout of pleasure almost one of pain as his body convulsed, he crested, and she felt the hot rush of his second release deep within her.

He slumped back in the chair and gasped for breath. He stared at her in wonder, his hand stroking her cheek, "How is that possible?" he whispered. "You are a sorceress who draws my lifeblood from me, my soul, and my essence. You conjure the seed from my body, like the tide drawn by the moon." He held her against him burying his face in her hair. "Always and ever, mine," he whispered.

CHAPTER 27

Connor drank his beer, cocooned in the noise of the other patrons of the Bucket of Blood, the nickname for the Coopers Arms, because of its patronage by prize-fighters. Garmon appeared, weaving his way through the tables, and pulled out a chair, signalling to a waitress for a pot of beer. He sat and leaned in.

"Did they swallow it?"

"Hook, line and sinker," said Connor with a smile.

Garmon grinned. "Excellent. I'll leave Diana to you. I will deal with Mowbray."

Garmon's beer arrived and the two men toasted the success of their enterprise.

Diana adhered to her promise to stay holed up at the Stanton's home all day, and it was the longest day she could remember. The time ticked past agonisingly slowly as she waited for dusk and the even more knuckle biting wait for the events of the evening to be over. The worst part was not knowing when and what might happen.

She had pleaded a headache to keep to her room, but by night fall she was climbing the walls with worry. When Anne knocked at her door to ask if she felt well enough to attend the theatre with them, she jumped at the chance. Anything to escape the nightmare of her own thoughts. She should be safe enough in the Stanton's company, even Uncle wouldn't be barefaced enough to seize her from under the Earl's nose.

Wearing lilac silk, she entered the Drury Lane theatre with her hosts, with her heart thudding fast. Not for the excitement of her first visit to the theatre, but because her thoughts were still on Anthony and what might or might not be happening elsewhere in the city.

∼

FOREWARNED BY MOR, Anthony received the expected note from Garmon that evening. He had already spoken with Conant to secure some men to accompany him. He set out for the rendezvous with three constables, and the useful street urchin who had identified Diana being hustled into a carriage by Mor a week ago, secure in the knowledge that Diana was safely at Anne's and out of harms way.

∼

ANTHONY ARRIVED at the arched entrance to St Giles in the Fields Churchyard on High Street, half an hour ahead of the rendezvous time. The gates were closed at this time of night and the spiked iron fence stretched in both directions. The area was not well lit and one of the constables carried a lamp to light their way. Trees flanked the church building, which ran perpendicular to the fence with its high square tower and rounded spire at the Western end that faced narrow Flitwick street.

Anthony sent one constable to the Western end and another to the Eastern end, retaining the third man with himself, standing in the shadows across the street with an excellent view of the entrance. He then sent the urchin into the churchyard proper to reconnoitre and report back on what he saw. The kid, whose name he had learned, was Ben, just Ben, pocketed the half-crown he offered and disappeared into the shadows.

He popped up ten minutes later with a report of the layout of the churchyard, including the presence of a rear entrance through a lychgate on the East side of the irregularly shaped block. He also imparted the fact that there were "Two coves wiv pops having a bear garden jaw in the cemetery. Reckon they's on the watch, guv."

"Thank you, Ben," said Anthony solemnly, and handed him a second half crown.

"You're a real gent, milord!"

The lad bit it from habit, pocketed the douceur, and with a dip of his hat disappeared.

Anthony then whistled up the other two constables who rejoined him. It lacked only a few minutes to the rendezvous time, so he walked up to the front entrance, trailed by the constables, and entered the churchyard. He circled the church building to the right, rounding the Western end and arriving on the south side where the cemetery was located. Taking up a position in the open area between the church and the cemetery, he waited. To all intents, his demeanour was casual, in reality he was on high alert. The constables spread out to watch from different directions and the two men that Ben had spoken of ambled over to wait and watch. No one spoke. They were waiting for Garmon.

The theatrical performance was no doubt one of the best of the season, but it failed entirely to distract Diana from her worry.

Leaving the box to stretch her legs in the intermission, her nerves were at breaking point and her attention so centred on her inner turmoil, that she failed to see the gentleman who approached her until his hand was on her arm.

"Diana, Mowbray sent me, he is bleeding badly, you must come at once!"

She stared up at Connor, her brain refusing for a moment to absorb his words, thinking that the horrors she had been imagining had overtaken her senses. He shook her arm and tugged at her. "Hurry, we must go at once!"

She allowed him to tow her along the corridor to the stairs, down them and out into the street, where he bundled her into a carriage before she had drawn breath to ask any questions.

Inside the carriage, her wits finally returned to her, and she said urgently, "What happened?"

"Garmon's men attacked him as I said they would. Why did he not heed my warning?"

"He said he would take someone with him. How badly hurt is he?"

"Bleeding out," said Connor grimly and for a moment she feared she would faint. Dropping her head between her legs to stave off the dizziness, she spoke, her voice muffled by her petticoats. "Where? Where is he? How far-?"

She raised her head, breathing deeply and swallowing. She had been unable to eat anything all day and her empty stomach had nothing to offer up but bile.

"Not far. In fact, we have come as far as we can by carriage, the streets are too narrow to allow a carriage to pass along them here. We must walk the rest of the way, come."

GARMON KEPT HIM WAITING. A tactic to try to unsettle him, but Anthony was a gamester and such tactics had no effect on him. Particularly when he knew that Diana was safe.

Garmon arrived eventually with a man who looked vaguely familiar, one of the men from Lovells no doubt. The two cemetery watchers nodded to him, and he turned his attention to Anthony.

"Three men a piece, your Grace. How did you know?"

"I have my sources," replied Anthony evenly. "Now, you claim to have Miss Lovell in your keeping. Produce her at once."

Garmon shook his head. "Did you bring what I want?"

"The deeds to the hell?"

"Yes."

"No."

Garmon raised an eyebrow. "I didn't think you would be so careless with your lady's health."

Anthony's heart skipped a beat as a thread of doubt entered his mind. *Could Garmon somehow have got hold of Diana? Surely not. If she had been taken, he would have been apprised by one of the several lookouts he had posted round Anne's house and charged with following her should she leave the building for any reason.*

"You will not harm her, she is your niece." Anthony stated flatly.

"You are assuming I have a shred of family feeling, Harcourt!" Garmon grimaced. "I thought you of all people would understand that for men like us, familial ties are an unwanted burden.

Anthony tightened his hand on the head of his swordstick. "You lie." He spoke calmly, but with just an inflection of doubt to ensure Garmon believed that he might still have leverage.

"Do I?" Garmon looked around. "Do you notice anyone missing from this little gathering?"

Anthony smiled sardonically. "Mor?"

Garmon bowed. "Precisely! He is even now collecting Diana."

"Collecting her from where?" Anthony frowned, the first real niggle of fear skittering down his spine.

"Why Berkeley Square of course."

Anthony shook his head. "She is well guarded. Mor will not be able to reach her."

"You underestimate him. He has a way with housemaids."

"Very well, produce Diana. When I am assured of her safety, we can negotiate. Until then, this is a stalemate. And if you harm so much a hair on her head you will get nothing from me except a warrant for your arrest, which these gentlemen," he nodded to the constables, "Will be glad to execute."

Garmon's face closed with grim determination. "You can't outflank me, Mowbray! You don't seem to realise I hold all the cards. You see, there is difference between us, you have something to lose and I do not!"

With a gesture, his men advanced on the constables their weapons raised.

"Shoot them if they so much as twitch!" said Garmon.

Garmon's men cocked their pistols and kept them trained on the constables.

Garmon smiled, it was predatory in the dark, his eyes glittered, his teeth showed white. "You will fight me to the death, Mowbray. Winner takes all." He drew a sword from his cane and flourished it. "En Garde!"

Anthony, ready for him, drew his own sword and touched it to Garmons. "As you wish, but I suggest we rid ourselves of our coats first."

Garmon bowed with punctilio and both men stripped rapidly to their shirt sleeves.

Anthony raised his sword, which showed silver in the sudden flood of moon light that lit up the churchyard. Garmon clashed his sword against Anthony's in salute, steel on steel, and the battle was joined.

CHAPTER 28

The carriage came to a halt as he spoke, and he opened the door, let down the steps and helped her to descend to the noisome street. The stench assailed her nostrils and her stomach heaved. She swallowed and covered her nose with her shawl. Lifting her skirts with her other hand she allowed Connor to drag her swiftly along the street to a narrow dark alley where the smell, if possible, was even worse. Only the moon peeking out from behind the clouds provide any light to see by.

They arrived at a narrow, dilapidated building, it hardly qualified as a house. The roof above the second floor appeared to have a several large holes, and the windows were either empty sockets or boarded up. The door was solid however and firmly shut. Connor banged on this peremptorily, and which was opened in a moment by a disreputable looking individual with a lean face, half covered in a scraggly beard. He held a stub of a candle in one dirty hand, and he grinned at sight of Connor, baring broken, discoloured, and missing teeth.

Diana's instincts told her that Anthony was not here and this was trap. Stepping back into the alley she drew the pistol

Anthony gave her and trained it on Connor, who turned, raising his hands placatingly at sight of the pistol.

"Now, sweetheart there is no need for that."

"Yes, there is. Where is Anthony? He is not here I'll warrant."

"He is. Upstairs, bleeding out. You'll be too late if you don't hurry."

She swallowed, refusing to believe him. "No. He. Isn't. Now, take me to him, or I'll kill you!" Her voice rose slightly, she was close to getting hysterical. She bit her lip to steady herself and cocked the gun carefully. "I won't miss at this range, Connor. Take me to him, *now*!"

Connor sighed. "Garmon made me do it. He found out I'd been to see you and -"

"Enough of your lies! Move. Take me to Anthony!" She gestured with the pistol. The fellow with the bad teeth had melted away at sight of the gun, they were alone in the alley.

Connor moved towards the other end of the alley, away from the way they had come in. The street forked, taking the left arm, they came out in a larger street and several paces further on to the junction of three roads and a fourth narrow lane way to which Connor led her.

Plunged once more in the noisome dark of a narrow, stinking alley he led her to a square labelled by the sign on one building wall, Kendrick Yard. Emerging past the building on the right, they came into the square proper. Just an open space, surrounded on three sides by buildings with a lychgate let into the fourth, that led, as far as she could tell, to a garden of some kind.

"What is this place?" she asked, looking around.

"The entrance to the churchyard, come." Connor approached the lychgate and opened it. It squeaked, and she winced. Hurrying to catch him up, she passed between the overhang of trees on either side of the path, and they emerged in a cemetery plot, dotted with gravestone. The outline of St Giles Church loomed ahead and to the right, a black shadow against the almost equally dark sky.

"Where-" she began, and then she saw. Surrounded by a dozen men in three pairs, one holding a pistol to the head of the other, two men fought with swords in an open area between the cemetery and the church. Anthony and Garmon. Both had stripped to shirt and breeches, their attention fully on each other.

Snagging Connor, she pressed the pistol to his ribs, much as he had done to her, there was some satisfaction in that, and whispered. "Stay here and stay silent!" She knew that if Anthony discovered she was here, it would distract him and that could be fatal to his chances. She drew Connor back into the shadows of the trees and watched, her heart in her mouth as the two men fought in deadly earnest. She was in no doubt that this bout was intended to be to the death. A shiver of fear skated over her skin and down her spine.

ANTHONY HEARD the screech of the gate opening but could spare no attention to seek its source. Lovell was fighting like a man possessed, and he was good, the best Anthony had fought in a while. Breathing hard, Anthony parried another savage thrust from Lovell and danced back out of the way. The trouble was his shoulder was weakened from the bullet he took from Diana. It hurt like the devil, and he was very much afraid if he didn't finish Lovell soon, the wound would break open and begin to bleed again.

He parried again and sought an opening to force the attack back on his opponent. Lovell was having too much of it his own way. Ignoring the screaming pain in his shoulder, Anthony parried, feinted, and then lunged, his blade met steel, but at the least, he forced Lovell to take a step back which was good. He followed it up with another lunge and for a moment he dared to hope his blade would find its target, but at the last-minute Lovell turned it aside, dancing to the left before turning and lunging back at him. The blades clashed and tangled. Both men stepped back and both tried again to stab the other.

Sweat got in Anthony's eyes, and he blinked, but in the momentary distraction, he failed to react quickly enough. Lovell's sword plunged towards him heading straight for his heart. He brought his sword up at the last moment, deflecting the blade to the right. But it kept coming with the force of Lovell's lunge and skated up his sword arm cutting the fabric of his sleeve and biting into the flesh beneath.

At the same time a shot was fired and Lovell jerked and with a curse fell to his knees, then forward onto the turf at Anthony's feet. In the dim light, Anthony stared down at the growing crimson stain on the back of Lovell's shoulder.

"Anthony!"

He looked up, and Diana in evening dress, her hair coming out of its pins, was sprinting across the lawn to his side, the pistol clutched in one hand. She was trailed by Connor Mor.

"Anthony! Are you alright?" she reached him and flung herself against his chest. He caught her with his good arm. The other was bleeding, he could feel the warm blood dripping down it into the grass.

"Diana," he said, dazed. "What the hell are you doing here?"

"Connor brought me," she said, her eyes glittering in the dark. She looked down at Lovell at his feet and fell to her knees. "Did I kill him?"

She touched Lovell and the man groaned, which was a good sign.

"Apparently not, love. At least not yet. We'd best get him to a doctor."

He looked up at the circle of men surrounding them, all of which seemed frozen with indecision about what to do. When Garmon went down, his men lost their focus. The constables coming to life seized them, but the men were slippery and evaded their clutches. The three constables he had brought with him, chased after the men, leaving them alone with Connor Mor and Garmon still prone on the ground. Mor stepped forward and knelt beside Lovell to examine the wound.

"Aye, darlin' you've not hit a fatal spot, that's fortunate. A good shot from that distance. Or did you mean to kill him?"

"Of course I didn't, I just wanted to stop him from killing Anthony. Uncle Garmon, can you speak?"

Garmon opened his eyes and blinked up at her. "I can, lass. You're a fine shot, I taught you well."

"I'm sorry, Uncle, but I couldn't let you kill Anthony."

"Aye, well you got your wish. I'll not kill him today." He threw Anthony a venomous look.

"You'll not kill him *any* day!" she said hotly. "Promise me, you'll call off your dogs."

Lovell closed his eyes. "Connor, get me out of here, I'll not gratify his Grace by bleeding out at his feet."

Mor helped him to his feet, whereupon Lovell stood swaying and glared at Anthony. "This isn't over, your Grace. I mean to get my hell back, come what may. Watch your back!" Then he turned and walked away, supported by Mor. The screech of the lychgate announced their exit from the church grounds.

EPILOGUE

Six weeks later the Duke of Mowbray married Lady Diana Barrington in a private ceremony at the Duke's home in Leicestershire. The coverage of the wedding in the Times included a description of the bride's gown and the particulars of the wedding.

The bride was given away by her paternal uncle Lord Barrington. She is rumoured to have a dowry of upwards of ten thousand pounds, being her father's only child. The circumstances of her recovery and return to the bosom of her family have been extensively covered elsewhere and will therefore not be expounded upon by this correspondent. The guests were predominantly made up of the Duke's family, and included the Earl and Countess of Stanton, Captain John Elliott and his wife, Lady Mary Wroxton and her husband, Lord, and Lady Barrington and their two daughters and the Honourable Ashley Morton.

"Well, I think we've brushed through it quite well, don't you?" said Lady Mary to the Countess over breakfast, putting the Times aside.

The Countess buttered her toast and cut it into triangles. "Everyone is so used to Anthony doing scandalous things, I suppose it is fitting that he should have set the world on its ears when choosing a bride. For one, I am just thankful they found each other. No matter how outrageous the circumstances, she has been the making of him."

"Do you think we will see them today?"

"I doubt it. They are not due to leave on their honeymoon until tomorrow and I distinctly heard Anthony telling Kilham they were not to be disturbed under any circumstances."

Lady Mary giggled like a schoolgirl and sighed, casting a wistful glance at her husband engrossed in his paper.

The Countess let her gaze stray to her husband who was deep in conversation with the gentlemen at the other end of the table and placed a comforting hand over the slight swell of her belly. Viviana had not joined them for breakfast, her husband Jack informing them that she was unwell this morning. Viviana was finding pregnancy hard, while Anne on the other hand seemed blessed. She would pay a visit to her sister-in-law after breakfast to see how she did and see if there was anything she could do to help.

UPSTAIRS in the privacy of their bedchamber, the Duke surveyed his sleeping wife and sent an unaccustomed prayer of gratitude to God for her existence. As he watched, she stirred and opened her eyes. She was flushed and tousled and altogether delicious.

"Good morning, my love," he said, a lump of tenderness making his voice croaky.

She smiled and leaned up on an elbow to kiss him. "Good morning, Anthony."

"You do realise I'm never being separated from you again?" he said pulling her closer.

"Good," she said. "The last six weeks have been hell. In particular having to pretend and be polite to the Barrington's. But I suppose I must be grateful to them for accepting me back into the family." Her wry expression gave the lie to that. "But I *am* grateful for the dowry. That was your doing, wasn't it?"

"Yes. I wanted to make sure that no matter what happens, you and our children will be taken care of. Not that I plan to squander any more fortunes. I've won and lost too many in my lifetime. My gambling days are done. The hell will enable me to generate sufficient income to pay off my grandfather's debts and the rest will be ploughed back into the estate so that it will become self-sustaining. I'll build a legacy for our son and any other children we may have, if we're so blessed."

"Anthony," she touched his face with a gentle hand.

"I will strive every day of my life to be worthy of you, my darling, but I can't pretend that the prospect of fatherhood doesn't terrify me. My own sire and grandsire are such shocking examples, I am afraid I will repeat their mistakes, and that is the last thing I want."

"You won't," she said, with such conviction he wanted to believe her.

"The difference will be you. You are *not* my mother."

"From the little you have said I understand your parents' marriage was not a happy one."

He grimaced. "No, it was not. They both hated and loved each other in equal measure, and their hatred led them to do terrible things to the other. My mother's affairs were as legendary as my fathers. They seemed to take such delight in hurting each other." He sighed. "Anne and I were unregarded casualties caught in the crossfire of their love affair. I doubt when they were in the midst of one of their wars that they even knew we existed. Mother was a master manipulator of men, and my father was her greatest victim. Not that I'm excusing his behaviour, he was just as bad she was in his own way."

"That must have been awful."

"It was. I will do anything to avoid having that happen to our children. Promise to remind me of that if I start to get out of control," he kissed her hand, squeezing it tightly. "I have a damnable temper, you've seen ample evidence of it and when the bit is between my teeth, I can do and say unforgivable things. I would never forgive myself if I hurt you or our children." He swallowed and wiped his cheeks. She reached up and did it for him and kissed his cheeks.

"You won't," she repeated softly.

He wrapped his arms round her and held her close. "If I do not, it will be because of you." He kissed her, and it was sometime before either of them said anything.

"It was a very long six weeks," she remarked dreamily.

"Agreed." He murmured kissing her neck.

"Well, you did ravish me against the door of the music room and over the back of the couch in the parlour." She reminded him.

"Yes, and in the rose garden and on the floor of the library. But I was driven to it by desperation." He nipped her ear.

She smiled and traced his lower lip with her finger. "It is very fortunate for us that the Countess was so understanding. I'm quite sure she nearly walked in on us in the parlour. And she absolutely knew what we had been doing in the music room, I caught her smothering a laugh behind her hand."

"Annie is the best of sisters, remind me to tell her so."

"She has the best of brothers certainly," she said curling into him.

"That she does not, but I will try to be from now on. You make me want to be better, Diana."

She slid her fingers up his forearm, over the scar from Lovell's blade and shivered. "Do you know where he has gone?"

He knew she was referring to Lovell. The man had vanished after leaving the churchyard. Anthony had used all his resources to try to track him down, but he had disappeared.

"No, love, but the moment he pops his head up again, I will know of it. He will not take us unaware, of that I swear."

She sighed and kissed him. "Good, I do not wish to have to shoot him again."

"It won't be you that shoots him next time," said the Duke grimly.

"Oh, let us forget him for the moment, I want to enjoy being the Duchess of Mowbray for a spell. I shall take some time to get used to it, you know."

"Take all the time you need, my darling. Would you like breakfast or do you wish to sample the dildo again?" he asked, his hands running up her thighs under the sheets.

She slumped back on the pillows and stretched decadently. "What more can you suggest we do with it?"

"Lots of things my darling," he said kissing her. "We've barely begun yet. Did I tell you I plan to fuck you in every room in this house, when we have it to ourselves."

"Oh, Anthony..." sighed the Duchess of Mowbray.

WREN ST CLAIRE

REVENGE
on the
DEVIL

A Steamy Regency Romance

VILLAIN'S REDEMPTION BOOK 2

ABOUT REVENGE ON THE DEVIL

A man with no heart.
Until he meets her.
A stubborn independent widow, in need of his protection, ironically from himself.

Seven nights of passion. Will either of them survive with their hearts intact?

Garmon Lovell has never allowed himself to love anyone. Until he meets her.
A man hardened by his past and obsessed with exacting revenge on those who have wronged him. When his men mistakenly capture Genevra Tate, a determined woman desperate to hang onto her late husband's Tavern, Garmon finds himself irresistibly drawn to her strength as much as her luminous beauty.
A passion like she has never known...but it will take more than passion to mend Genevra's shattered heart.
Genevra swears she will never trust a man again. To buy a stay of execution on her husband's gambling debt, Genevra offers the only currency she has: a night in Garmon's bed.

ABOUT REVENGE ON THE DEVIL

The sparks that fly between them could set London on fire.

As the hard man falls hard, Garmon's tender care for her, threatens Genevra's vulnerable heart. Yet when disaster strikes, is there anywhere else to turn, but to the man who swears he will kill and die for her?

Revenge on the Devil is the searingly passionate 3rd book in the Villain's Redemption Steamy Regency Romance series. If you like strong but soft-centred heroes, steamy passion, tender and touching romance with all the feels, then you'll love Wren St Claire's heart-rending Steamy Regency Romance.

What readers are saying about Revenge on the Devil
10* please! This is awesome!

Reviewed in the United Kingdom on November 6, 2023
Verified Purchase

If you want a hot steamy romance with plenty of deadly excitement (and who doesnt?!) then this is for you. I went through every emotion reading this and was reminded of one of Grimms dark fairytales! Please give this book a try and once you've done so read the whole series cos they're all brill!!!

"Hot and tender, this book will melt your heart – and your kindle!" readers comment.

"This was such an amazing story! It's rare to find such a good book with the ability to move me to tears, has the steam and makes me happy all in the same book." - readers comment

REVENGE ON THE DEVIL

Chapter 1

June 1815

Genevra Tate looked up from her vigorous polishing of the beer engine handle, as a new customer strolled into the tap room. Welcome summer sunlight, streaked through the mullioned windows, across floorboards worn and grey with scrubbing, taking the morning chill off the air. It was mid-morning and only a handful of the regulars were present, muttering into their tankards of porter or sharing a coffee-pot and late breakfast.

She tracked the stranger as he wandered in, looked about and spied her at the bar. He smiled, drawing an answering smile from her. He was tall, well-made and handsome, with unfashionably long dark hair and a dark stubble on his jaw. His clothes were casual but of good quality, he had eschewed a hat, jacket and neckcloth in deference to the summer heat, and wore only a shirt and waistcoat with well fitted breeches and boots.

"Good morning, sir," she said. "Would you care for a drink?"

"I would at that me darlin'," he said with a striking Irish accent. As he came closer, she got the full effect of his startlingly dark blue eyes. "A half pot of porter," he said leaning on the bar and smiling with blatant admiration.

Genevra fetched a pewter pot and pulled the handle of the beer engine to dispense the porter, the dark liquid forming a thick, delicious, creamy head on top. Pausing at halfway to let it settle, she looked up at her customer and said encouragingly, "Would you like a bite to eat with that?"

"No, thank you sweetheart. I've just eaten."

She topped up the rest of the pot.

"Ah, thank you," he said, receiving the pot from her and taking a long draught. "That's a fine drop."

"Whittaker's" she said, flicking a stray strawberry blonde curl behind her ear as she wiped down the bench.

He nodded. "Would Jacob Tate be around me darling'? I've a mite of business with him."

Genevra's heart skipped a beat. "What would your business be with Jacob?"

"That would be my business, love. Can you direct me to him?"

"He's buried in the St Giles Church cemetery six feet under!" she said with perhaps more venom than the situation warranted. *After all the man was dead and couldn't hurt her anymore.*

Her customer pursed his lips in consternation. "Can you tell me who the publican of this fine establishment might be then?"

"That would be me. Genevra Tate. Jacob's widow." She held out her hand. "And who might you be?"

"Connor Mor at your service Ma'am. Delighted to make your acquaintance. Forgive me manners, I tort you was the bar maid."

"It's a common mistake Mr Mor, how may I help you?"

He leaned in and said softly, "It's a matter of some delicacy, you may want to do this in private Ma'am."

She eyed him suspiciously for a moment and then waved him round the bar to the office behind it. She showed him into a small square wood panelled room, dominated by a scratched desk and two battered chairs.

"Well?" she said, her arms crossed.

"It's a matter of some debts," he said apologetically, and her heart sank. *She had enough debt as it was. What had Jacob done?*

"How much? And to whom?"

"The debt is owed to Mr Garmon Lovell, of Lovells' gaming hell in St James Street." He handed her a slip of paper he had taken from his waistcoat pocket.

She took it with a hand that trembled slightly and opened the paper. She couldn't believe what her eyes were seeing.

"Five hundred pounds?" Her voice squeaked in outrage. She thrust the paper back at him. "I do not believe you. My husband could not have incurred such a monstrous debt."

He refused to take the paper. "I assure you that he did Mrs Tate."

"Where's the proof?"

He took another piece of paper from his pocket and held it up for her to read. It was an I.O.U. signed by Jacob for five hundred pounds to Garmon Lovell and dated to January 9th, 1815. It was undoubtedly Jacob's handwriting. She groped for the chair behind her and sat down heavily. "My God," she whispered. "It's a fortune!"

"You note the date Mrs Tate. That is six months ago. Mr Lovell has been very patient, but he really must insist the debt be paid in full by the end of the week."

"The end of the week?" she jumped up. "That's impossible! I had no notion of this debt until this very moment. I cannot summon five hundred pounds out of thin air! You must give me time- I -"

"As I pointed out Mrs Tate, Mr Lovell has been very patient. He requires that the debt be paid immediately. I will call again at the end of the week." His expression had hardened, and she shivered. "I can assure you, that should you not have the required funds Mr Lovell will take steps to recover the amount from you by means you will not like." He shook his head. "I should not like to see violence perpetrated against such a lovely lady as yourself my dear, but business, as they say, is business."

She shuddered, terror slicing down her spine. "Get out!" she said, pointing to the door.

He bowed. "Good day to you Mrs Tate. Thank you for the fine porter. I will see you on Friday."

He turned to leave the room, and she followed him. "It's four pence!" Holding out her hand. He turned, fished in his pocket and dropped the coins into her palm.

"Good day Ma'am."

He turned and sauntered out, cool as you please. She fumed and then reaction set in, her knees gave out, and she went back into the office, collapsing into the chair shaking with terror.

The look in Mr Mor's eyes as he threatened her with violence just brought it all back. She bit her lip hard, to stop its trembling, and blinked back tears. She would not cry, *damn it!* Jacob was dead and could not harm her anymore. Yet he could reach beyond the grave to haunt her with his unpaid debts, bringing terror and financial hardship to her door. *When would it end? When would she be rid of him? He was like a curse.*

"Mrs Tate?" Annie one of the barmaids called out from the tap. Pulling herself together with an effort, she plastered a smile on her face and went to the door.

"Yes Annie."

"There you are! Joe says can you come down to the cellar, something about rats?" Annie shuddered. "I'll mind the tap for you."

"Thank you, Annie," she said wearily and headed towards the cellar to manage the immediate crisis. Mr Lovell's debt would have to wait until she had a spare moment to address it.

Chapter 2

A few hours earlier

The room in which Mr Garmon Lovell sat, was quite pleasant, particularly given its location in Monmouth Court, Saint Giles in the notorious district of Seven Dials. A fresh coat of paint to the walls, panes of glass in the windows and a sturdy door with a lock, did much to restore the room and the building in which it was situated above a bookshop and printers, and gave it a certain éclat.

The row of urchins before him certainly thought so and were suitably overawed. This collection of the scaff and raff of the street were, to a child, small, under-nourished, filthy and scabrous. They also stank of the Thames in which they spent quite a bit of their time. That notwithstanding, they were valuable to Garmon as the cogs of his vast information network. He paid them five pence a day and a meal, to fatten them up, but he suspected most of the money and the food went to their families, because the little varmints continued to be skinny and malodorous no matter his efforts. Having briefed them for their day's work, he dismissed them. He listened to them pad downstairs on dirty, bare feet and into the street where they would disperse to their posts for the day, returning at dusk to receive their wages and meal and be replaced by the night shift.

The idea of using street urchins for his spy network was not his. He had learned it from his mentor, the Chevalier De Salle– purportedly a French émigré fled the terror in Paris-, on the streets of Brussels, where he served an apprenticeship as a youth and young man, learning the ways of an adventurer, which including aping the manner of a gentleman, as well as how to fleece an ignorant nobleman and survive the scaff and raff of Brussels' backstreets.

De Salle owned Brussels in those days, much as Garmon now owned London. He wondered if the old reprobate was still alive. He'd lost touch with him when Brussels was annexed by the French in 1795, and they were forced to flee the city. He returned to London, De Salle's intention was to go to Italy, he had been tempted to go with him, but a strange homesickness sent him back to St Giles to find his own way.

Dismissing the reminiscence, he returned to his work of sifting through titbits of information that he had gleaned from his various sources, putting together connections and opportunities which were his stock-in-trade. This was his new enterprise, having been robbed of his gaming hell by the Duke of Mowbray. He still had every intention of getting the hell back, now that he was healed of the bullet the Duchess of Mowbray had put in his back. She had damned near killed him with that shot, if it weren't for Connor he would have died of the fever.

Vengeance was a dish best served cold, and Garmon's fury had cooled to arctic temperatures by now. He meant to exact a price against his treacherous niece and her iniquitous husband that neither should ever forget and get his hell back in the process. They would both learn the price of crossing Garmon Lovell.

The door opened to admit a swarthy man of solid, muscular build, escorting none too gently, a thin man in a jacket shiny with age and a battered crown beaver hat. He removed it at sight of Garmon, revealing a thinning crop of greying hair, combed over his balding forehead. His eyes watered behind their spectacles, and he clutched his hat nervously. Garmon nodded to Rooke, who released the thin man's arm and stepped back, blocking the exit with his large frame.

"Mr Whiteside, it is quarter day. Where is my money?"

"Mr Lovell, Sir, I just need a little more time-"

"How much does he have Rooke?" Garmon asked.

Rooke stepped forward and laid a roll of bills on his desk. "Just shy of fifty pounds by my reckoning."

"It's all I have Mr Lovell!"

"But not enough..." Lovell counted the bills rapidly and shoved them in a drawer of his desk. "Rooke, retrieve whatever you can to make up the shortfall. The house if necessary. Good day Mr Whiteside."

"Not the house–where will I live?"

"Not my problem, Mr Whiteside." Garmon returned his attention to the pile of documents before him.

"Please Mr Lovell, I'll do anything, just don't take the house-"

"You had your opportunity; I have been more than patient. Mr Rooke, please remove Mr Whiteside from my presence."

Rooke stepped forward and seized the man's arm as he cried out a protest. Rooke hustled him towards the door and the man's glasses fell off in the scuffle, clacking on the floorboards. "Please! Wait! I–I have something you may want-"

"I want my money," replied Garmon.

"I have information!" The man tried to pry his arm out of Rooke's grip, but the attempt was futile.

"Well?" Garmon sat back sceptical. "Out with it."

"You will leave my house alone?"

"Depends on the value of your information."

"I want a guarantee-"

"You're in no position to be making demands Mr Whiteside. Leave here with your information and without your house, it's all one to me." He waved a hand. "Rooke." The big man seized his arm again and Whiteside began to babble.

Garmon listened to him for a few minutes and then waved him away. "I already knew most of that, and the rest is incorrect. Take him away Rooke and bring me the title to his house. Send the men in to sort through what is there, anything of value bring to me, the rest they can have."

"Yes Mr Lovell." Rooke bundled up the still protesting Whiteside and manhandled him out the door. His protests could be heard all the way to the street. Garmon shook his head and returned to the pile of documents before him.

A little while later Mr Rooke came back with the title deeds for the house and a collection of valuable trinkets.

Garmon shoved the deed in a drawer, sorted through the trinkets and instructed Rooke to exchange them for money from Old Harry in Bent Street.

Rooke nodded. "Cruikshank's been spotted over at Temple Bar this morning."

"Good send a couple of lads to fetch him I want a word."

"Already done, Mr Lovell. He should arrive at any moment."

"Excellent, escort him in, will you? He might need a little persuasion."

"Yes sir."

He came back shortly with a very tall, very thin man dressed rather dapperly in a coat of navy blue over fawn-coloured pantaloons and a floral waistcoat.

"Ah Mr Cruickshank, nice of you to drop in," said Garmon with heavy sarcasm.

Straightening his neckcloth and shucking his cuffs, Cruikshank grimaced. "There was no need for violence Mr Lovell. No need at all."

"There was every need Cruikshank. You've been evading my men for weeks. You owe me one thousand pounds. Pay up!"

Cruikshank eyed him with mild alarm, nowhere in proportion to the fear he should be feeling. The man had the hide of a rhinoceros.

"We are both businessmen, Mr Lovell. You know full well you can't expect a fellow to produce a sum like that out of thin air."

"You have had several months to make good on your debt Cruikshank, do you fancy a spell in debtor's prison?"

"Now do be reasonable -!" He said visibly blenching.

"I have been more than reasonable Cruikshank." he advanced on the man and despite Cruikshank being several inches taller, he shrank back from Garmon's menacing glare. Coming up against Rooke standing like a brick wall behind him. He glanced up at Rooke and gulped.

"Mr Rooke, I think Mr Cruikshank is unaware of the seriousness of the situation. Perhaps you could enlighten him?"

Rooke reached a big hand around and gripped Cruikshank by the throat and squeezed. The man's face began to turn purple, and he uttered some choking sounds, his hands scrabbling in effectually at the hand on his throat., his feet dangled a few inches off the ground. He wasn't taller than Rooke.

Just as he judged Cruikshank was losing consciousness he waved at Rook to ease his grip, which he did.

The man coughed and wheezed for a bit, while Rooke kept him upright.

"I trust I've made my point?" Garmon leaned against his desk watching this display of distress dispassionately.

"You–have that!" wheezed the other man.

"Good next time it won't be you my men bring me, but your son. How old is he? Eight? Ten? Just the right age to be a mud lark. Don't you think? He'll have to earn his living somehow, as he will be an orphan by the end of the week."

"No! You wouldn't!"

"You know better than that. How many men have wound up in the Thames who crossed me? Care me to list them?"

Cruikshank swallowed painfully. "No."

"Good, then pay up by the end of the week, or you'll be joining that illustrious list!" Garmon smiled, but he knew it didn't reach his eyes, it was a grimace, designed to put the fear of God into anyone who witnessed it. He'd practised it for years in his teens and got so good at it, he'd induced many men to lose control of their bowels on sight of it.

"And if you think to disappear, think again. Your son is sojourning with us until you pay up in full."

"He's not! he's with his mother in S-"

"Soho. Yes we picked him up this morning. Don't worry we will take very good care of him. Won't we Mr Rooke."

"That we will Mr Lovell," rumbled Rooke in Cruikshank's ear. He jumped and shuddered. "You're a cruel man Mr Lovell!"

"I'm a businessman. Which you also claim to be . But unlike you, I pay my debts. Now do you require any further persuasion to my point of view?"

Garmon advanced on him again and grabbed his hand, twisting the fingers. "I understand you're fond of playing the piano, Mr Cruikshank. Difficult to do with broken fingers."

Cruikshank yelped and whimpered. "I understand Mr Lovell. Truly. You'll get your money. I promise."

"Don't promise, just deliver. You know what will happen if you don't." Garmon let his fingers go.

"I do. I do." He nodded cringing and holding his fingers.

Some hours later the door opened again and Connor ambled in. Garmon looked up Garmon sat back in his chair. "Well did you get the money?"

"Not yet. According to his so-called wife, Tate is dead. I told her I'd be back on Friday to collect. Naturally she claimed not to have the money."

Garmon waved a hand dismissively, he had more things on his mind than another petty debt. "I want you to take a note to Diana from me."

"Alright, but why?" said Connor with a puzzled look.

"I have a plan to get the hell back and this time it's going to work!' he glared at Connor.

Connor flushed. "It wasn't my fault Diana smelled a rat. I did warn you she wouldn't fall for it."

Garmon got up from his desk and paced to the window and back, too restless to sit still. Just thinking about that devil Mowbray and his wretched little ungrateful witch of wife made his blood boil.

"So, what is the plan?" asked Connor.

With his back still to the room Garmon said, "I plan to lure Diana to the hell ostensibly to meet me. Instead, I want you to kidnap her. We will hold her to ransom until Mowbray surrenders the title deeds to the hell. He dotes on her; he'll do anything to get her back."

"No."

Garmon rounded on Connor. "What do you mean, no?" His heart thudded in his chest, two parts fury to one part anguish at this betrayal.

Connor looked at him steadily. "I mean no. I won't do it. I'll do a lot of things for you Garmon, I've even killed for you. But I won't do this. She's your niece for fucks sake!"

Garmon strode over to the desk and pounded on it with his fist to stop himself hitting Connor with it. "Yes, my treacherous, ungrateful niece! The little bitch betrayed me!" He breathed hard, his vision blurring.

"She's happy Garmon. After everything she went through I'd've thought you of all people would be happy for her. God, have you got no heart? I thought you cared for her!"

"Clearly you do!" Garmon's eyes narrowed.

Connor flushed. "Yes, I do, and there's no need to glare at me like that, it never went further than the odd kiss and grope, she wasn't interested in me and whatever you might think of me I don't force myself on unwilling women!"

Garmon's shoulders twitched and a pang from the bullet wound made him wince. "So, I should fucking hope. You knew what my rules were about Diana, no one was to touch her and that included you! If I'd known I'd've, had you fucking flogged!"

Connor's face twisted into a grimace. "Yes, you always hide behind your bully boy's, don't you?" Connor shook his head, turning away. "Since you lost the hell, you've lost your mind! I've about had enough of your obsessive madness." He turned back. "I won't let you hurt Diana anymore. Find another way to get the hell back, but don't use her to get it!"

"I'll do as I see fit, and you'll do as you're told!" snapped Garmon.

Connor smiled and it wasn't pretty. "I'm not eight years old any more Garmon, you can't beat me into submission. Get someone else to do your dirty work from now on. I'm out!" he turned and slammed out of the room, his booted feet loud on the wooden stairs. The bang of the back door slamming out into the street left Garmon shaking with rage. He almost went after him, but pride held him in place. *He'd be back. Connor wouldn't leave him. Connor was loyal.*

He swallowed the hard lump in his throat and went to the locked cupboard against the back wall, taking out a key with hands that shook, he fetched out a bottle of whisky and a glass, poured himself a generous tot and tossed it off in a swallow. Connor's voice echoed in his head: *since you lost the hell you've lost your mind.* It was true he hadn't been himself since then. He had lost a piece of himself. He wasn't whole without the hell. It was his identity. *Fuck!* A shudder, remnant of the old fear ran through him, and he reached for the bottle. A second glass steadied his nerves and he put both the bottle and glass back and relocked the cupboard.

Chapter 3

Five months ago

"Jacob!"

The voice behind him made him stop and turn. Moonlight shone on the water of the Thames lapping against the embankment. It was late and he was drunk. He peered at the man walking towards him, he looked eerily familiar, but it couldn't be. He was safely locked up in prison, where Jacob had put him! He took a step, listing with the slope of the embankment. *Fuck he was drunk!* Jacob staggered trying to recover his footing.

The man came to a stop in front of him and the moonlight revealed his features, familiar as his own.

"Elijah!" His heart thudded uneasily in his chest. He forced a grin. "How did you get here?" He put out his arms to hug his twin and Elijah grinned back, a baring of teeth, more than a smile.

"I escaped, no thanks to you! Prick!" Elijah's fist connected with his stomach and sent him flying backwards into the mud.

Pain and nausea swamped Jacob's body, and he turned, struggling to his knees and vomited into the mud.

Elijah's laugh brought him to his feet with a roar of rage, and he swung wildly. Elijah dodged and laughed again. Jacob staggered after him, sobering by the moment, his vision narrowing to dark, red rage.

"You gave me up, you bastard!" Yelled Elijah. "I'll kill you for it, you drunken, sodding fuck!"

Jacob fumbled in his coat pocket and brought out a knife, flicking it open he advanced on his brother. "I don't think so Elijah!"

Elijah closed with him trying to wrest the knife from his hand. The two men swayed and scrabbled, scuffling in the mud, each trying to overbalance the other. Elijah twisted Jacob's arm up his back and with a cry he let go the knife before the bone snapped. Elijah got his arm over Jacob's throat and squeezed.

Jacob's head pounded as he gasped for breath. He stomped on his brothers in-step with his boots and wrenched himself out of his grip. Turning he punched him in the stomach and Elijah stumbled backwards with an ooff, tripped over some driftwood and fell backwards into the water. Jacob waded in after him. Pulled him up by his shirt and hit him square in the face. Elijah's eyes rolled back, and Jacob let him go. He flopped back into the water, and his head hit something with an audible crack. His body rolled sideways in the water his head going under. Jacob stood, his head hanging while he tried to bring his own breathing under control. He grasped Elijah's shirt pulling him up again and shook him. His head lolled drunkenly, bloody water streaming off his collar length hair. Jacob dropped his hand into the water and found the rock his brothers head must have hit.

"Fuck!" Jacob howled. He dropped to his knees in the water and shook his brother again, but there was no response.

Panic skittered over his skin, and he looked around. He didn't think anyone had seen what happened. Feverishly he tore his brothers tattered and filthy clothes from his body and stripped off his own. Dressing the other man in his clothing took some time, and he kept looking around to ensure no one was about. When he had dressed his brother in his trousers, shirt and waistcoat, he towed the body out further into the Thames, where the current caught it, and it floated away from him.

He watched a moment or two, then sniffing, he sloshed back to the shore and put on his brothers wretched clothes, a stained and tattered shirt, and breeches, not much better. He had kept his signet ring, boots and his purse. He turned and hurried from the embankment up the steps and into the darkness. He needed to find a boat to take him up the river, away from here.

Chapter 4

Generally, after a day of back-breakingly hard work, Genevra fell into bed and slept like the dead, but thanks to the Irishman's visit, sleep eluded her. The worry she had managed to keep at bay for the rest of the day, spiralled out of control as she fell into the pit of dark despair at 3:00 am.

The night terrors she used to suffer when Jacob returned drunk from some spree with his mates, returned with a vengeance, and she lay shaking under the covers, rigid with fear, a prey to a rigour mortis of panic. Unable to breathe, unable to move, she rode out the attack which left her limp and sodden with sweat and tears. She fell into a deep slumber just before dawn and was awoken by the clatter of the dray horses on the cobbles beneath her window, bringing today's deliveries.

Dragging herself out of bed, she washed hurriedly in the cold water and scrambled into her clothes, shivering. Bundling up her hair into a knot on the top of her head she bolted downstairs to receive the delivery and thus her day started all over again.

As the day wore on, her determination that she would not surrender to the terror again grew. She had to be free of this insidious creeping fear before it stole her sanity and her life. And she had to find a way to stave off the debt to this man Lovell. She didn't have five hundred pounds to pay him and even if she did, she had other debts to service as well.

The Tavern was doing relatively well as to daily trade, but Jacob had mismanaged the funds so badly, that when he died, she had discovered a drawer full of unpaid bills. And of course, as soon as word of his death got out, every supplier to whom they owed money had begun to dun her. So, she had done the only thing she could do, turned to her wretched stepfather for a loan. Which he had gleefully agreed to provide, in return for exclusively selling her father's brew, Whittaker's. The move had at least consolidated her debts, but it hadn't made them go away.

She was whittling the debt down, but she wasn't out of the woods yet. Just as she was beginning to think she could be free and clear inside of six months, if trade continued as it was, or sooner if trade improved, this wretched debt from Lovell comes to light. She had to find a way to buy time to pay the debt. *But what did she have to barter with?*

She had never heard of Lovell, but a casual enquiry of her Tapster, Joe, elicited some disturbing information.

"Lovell?" said Joe pausing in the act of connecting the hose pump to the cask of beer. "Aye I've heard of him. The hell is popular with the swells. By all accounts he grew up in St Giles, son of a prostitute or some such, but his talent for cards earned him enough to set up the hell."

"How old is he?" Genevra stopped stacking bottles of wine to push the pins back into her bun which was threatening to fall. She was wondering if the Irishman was actually Lovell himself, under a false name.

Joe shrugged. "Forty maybe?" *No, the Irishman wasn't that old, closer to her own age she guessed.*

"Does he have a family? A wife?"

"Not that I've heard of. Why do you ask?"

"Jacob had some dealings with him, I was just curious," she said carelessly.

"Well, I'd stay out of it. By all accounts he's a dangerous man to cross, with a long reach as I understand, and a might of men at his beck and call to do what he wants. He's not the sort you'd want to be mixed up with," Joe said, straightening and giving her a fatherly look of concern.

She forced a smile. "Thanks Joe, I appreciate the warning, but I'm not about to tangle with him," she lied. "I was just curious when I came across his name in some of Jacob's papers that is all."

An idea, distasteful as it was, was forming in her mind. There was one thing she could offer that might persuade the man to give her more time. *Could she, do it? The idea of offering herself to man of violence...* She shuddered and swallowed as her stomach knotted up. *No, she couldn't, anything but that. Perhaps there was some other service she could perform for him? But what?*

She would first try to play upon his good nature, if he had any. Joe's words and the words of the Irishman, suggested that he didn't, *but no man was all bad, was he?*

Except Jacob. Her heart sank. In a world in which Jacob Tate existed, good men were few and far between. It was probably too much to hope that Garmon Lovell had a smidgen of compassion in his apparently ruthless heart, but she had to try to find it if he did.

She would leave it until Thursday night to pay him a visit and hope her courage didn't fail her. She had to save the Tavern, not only her own livelihood, but those of her staff, depended on it. If Lovell should foreclose on her, she would lose everything she had fought so hard to retain and could end in debtor's prison. It didn't bear thinking of.

But then neither did offering her body to a man she didn't know. One who was likely to be as bad, if not worse, than Jacob. *No one could be worse than Jacob, could they?*

If she had survived Jacob, she could survive this. One night in exchange for financial freedom, what could he do to her in one night that was any worse than what she had been subjected to for years? It was worth it. It had to be. If her courage held... Was she brave enough or would fear continue to control her? Take away her choices? She could do it. She had to.

∼

Two nights later, Connor hadn't returned, and Garmon's temper was at breaking point. He had sent his boys out to find Connor, and they had come back saying no one had seen him since Monday. He hadn't returned to his lodgings, nor had he been seen at his usual haunts, such as the Bucket of Blood.

Garmon's shoulders twitched, and his wound ached. *Where was he? Had he left London altogether? And if so, where could he have gone?*

A pain in his chest persisted, and he blamed it on the stew he'd eaten for dinner.

He couldn't wait any longer to execute his plan against the Mowbray's. It would have to be tomorrow night.

∼

Diana, Duchess of Mowbray, received the note from the hand of a dirty urchin in the middle of Bond Street, and the creature was gone before she could question him, leaving her with a grubby piece of paper and lingering odour of the Thames in his wake. *One of Uncle Garmon's mudlarks.* Opening the crumpled sheet, she read the note and then stuffed it in her reticule.

"Who was that, your Grace?" asked her maid.

"No one my dear," said Diana frowning. *What was Uncle Garmon up to this time?* She debated whether to show the note to Anthony and decided against it. She could deal with Uncle herself. If she brought Anthony into it, he'd likely kill Garmon (or die trying), and she wasn't about to let that happen.

~

Genevra surveyed her appearance in the glass. Her deep blue eyes seemed too big, dominating her face. Did the weariness in her bones show in her eyes? She tried smiling to dispel the heaviness in her quaking heart. *She would not be afraid.* She had to do this. The alternative was unthinkable. One night wouldn't kill her. She had survived much worse. She straightened her shoulders and smiled again, bobbing a curtsy to her reflection. Her heart lifted a little, but she was still conscious of a brittleness in her nerves. *She was afraid, but she wouldn't surrender to it.*

She had donned her best gown, a cream satin that complimented her creamy skin and gave her hair a luminous glow. Romantics called her hair colouring strawberry blonde, she had always just thought of it as carrot coloured, she wasn't accustomed to thinking about her appearance a lot. But looking in the mirror she had hopes that she was tempting enough to persuade Lovell to look upon her situation with compassion. Not that Mr Mor had shown any. *Like master like servant?*

It was a gown she hadn't worn in a while, *when did she have time for evening gowns these days?* And the bodice was a little tight, causing her breasts to appear as if they were about to burst from their confines. Which, given the nature of her errand, was probably not a bad thing. All the same, it made her a distinctly uncomfortable. She wasn't a whore and behaving like one, even for a cause such as this didn't sit well.

Her mother would be mortified and her stepfather–the thought of Hiram's face if he should get wind of this escapade made her smile and strengthened her resolve. If there was one thing she was determined on, it was that Hiram would not continue to exert control over her future. She would pay his blasted debt down as soon as she possibly could, and if getting a stay of execution on this one from Lovell would allow that she could do whatever it took to achieve it.

What she refused to think about was what her real father would think of this. On that thought, she very firmly shut the door. Papa wasn't here to save her. He was dead and gone these many years. There was no one to look out for her except herself, and she had people she was responsible for. *She could do this. She had to do this.*

A simple gold locket that her parents had given her on the occasion of her marriage, and her only piece of jewellery, nestled just above her cleavage and drew further attention to the generous pillows of her breasts.

Her heart quaked, and she wondered briefly if she should change into something less blatant. But her experience of men told her that the more alluring she looked, the more likely she was to get what she wanted. Men were incurably weakened by female charms. Even Jacob had been vulnerable to seduction unless he was so blind drunk or furious that nothing and no one could reason with him.

She had dressed her strawberry curls in an elegant knot on the top of her head, but try as she might, she couldn't prevent the wisps of curls falling round her face. Her gloves, she found were grubby and had holes in the fingers, so she couldn't wear those. Her reticule was still clean and intact, but her evening slippers had also suffered some accident while stored, the ribbons were ruined and the fabric stained, forcing her to exchange them for a sturdier pair of kid boots.

She flung her cloak over the ensemble and strode purposefully towards the door.

Half an hour later she stepped down from the hackney carriage in St James Street and approached the discreet entrance to the four-story mansion that was, she was reliably told, Lovell's gaming establishment. The building was well maintained and lights in the windows told her that it was occupied. She paused looking up at the entrance.

A carriage drew up behind her, but before she could even turn to see who it might be, an explosion of pain to the back of her head made everything go black. The last thing she remembered as she crumpled towards the pavement was of hands grabbing her round the waist and lifting her bodily off her feet.

∼

Diana was attending the theatre with her husband and the Stanton's that evening. So typical of Uncle Garmon's arrogance that he thought she could just drop everything to obey his summons. With his note burning a hole in her reticule, she vowed to deal with him tomorrow.

∼

Genevra woke to a thumping ache in her skull and the realisation that she was bound to a chair and gagged, with a musty hessian bag over her head, through which she could see nothing except a faint light from candles. She made a noise in her throat and pulled at her bonds, shaking the chair in her efforts to rise, which failed. Both her wrists and ankles were tied, and she was, in-turn, tied to the chair. The gag tasted foul and for a panicked moment she thought she would be sick and choke to death.

Just then a door opened, and a man's voice said, "Good God!" the next moment the bag was ripped from her head and a brown haired, handsome male of forty-something years, judging from the grey at his temples and the lines round his hazel eyes, was glaring at her. He rounded on the two men behind him.

"You imbeciles, it's the wrong woman! Fuck, do I have to do everything myself!" He turned back to survey Genevra, and she made an urgent noise in her throat. "Ungag and untie her for God's sake and get out!" the men hurried to obey him, muttering profuse apologies.

"Sorry Mr Lovell sir!"

So, this was Garmon Lovell. Her heart thudded in panic, fury poured off the man in waves, *why had he had her kidnapped? But he'd said she was the wrong woman. Why was he kidnapping women off the street?*

She took a deep breath when the gag was removed. Which made her cough and the sore spot on the back of head throb. As her hands were freed she brought them to her face to cover her mouth, embarrassed.

"Get out!" said Lovell, his eyes flashing green in the candle-light. She jumped then realised he was speaking to his men and waving them out as they obsequiously backed out and shut the door.

His mouth compressed in a line of consternation and his brows drew down in a frown as he regarded her distress. He turned away and got out a decanter and glasses pouring out two generous tots of golden liquid.

"Here," he said, handing her a glass. "I'm sorry."

She wiped her streaming eyes with a handkerchief from her

reticule and sniffed the glass cautiously. Whisky. This had not gone at all how she had imagined. She glanced around the room, where was she? In the gaming hell? Her heart was still thudding hard, and her nerves were jangled to pieces. *What now?* How could she recover from this. She felt all off kilter.

She swallowed a mouthful of the whisky and discovered it was a good drop. It burned all the way down but settled her nerves in the process.

"Thank you," she said putting down the glass on the low table to her right and taking a better look round the room. Apart from the chair and table beside her, it contained a desk with a chair and cabinet against the wall. It was very plain, not the sort of room she imagined would be inside a gaming hell like Lovell's.

"My apologies ma'am, you were in the wrong place at the wrong time, and I employ fools!" He said, casting his eyes over her. It was difficult to discern what he was thinking. His eyes appeared more green than hazel in the candlelight now. *What would he do with her?*

His scrutiny was thorough and unsettling.

Her skin prickled as she wondered if he was looking for injuries or appreciating what he was looking at. She pulled her cloak over her exposed bosom, suddenly conscious of her assets being in full view.

"May I know your name?" he asked.

"Mrs Tate," she said and waited for him to connect the dots.

"Mrs-" he frowned in an effort of memory. "Ah Jacob Tate's widow I presume?"

"Yes," she said.

"And what were you doing outside Lovell's at 8:00 pm in-" he paused and took in her appearance. "An evening gown?"

"Calling upon you Mr Lovell," she said striving for some composure. If she was to prosecute her case she needed her wits about her. "Before I was assaulted by your men. Do you make it a habit to kidnap women off the street?"

"No, I do not. As I said, you were not the target of my men. They mistook you for someone else."

"My misfortune is some other lady's fortune then?" she said with a slight edge to her tone.

He raised his eyebrows. At least his temper seemed to have cooled somewhat. Her skipping pulse settled down, and she took another sip of the whisky. He filled a glass for himself and offered to refill hers. She held it out and let him. She needed all the Dutch courage she could get in this situation. He didn't seem inclined to throw her out, so perhaps she would have an opportunity to ask for clemency after all?

She took another sip of the really quite excellent whisky and tried for a nonchalant tone, "I certainly didn't expect to be ushered into your presence bound and gagged."

He smiled at her mild joke and bowed his head, "you have my deepest apologies. Were you hurt?"

"I received a blow to the back of the head, which is somewhat painful, yes."

He frowned and set down his glass, stepping towards her and skirting behind her chair.

"Tip your head forward," his voice was crisp with command, and she obeyed without thinking. His fingertips touched the back of her skull lightly and a shiver prickled over the nape of her neck and down her spine. A whiff of his scent, something woodsy and spicy assailed her nostrils. A finger trailed down her nape and her whole body jerked in reaction as an unaccustomed heat bloomed between her legs. She gasped and the finger withdrew abruptly.

"I apologise for my men's brutality, but I doubt that the blow has done any lasting damage." He moved back to the desk where he resumed his glass of whisky.

Perhaps it was the scent of his cologne or the effect of his touch, but the man before her was suddenly better looking than she could have hoped for and the way he was looking at her made her pulse dance in nervous anticipation.

"What were you wanting to say to me?" He leaned on the edge of the desk and crossed his ankles, a slight smile curved his lips, and her heart skipped a beat for an entirely different cause than fear.

She swallowed and summoned her best smile. "You must understand, Mr Lovell, that I had no notion of the debt my husband owed you until Mr Mor came to see me the other day."

"So, you say, but what proof do I have that your husband is dead? Perhaps he sent you here in the hopes that you will soften me up?"

"I can assure you my husband is dead Mr Lovell." she said through clenched teeth. "If you wish me to furnish you proof, I will gladly take you to the St Giles Church cemetery where you can view his gravestone. He was unequivocally dead as a door nail when they drew his body from the Thames with his face half chewed off!"

He raised his brows at this graphic description but seemed unmoved by it. *But then if he'd grown up in St Giles, he would be used to such horrors daily.* He bowed politely. "You have my condolences Mrs Tate."

"Save your breath! I was never so glad of anything in my life!" she said frankly.

"I see. How long has he been ah–dead?"

"I don't know precisely. He disappeared back in February. They fished his body out of the Thames just over three months ago. I was able to identify him by his clothes, what was left of his face and the general shape of his form, despite its bloated condition. His signet ring was missing, but no doubt the assailant who killed him stole that."

"I see. And might I enquire why you were so elated to be rid of him?"

"I'd rather not go into that, suffice it to say that I was not happy in my marriage Mr Lovell."

"How long were you married for?"

"Five years." She swallowed, her jaw clenching.

"I see the subject is distressing for you," he said quietly. "Perhaps we should return to the point at issue?"

She took a breath and shook her head to shake off the memories and straightened her shoulders. "As I said, I am not in a position to repay such a huge sum immediately. If you will give me some time -"

"The debt is outstanding by several month's madam." His voice was gentle, but it held an implacable note that sent a tendril of fear skittering down her spine.

"I know, but as I said, I wasn't aware of it until the other day." Time to implement her plan, if she dared. Panic ripple through her body and her stomach knotted. *I can't do this!.*

But then she thought of the Tavern and her staff and everything she had worked so hard for, and stubborn resolution came to her aid and stiffened her backbone. *At least the man wasn't ugly, old or obese. In fact, he was quite handsome and well-made, with broad shoulders and a flat stomach. She could do this. She had to.*

She set the glass down on the table and undid the clasp of her cloak, letting it fall back over the chair and rose.

"Surely you must agree that to find such a vast sum as that is not possible in the twinkling of an eye. I have a business to run, and if you will but give me a few months -"

"What business?"

"The Globe Tavern on Brewery Yard, I thought you knew that was my husband's business?" It was the business she was trying to save, if he foreclosed on her, she could be declared bankrupt and sent to debtor's prison. She suppressed a shudder at the thought.

Yes, she had to do this, that alternative was worse, far worse than whatever Mr Lovell could do to her. He was more attractive than she could have hoped and if his temper was uncertain, she could only hope he wouldn't turn it against her. She wasn't sure what she would do if he did and at all costs, she must not show her weakness.

His eyebrows rose and a thoughtful expression came over his face. She wasn't sure if this was a good or a bad thing.

"My business is reasonably profitable sir, I can, if you give me sufficient time, repay the debt either by instalments or if you wish to wait, the full sum in one go. But it will take me some months to accumulate such a large amount." She waited with bated breath and a fast-beating heart for his reaction.

He pursed his lips and regarded her with a sapient eye. "And why would I do you this favour?"

Because your men assaulted me in the street and kidnapped me! But she knew that even if she took the case to the magistrate she would be unlikely to get any redress. Joe had made it clear the Mr Lovell's power reached far and wide, including Bow Street. She swallowed and straightened her spine, taking a steadying breath.

This was it, she had better make it convincing. Putting up a hand to the locket, she toyed with it lightly, drawing attention to her breasts and like an obedient dog, Mr Lovell's eyes followed her fingers and snagged on her cleavage. She took a breath, heaving them slightly and glancing at him under her lashes, she dropped her voice a little and said softly, "Perhaps we could come to some arrangement?"

He put down his glass and rose, stepping towards her, and she discovered that he was a full head taller than her. Since she was tall for a woman this was unusual and gave her an oddly vulnerable feeling.

Revenge on the Devil available from Amazon.

Turn the Page to discover your next FREE book…

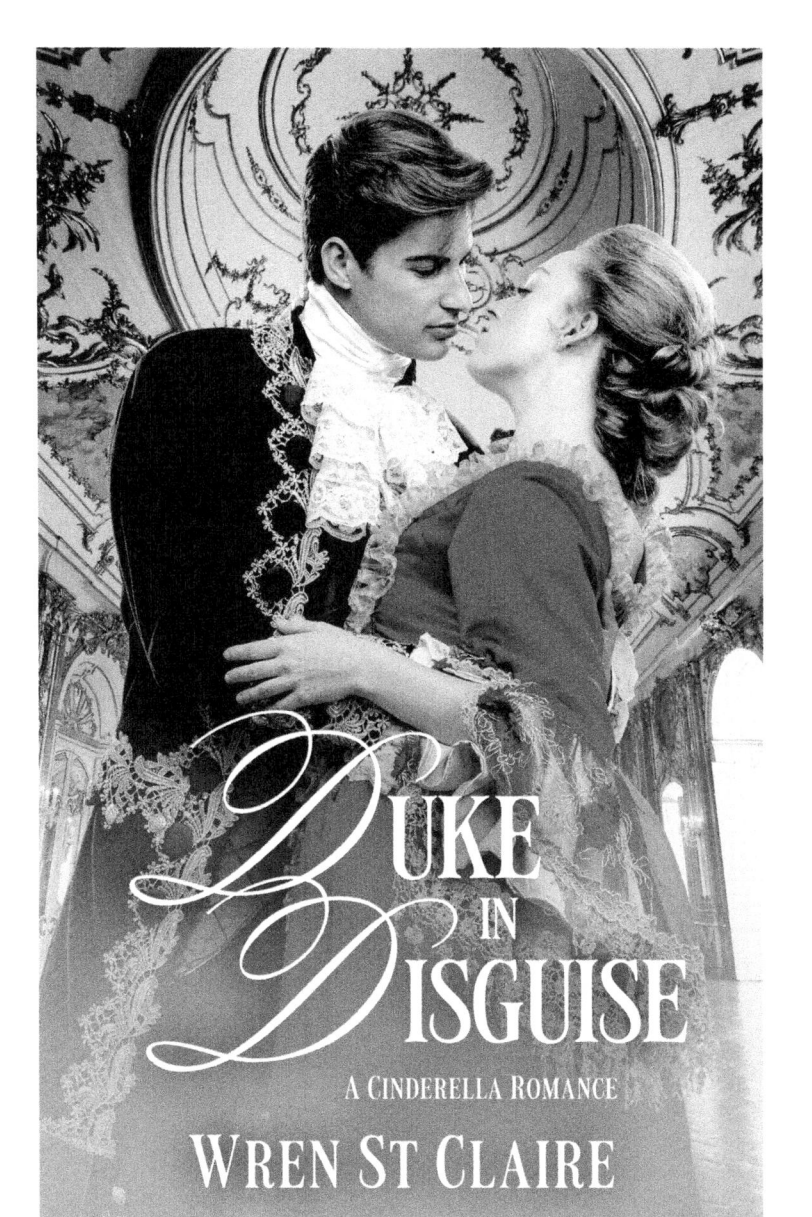

Duke in Disguise

A Cinderella Romance

Wren St Claire

DUKE IN DISGUISE - FREE BOOK!

Duke in Disguise: A Cinderella Romance A Steamy Georgian Fairy Tale Romance

A feckless hero, a cinderella heroine and an HEA. Romantic and 3 Flames Steamy!

Miss Jocelyn Eden, is an unpaid drudge in the house of her Uncle a strict Methodist. When she is separated from her family during an evangelical mission to the gin-swilling prostitutes of St Giles, London, she is rescued by a handsome, charming and very drunk stranger, dressed only in torn shirt and stained breeches.

Her mysterious rescuer is Costin Layne, a Duke in disguise and refugee from his mother's plot to marry him to a woman he detests.

As these two embark upon a clandestine relationship and fall hopelessly in love, the machinations of their respective families threaten to tear them apart.

But Costin will go to any lengths to give Jocelyn the happily-ever-after she deserves, complete with ball gown and ~~Prince~~ Duke, no matter the price he has to pay.

WANT A COPY OF DUKE IN DISGUISE - FREE?

Go to Wren St Claire to sign up for my newsletter and get your FREE copy of **Duke in Disguise** and lots more goodies.

ACKNOWLEDGMENTS

I would like to thank all my beta readers for your feedback which helped to make this a much better book!

In no particular order : Nilambari, Ruchika, Kesha, Olivia, Enna, Mari, Germaine, Kelsey, Estee, Sarah, Rashi, Gloria, Zara and Ginny.

Special shout outs to:

Gloria for encouraging me to publish book one and providing excellent feedback for that book, which has resulted in me writing books 2, 3 and 4! (3 and 4 are in the works now).

Sarah, Kesha, Olivia and Mari for re reading the revised version and providing feedback, thank you.

Olivia for line editing both versions and for help with commas and apostrophes, you're awesome. Any remaining errors are all mine!

Ginny (fellow writer) for encouragement and support.

And Nilambari for her enthusiasm for this book and wonderful review.

You're all awesome, thank you so much!

ABOUT THE AUTHOR

Email me at author@wrenstclaire.com

You can find me hanging out (under my real name) in the HR Facebook groups Ton & the Tartans and Upturned Petticoats and Undone Cravats.

Follow me on Facebook, Bookbub or visit my Website to find out what I'm working on next, or my Amazon Author page to find all my books.

ALSO BY WREN ST CLAIRE

Prequel The Villain's Redemption Series
The Devil's Mistress

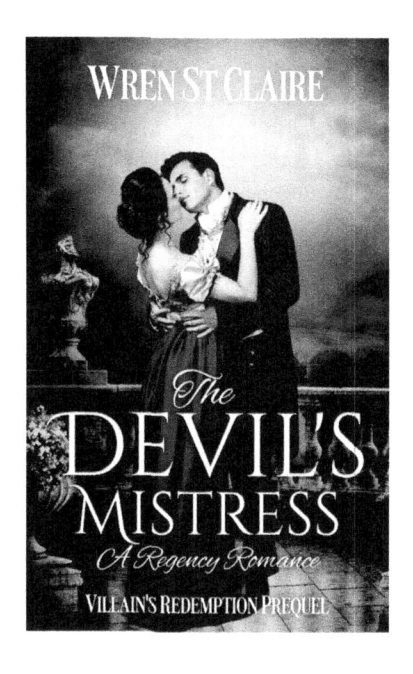

She is his brother's fiancé. Forbidden.

Viviana Torrington longs to be understood.

The toast of the Ton, spoiled beauty, Viviana, wants a man who will see past her wicked nature to the vital, passionate woman beneath, and love her with all her faults. At the end of a stellar season, Viviana accepts the proposal of her most eligible of suitors, but realises her mistake when she meets his irresistibly attractive, charismatic and commanding younger brother, Captain Jack Elliot.

He wasn't looking for love, until he met her.

More than her stunning beauty, Jack saw her vital, shining spirit and knew he'd met his fate. But she is engaged to his brother who loves her, the last thing Jack is willing to do is break his brother's heart.

There is only one recourse open to a man of honour. Leave.

But when Viviana tries to follow Jack, she is kidnapped by another suitor, who wants her and her dazzling fortune, for himself.

How many hearts can one woman break, in her search for redemption and love?

The Devil's Mistress is the delightful first book in the Villain's Redemption, Steamy Regency Romance series. If you like flawed heroines, sizzling tension and irresistible heroes, then you'll love Wren St Claire's passionate romance.

What Readers are saying:

"Wren St Claire's writing brings Kerrigan Byrne, Elisa Braden and Elizabeth Hoyt to mind. Her stories are so rich and she has a great way of making the reader root for morally grey characters." Reader's comment

Masterful, moody and magnificent!

Reviewed in the United Kingdom on November 4, 2023

Verified Purchase

"Beautifully written, passionate and totally captivating. Haven't read a historical romance for ages but loved this - now onto book 2! HIGHLY RECOMMENDED."

Book 1 in the Villain's Redemption Series

Taming the Devil

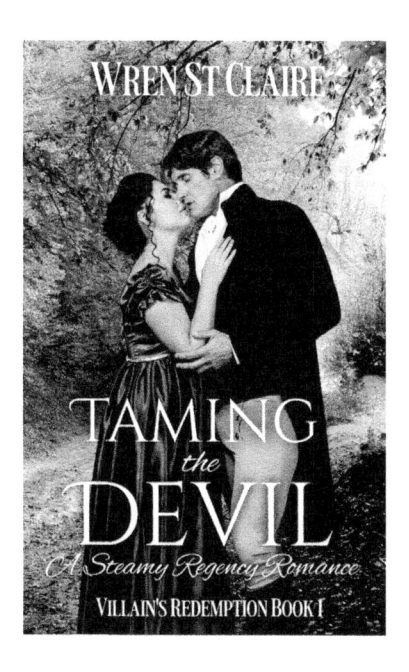

She destroyed all his plans with one shot from her pistol...now he will turn the world upside down to have her.

Miss Diana Lovell is a woman thirsting for revenge. She blames the late Duke of Mowbray for her father's demise and ruining her life. She reasons that the current Duke is cut from the same cloth as his grandsire and she means to get what is hers by right, no matter the cost. But she doesn't bargain on the magnetic attraction that sparks between her and the current Duke and finds herself drawn into an intimate and dangerous proximity with a man she cannot resist or get away from.

Sir Anthony "Devil" Harcourt is now the 7th Duke of Mowbray, but with the title comes a mountain of debt and a reckoning, as the sins of his grandfather come crashing down upon him in the form of a beautiful virago bent on revenge and obtaining what is hers. Anthony's cold heart is not easily softened, yet the moment he sets eyes on Diana he knows he will never let her go. The trouble is the lady has other ideas.

Passion explodes when these two souls collide and bitter, cynical Anthony discovers that love may be possible after all, if he can only redeem himself sufficiently to deserve it.

Taming the Devil is the sizzling HOT second book in the Villain's Redemption, Steamy Regency Romance series. If you like wicked heroes with a dark past, spicy, passionate romance and feisty heroines, then you'll love Wren St Claire's deliciously wicked romance.

Book 2 in the Villain's Redemption Series

Revenge on the Devil

A man with no heart.

Until he meets her.

A stubborn independent widow, in need of his protection, ironically from himself.

Seven nights of passion. Will either of them survive with their hearts intact?

Garmon Lovell has never allowed himself to love anyone. Until he meets her.

A man hardened by his past and obsessed with exacting revenge on those who have wronged him. When his men mistakenly capture Genevra Tate, a determined woman desperate to hang onto her late husband's Tavern, Garmon finds himself irresistibly drawn to her strength as much as her luminous beauty.

A passion like she has never known...but it will take more than passion to mend Genevra's shattered heart.

Genevra swears she will never trust a man again. To buy a stay of execution on her husband's gambling debt, Genevra offers the only currency she has: a night in Garmon's bed.

The sparks that fly between them could set London on fire.

As the hard man falls hard, Garmon's tender care for her, threatens Genevra's vulnerable heart. Yet when disaster strikes, is there anywhere else to turn, but to the man who swears he will kill and die for her?

Revenge on the Devil is the searingly passionate 3rd book in the Villain's Redemption Steamy Regency Romance series. If you like strong but soft-centred heroes, steamy passion, tender and touching romance with all the feels, then you'll love Wren St Claire's heart-rending Steamy Regency Romance.

10* please! This is awesome!🖤

Reviewed in the United Kingdom on November 6, 2023

Verified Purchase

"If you want a hot steamy romance with plenty of deadly excitement (and who doesnt?!) then this is for you. I went through every emotion reading this and was reminded of one of Grimms dark fairytales! Please give this book a try and once you've done so read the whole series cos they're all brill!!! 💕🔥🗡️🍃"

"Hot and tender, this book will melt your heart – and your kindle!" readers comment.

"This was such an amazing story! It's rare to find such a good book with the ability to move me to tears, has the steam and makes me happy all in the same book." - readers comment

Book 3 in the Villain's Redemption Series

Saving Mr Rooke: A Sweet and Steamy Age-Gap Novella

He rescues kittens and damsels in distress, now she must save him… from his dark past…

When her stepfather tries to force Bethany Whittaker to marry his business partner, Beth does the bravest and most foolish thing she has ever done in her life: she runs away. Unfortunately, her grand plan to catch the stagecoach to Bath, comes a cropper at the first hurdle and she finds herself at the mercy of the worst London at night has to offer a defenceless young woman alone.

Fortunately for her, Mr Sebastian Rooke has been instructed by his employer to find and protect her. Rescuing Beth from the consequences of her own folly is a simple matter for Mr Rooke, getting the enchanting and innocent young woman out of his mind and heart is not.

Saving Mr Rooke is the enchanting extra instalment in the Villain's Redemption Steamy Regency Romance series. This one is like a warm hug but with all the spice! If you like sweet but determined damsel in distress and big, over-protective, soft-hearted heroes and a generous dollop of passionate romance then you'll love Wren St Claire's Sweet and Steamy Regency Romance.

5.0 out of 5 stars

WOW! Beautifully written, passionate and highly romantic. 10* please!

Reviewed in the United Kingdom on November 6, 2023

Verified Purchase

Astoundingly sensual. The chemistry and achingly electrifying attraction make this a fantastic read. I'd go so far as saying this is one hell of a turn on - the kind of romantic desire and reverence every woman yearns for. LOVED THIS.

Book 4 in the Villain's Redemption Series

Seducing the Sea Devil

WREN ST CLAIRE

SEDUCING *the* SEA DEVIL

VILLAIN'S REDEMPTION BOOK 4

An Irish Rogue finds himself press-ganged by a bunch of desperate women.

Heaven or hell?

When Connor Mor leaves Garmon's office that fateful Monday in June 1815, he walks into an ambush set by a bunch of desperate female pirates, bent on pressing men for their crew. When he wakes up on the Sea Devil they are already in the North Atlantic Ocean and there is no way he is getting back to London in a hurry.

Mor gets his comeuppance at the hands of ruthless Pirate Captain Callista Montmayne

Meeting the Sea Devil's Captain, Callista Montmayne, a blonde, blue-eyed, force of nature, dressed in breeches and a battered tricorn hat, he sees an opportunity to seize control of the ship through seducing it's gorgeous captain. He doesn't bargain on Callista's strength and single mindedness.

Callista Montmayne is a woman bent on revenge and nothing and no one is going to distract her, not even a handsome Irishman who thinks he's God's gift to women. But that doesn't mean she can't enjoy what he's got to offer in her bed.

As Callista turns the tables on Connor, they negotiate shipboard politics and the dangers of the sea, to maintain her power base and chase down notorious slaver-captain, Raphael Jose Perez. Callista's obsession with catching Perez is all consuming and leaves no room for love in her damaged heart. Which is a problem for Connor, because he's fallen for the captain, hook, line and sinker.

Seducing the Sea Devil is the final (for now) flaming HOT volume in the Villain's Redemption Steamy Regency Romance series. This one is dark and gritty, action-packed adventure, with all the spice! If you're hankering for a heroine who can hold her own in a man's world, while sheltering her vulnerable heart from pain, you'll love powerful and passionate Callista. If you want a hero secure enough to handle her, you'll adore Connor. And you'll love Wren St Claire's passionate, high-stakes pirate adventure Regency Romance.

So good!

Reviewed in the United States on January 13, 2024

Verified Purchase

"What a totally original story. Brilliant. I absolutely loved Callista and Connor and the whole cast of characters. Each had their own dimension and contributed to the story. The plot was wonderful and unlike any I have read before. Wren St.Claire has a wonderful imagination and is so gifted. She brings intensity, emotion, drama, and love in all of her books. Wonderful!"

"For those who love the swashbuckling adventure of Pirates of the Caribbean and the grittiness of Black Sails but with hot romance..." Reader's comment.

"Wren St Claire's writing brings Kerrigan Byrne, Elisa Braden and Elizabeth Hoyt to mind. Her stories are so rich and she has a great way of making the reader root for morally grey characters." Reader's comment.

Other Regency Romance

The Assassin's Wife

The Missing Heir

Printed in Great Britain
by Amazon